P9-DWO-445

SIX-POUND WALLEYE

Also by Elizabeth Gunn
TRIPLE PLAY
PAR FOUR
FIVE CARD STUD

SIX-POUND
WALLEYE

A JAKE HINES MYSTERY

Elizabeth Gunn

Walker & Company ☀ New York

First published in the United States of America in 2001 by
Walker Publishing Company, Inc.

Published simultaneously in Canada by Fitzhenry and Whiteside,
Markham, Ontario L3R 4T8

Library of Congress Cataloging-in-Publication Data

Gunn, Elizabeth.
   Six-pound walleye : a Jake Hines mystery / Elizabeth Gunn.
      p. cm.
ISBN 0-8027-3356-5
1. Hines, Jake (Fictitious character)—Fiction.
2. Police—Minnesota—Fiction. 3. Minnesota—Fiction. I. Title.
PS3557.U4854 S59 2001
813'.54—dc21

                                                    2001017533

Series design by M. J. DiMassi
Printed in the United States of America

2   4   6   8   10   9   7   5   3   1

Acknowledgments

I am indebted to Dr. Paul Belau, Olmsted County Coroner, who kindly shared his extensive knowledge of autopsy procedures with me. Forensic scientist Nat Pearlson, of the Bureau of Criminal Apprehension in St. Paul, helped me understand rifles and their ammunition. Dave Thomson, of Dave Thomson Consulting in Rochester, Minnesota, and Rhonda Fay, of the support staff at the Rochester Police Department, have been wonderfully forthcoming about the bumpy road law enforcement must travel to reach paper-free record keeping. To Sgt. Mike Vik, of the Rochester Police department, I owe my understanding of the rigorous physical training undergone by members of the Emergency Response Unit, and the extraordinary volunteer effort that reclaimed the Peacekeeper. My guides to ice fishing, and the charms of the Winter Festival on Lake Pepin, were John and Lois Sibley.

SIX-POUND WALLEYE

1

I got nothing but grief around here yesterday," the chief said Tuesday morning. "What the hell's making everybody so grouchy, I wonder?"

"It's just February," I said. "They're all suffering from light deprivation."

"Light deprivation?" He sat back abruptly, punishing the springs in his big swivel chair. "Who thought up that excuse?"

"It's not an excuse, it's a syndrome. Doctors have an acronym for it now—SAD."

"Are you serious? SAD?"

"Yeah, it stands for, uh, seasonal affective disorder. It's caused by this soupy overcast we get in Minnesota in the winter. Vince Greeley said the other day, 'I don't think I've seen sunshine since the dog was a pup.' "

"Light deprivation. I'll be goddamned. What a useful discovery!" He slammed a drawer shut, and the windows shook. "I wonder how I should enter it in the log?" He manhandled a lot of loose reports into a stack and smacked his big glass paperweight on top of the pile. "Lessee, I guess I'll say, 'The support staff threw a shit fit when asked to straighten up the supply room, so Chief McCafferty, *shrewdly* identifying the problem" —he raised his left hand in a mock-effete gesture, with the massive pinkie extended—"identifying the problem as light deprivation, took all the money out of petty cash and sent them to the tanning salon.' "

"Hey, great idea. Maybe I'll go too. And take my significant other."

"What, Trudy's testy too? Your dream girl?"

"Spoiling for a fight. This morning I asked her if she wanted to go ice fishing next weekend, and she yelled at me and threw my boots out the door."

"Threw your *boots* out? Right out in the snowbank?" He grinned hugely. "But was she yelling yes or no?"

"What's the difference, if she's that mad?"

"Quite a bit, if you really want to go ice fishing." His smile fading, he stared out the window at the dirty-dishwater clouds hanging low over Rutherford, grew pensive, and sighed. "Personally, I'm beginning to think maybe men and women should just try to resign themselves to the fact that they don't speak the same language."

I sat very still and concentrated on the bright spot where his brass penholder reflected the ceiling light. If I was going to hear any details about Frank McCafferty's sex life, I wanted to be ready to zone out.

I should have known better. Frank and Sheila were just worrying about P. K. again. Patrick Kevin McCafferty, their first-born, was an endless source of anxiety to them. The dreamy son of tightly organized parents, surrounded all his life by feisty, competitive sisters, P. K. was almost always the one in hot water over late assignments and lost equipment. "He always looks as if his shoes are untied," Frank said once, "even when they're not."

"He wants to quit the hockey team, can you believe it?" Lately P. K. had shown a surprising talent for winter sports. "Him and his buddies, Owen and Butch; they've all decided to quit. And what drives me crazy is, Sheila says it's okay, let him do it if that's what he wants."

"But you think that would be bad, huh?" I tried for a neutral tone. Frank's passion for team sports was well known.

"Do you know how many kids would kill for a spot on the hockey team? And he showed real promise in preseason practice."

I went to one of those preseason practice games. I thought P. K. looked tentative.

"He had a good shot at making the starting lineup," Frank said sadly, "till his attitude changed."

"Why was that?"

"I don't know. He just got lazy, I think."

"Maybe he's scared."

"Scared?" He looked at me as if I'd worn nail polish to work. "Of what?"

"Oh, I don't know. Maybe of being in a cold, slippery place with a lot of crazed teenagers who are trying to break his face with sticks."

"Aw, shit." He closed the subject by grabbing up a long to-do list and a blue pencil. Now, I thought, peeking at my watch, maybe we can get down to it. Frank McCafferty was my field training officer when I joined the Rutherford Police Department, and my progress toward head of the investigations unit has followed more or less in lockstep behind his own steady advance to chief. I know him well, so I can tell right away when he's tap dancing, which is his own expression for maneuvering around a problem he's not ready to face. He had been tap dancing ever since he called me in here this morning. I figured he wanted a favor that he knew I wouldn't like, and I was hoping he'd quit kicking his desk now and tell me what it was. Eight-fifteen was scrolling past, and I had chores waiting in my office.

"Where were we? Paperless records, how's that coming?"

"Rosie's handling liaison between investigative section and the computer guy. She claims they're on schedule."

"On schedule meaning what?"

"Meaning at some point, we hope in our lifetime, we're gonna quit filing paper records and get all our information off a screen. But first—" I held up my left hand and got ready to tick off the fingers with my right.

"I know, I know," the chief said, waving me off. "Insufficient radio bandwidth. Codes that don't match the state system."

"Plus some of the software's still being written. Rosie says this Stacey Morse who's building the system is very confident, though. And the people in the records room are sold on it. They've been keeping duplicate records for months, and they're still not discouraged, can you beat that? They seem to be convinced the extra work is gonna pay off down the line."

"Well, good. Good! Now, what else? Oh, yeah, Stearns's retirement."

Oh, shit.

"He's put in his notice for the end of this month. So we need to give him a send-off, around the twenty-seventh or twenty-eighth. It doesn't have to be anything elaborate," he said hastily, seeing me start to twitch, "but he's put in his full thirty years and then some, so it oughta be a decent party. The main thing is, we want a good turnout. I'd like to ask you to take charge of it, Jake."

"Why me? I hardly know the guy."

"Why not you? You know him as well as anybody."

"What about Mary Agnes Donovan? She used to ride with him."

"She's got four boys in school, between first grade and ninth. She hasn't sat down since September. She'll be glad to give you some help with family names, though." So he had already tried Mary Agnes.

"He must have some friends in the squads, doesn't he?"

"Everybody in his age group retired a couple of years ago. Stearns kept working."

"Why did he, I wonder? He seems to hate his job."

"You got something against this guy, Jake?"

"He never smiles. He never talks. He seems like an empty space in a blue suit."

"He's done his job in this department for thirty-two-plus years. You want to give him the finger now because he's not a cheerleader?"

"I guess not. But Jesus, Frank, you think everybody's ornery now, wait'll you hear the bitching that starts when I tell them to pony up for a fun evening with Al Stearns."

"Figure out something good to do, then. Have a roast, tell some funny anecdotes from the old days."

Funny anecdotes about Al Stearns? I stopped twitching and began to sweat.

The boss turned the full force of his motivational rhetoric on me. "We always give the long-timers a big send-off." He waved his arms. "Even Piggy, for chrissake, got a cake and a gift—" Piggy Dolan was a hapless drunk who, because he never had any money left after a bender, used to work off his fines doing janitor work around the jail. Finally Frank and the Sheriff fixed up a storeroom for him to stay in and more or less put him on steady.

"Piggy was easy. Everybody's pet."

"And Stearns isn't so easy. Does that make it okay to let him walk away without a word of appreciation after all these years?"

"No, but—" I felt like I was trapped in an old Pat O'Brien movie, being told to go out and win one for the Gipper.

"And you know damn well it can't be me doing the organizing. Then the department's forcing it, and nobody'll come. It has to be somebody from the ranks, but somebody with status."

I opened my mouth to say that if I ever had any status, this party was made to order to blow it away. But an odd sort of bustling and clamor had started in the hall outside. Voices repeated something loud and urgent, and then Frank's phone rang. He picked it up and said "McCafferty," listened a couple of seconds, put it down hard, and said, "Dispatch says we got a doubleheader."

I sprinted through the secretary's office, into the hall. My assistant, Kevin Evjan, was coming out of my office. "I'm here," I said. "What?"

"Doubleheader," he said. "A little kid's been critically injured in his yard out southeast, and there's a big fight at Central School."

"Get everybody in my office. Now."

I grabbed my briefcase off the console and began stuffing it with gear: notebook, tape recorder, camera, film. Outside the building, sirens screamed away from downtown in two directions. Rosie Doyle came in, vibrating with curiosity, asking, "What's up?"

"Wait'll everybody's here," I said, pulling on my jacket, checking the pockets for pens, tissues, surgical gloves.

Bo Dooley came in and stood, cool and silent, against the wall just inside the door. Ray and Darrell followed him in, muttering to each other. Rosie pushed into their conversation saying, "What? What?" and the three of them began passing useless fragments of gossip around. Then Kevin brought Lou, who was saying irritably, "Don't push, dammit! What's all the commotion?"

"You took the call," I told Kevin, "tell us what you know."

"A little boy, waiting for the school bus in front of his house—" he squinted at his notes and read an address in a southeast residential section. "He fell down, nobody could rouse him, so they called nine-one-one. But now the ambulance crew bringing him in sent a message that there's a hole in his back, and they think he might have been shot."

"Victim's name?"

"Billy Schwartz, or Schatz. Headed for ER at Methodist."

"Okay. What's the other call?"

"Two teachers called almost simultaneously, asking for help to break up a helluva fight in the parking lot at Central School. There's a couple of kids on the ground, and the fight is spreading. Dispatch sent four squads."

"Okay. We'll split into three teams. Rosie and Darrell, go to Central School. Find the principal and help him any way you can, whatever he asks for. Soon as the squads get the fighting stopped, try to find out who started it and why. You'll probably get a dozen different versions; write 'em all down. Find out if there's weapons involved, drugs, liquor, any of that. Remember we take school fights seriously now; check your weapons and take plenty of ammo."

Rosie and Darrell looked at each other with raised eyebrows.

"Kevin and Ray, get out to the boy's house. Find out before

you leave which squads are on the scene, tell them to wait for you there. Help them secure the area. The place where the kid fell down is going to be trampled all to hell, but get a tape around it anyway. Then start talking to everybody you find there, see if anybody saw a gun or knows what happened. I'll be there ASAP.

"Bo, you come with me to Methodist. We'll meet the ambulance and find out what we can from the drivers and the hospital people. Lou, you stay here and cover home base. Hear that, everybody? Lou's home base. Any questions after you get where you're going, phone Lou; he'll find me or the chief and get your answer. Keep your phones with you and turned on so we can reach you! Let's go."

The other two teams headed for the basement garage to check out department vehicles, but I told Bo, "Let's take my pickup. I'd like to get over there and catch that ambulance crew." Bo grabbed his coat out of his office and followed me down the broad front stairway. We crunched across dirty ice to the sidewalk, turned our backs to a bitter northwest wind, and scuttled two frosty blocks to the employee parking lot. My truck wasn't even stiff yet; I'd only been at work half an hour.

"Pickup starts nice," Bo said.

"Pretty good down to about zero."

"What weight oil you got in 'er?"

"Ten/thirty. Plus I just drove it forty miles to work, so it's pretty well limbered up." Minnesota winter car talk disposed of, we drove the remaining six blocks in silence. Bo's not a chatterer, and I had plenty on my mind.

The ambulance screamed up to the ER door while we were parking. I watched the people piling out of it. "The man and woman following the stretcher look like the parents, huh?"

"Uh . . . yeah. You gonna talk to them?" Bo hopped out his side. "I'll go catch the crew."

I grabbed my briefcase and followed the couple clinging to the gurney. They tried to stay with the cart as it was wheeled into a curtained cubicle, but an aide in a pink-striped pinafore took them firmly by their arms and ushered them into a waiting room. When they paused uncertainly by a group of couches, I stepped in front of them and held up my badge. While they looked at it, I said my name and gave them each my card. My face is not the standard blue-eyed white-guy face people expect to see on a Minnesota cop, and now that I'm a detective, wearing street clothes, I have to be careful not to be taken for a door-to-door salesman. My card, with my picture on it, lends a little extra credibility, and gives people something to do with their hands.

The man read aloud, "Lieutenant Jake Hines. How come you're not in uniform if you're a cop?"

"I'm an investigator."

The woman's eyes came alive, and she asked me, "Oh, have you found out what happened to Billy?"

"No, ma'am. I came to ask you that."

"Well, it's not much use asking *me* anything. I don't seem to know *what's* going on." She tugged impatiently at her coat, which kept slipping off one shoulder. She was too distracted to notice that it was buttoned crooked. "I just walked out the door of my house to hand my little boy his lunch money—" She had obviously been crying earlier, and talking set her off again. Tears poured out of her eyes and ran down her cheeks.

"All of a sudden, right there while I was watching him, he fell down on the ground. I said, 'What happened? Who hit him?' but nobody said anything. And Billy just laid there . . . as still as if . . ." Big drops of water had begun falling off her chin, spotting her coat collar and splashing on her hands. She seemed not to notice. "All those people around, but not one of them could tell me what happened! Can you believe it? Nobody knew what was *wrong with him—*" She choked up entirely then and turned blindly toward her husband, her hands groping the front of his jacket for support.

He put his arms around her awkwardly, not holding her close but patting her back and shoulders, making little chirping, clucking sounds, as if soothing a small animal. He murmured something into her hair, met my eyes above her head, and said, "He's gonna be all right, isn't he?"

"I sure hope so, Mr. . . . is it Schatz?"

"Sheets. Fred Sheets. These doctors here, they any good?"

"Very good. They'll do everything possible for your son, I know that."

"Okay, then. Hear that, Angie?" He gave her a tiny shake. "Man here says these docs are okay."

"Do you have any idea what happened to your son, Mr. Sheets?"

"No."

"Where were you when he fell down?"

"In the house, asleep. I work late. Angie come runnin' in the house yelling, 'Billy's hurt, get up and help me!' First I thought I was dreamin'! Then I grabbed my pants and run out in the yard—" He shook his head in a dazed way. "Bunch of people millin' around out there, a dozen kids and the bus driver and the lady from next door, and there was Billy, just layin' on the ground—"

"Did you touch him?"

"I shook his shoulder a couple of times and said his name. When he wouldn't open his eyes I tried doing that mouth-to-mouth resuss—whatever they call that." He shrugged uncomfortably. "I took a course in it last year, at the Hilton where I work. I'm just on the night maintenance crew, but they made me take it anyway." He shook his head. "I probably didn't do it right. He never woke up or nothing."

"I'm sure you did fine. Could you tell if he was breathing?"

"I wanted to check, but I was afraid to stop what I was doing. And Angie was back inside the house by then calling nine-one-one. Weren't you, hon?" The back of his wife's head went up and down a couple of times. "So I kept on breathing in and out and pushing on his chest till the ambulance came." His eyes filled and his nose got pink. "It was all I knew to do."

"Sounds like you did the very best thing. He wasn't bleeding?"

"No."

"You didn't see anything to indicate that he'd been shot?"

"No. Are you sure he was shot? I know the ambulance crew said they thought he had a hole in his back, but—"

"But that can't be," his wife said, pulling away from his chest, shaking her head fiercely, "because I was right there watching him when he fell down, and I never saw him get shot. I may not be an expert, but I'd know if my own child got shot, wouldn't I? He never got shot!"

"You never saw anybody with a gun?"

"No. Why would anybody have a gun? It was just kids getting on the school bus, and one or two mothers."

"How long were you doing CPR," I asked Fred Sheets, "before the ambulance arrived?"

"Well, two squad cars got there first, one right after the other. I hadn't been working on him more than a minute or so. The first cop jumped out of his car and come over, and I stood up right away and told him what I'd done. He started trying to find Billy's pulse and then the second car came. The first cop yelled something, and the second one ran and got a kit of some kind out of the trunk of his car. They started taking Billy's clothes off, and I said, 'Hey, whaddya doin'? It's cold out here!' but the first cop said, 'He's not breathin', we gotta get his heart started!' and then for some reason he started asking me how old Billy was and damn if I could remember! What difference did that make, anyway?"

"I suppose he wanted to use a defibrillator on your boy. The ones they carry in the squad cars aren't supposed to be used on anybody under eight."

"Oh. Anyway, just then the ambulance got there, and they put Billy on that rolling stretcher thing and put him in the van."

"And then you all came directly here, right?" I turned to a clean page in my notebook and asked him, "Do you have any guns in your house, Mr. Sheets?"

"What?"

"Do you own any firearms?"

"You think I shot my own son?"

"I didn't say—"

"You got the balls of a goddamn brass monkey, you know it, mister? Asking me a question like that at a time like this. What kind of a cop are you, anyway?"

"I'm only trying to find out—"

"You're only trying to push your weight around because you think you can!" He pushed his wife away from his chest and shouted, directly into her face, "We got another power-hungry bureaucrat here! My son gets hurt, and he thinks that gives him the right to ask nosey questions!"

"Oh Fred, don't start that now," his wife said faintly. He pushed her away and faced me with his hands balled into fists. "You don't even look like an *American*, for chrissake!"

A little blond aide came hurrying through the door, saying, "What's the problem in here?" Over her shoulder I saw a fortyish man in scrubs standing in the hall, consulting a piece of paper he was holding. I turned away from Fred Sheets, who was still yelling at me, and walked quickly out the door. Pulling it shut behind me, I read the doctor's name tag and said, "Are you treating the little boy who was just brought in, Dr. Pike?"

"Yes. Are those the parents?"

"Yes."

"What are they yelling about?"

"Just a misunderstanding. He's worried about his son."

"Ah. Who are you?"

I held up my badge and said, "Lieutenant Jake Hines. Investigative section, Rutherford PD. You don't look like good news."

"Their son's a DOA."

"Aw, shit. Do you know yet what killed him?"

"He was shot. His heart's torn open, and he's got a chest full of blood."

"Did you find a bullet?"

"Lieutenant, if you don't mind, I think I ought to talk to the parents of the boy before we get into any more details."

"Okay. You want me to call the coroner?"

"Yes. Tell him the hospital will want to do an autopsy as soon as possible, probably this afternoon, at the Medical Science Building. I don't know what time yet, but he can get that from the lab within a few minutes."

"Uh . . . lately we've been sending them to BCA if there's any suggestion of foul play."

"Methodist Hospital will do this one. He died under our care. It's imperative we establish the cause of death."

"I see." Caught between this prestigious medical center and the science heavyweights at the Bureau of Criminal Apprehension, I decided to keep my head down.

"Are you going to stay with the parents while I tell them?" the doctor asked.

"Unless you tell me to get out."

"Suit yourself. Somebody should be with them. I can't stay long, we're having a busy day."

We went back in the waiting room, where Fred Sheets was telling the aide, " . . . pisses me off to no end. I can't even get on at the Post Office, for chrissake, and here's a guy with a face like the goddamn United *Nations*, and he claims to be a cop! What kind of a country—"

I said, "Mr. and Mrs. Sheets, this is Dr. Pike." Angie Sheets jerked on her husband's arm, and he stopped talking abruptly and turned toward us.

The doctor said, "Shall we sit here?" When they were all seated facing each other, the doctor said, "I want to tell you what we believe happened to your son, and what we've been doing to try to help him." They faced him attentively, like good children in school. "You know he has a hole in his back."

"We don't know how that happened, " Angie said.

"We believe he was shot," Dr. Pike said.

"Shot?" Angie said. "With a gun?"

"Yes. The bullet entered—"

Angie leaned forward, took hold of the doctor's arm, and shook it firmly, demanding attention. "I was right there," she said. "He didn't get shot. Nobody had a gun."

The doctor lifted her hand off his arm, put it back in her lap, and held it there. "Just listen a minute," he said, "will you?" He didn't sound angry, but he was not friendly either. Angie took her hands away from him and tucked them into her armpits. She humped up a little, drew into herself, and looked smaller and dingier.

"The bullet entered his back about—" He turned to me suddenly, said, "May I?" turned me around, and poked a finger high on my back, below my left shoulder. "About here. It made a small, clean entry hole with very little blood. What blood there was, probably, was absorbed by his clothing. The bullet hit his heart, and delivered enough of an insult to stop his heart beating."

"You mean went through it?" Fred quavered.

"I think so. Anyway, the ambulance crew couldn't find a pulse or heartbeat, so they entubated him, you saw that, didn't you? They put an endotracheal tube in his throat and hooked him up to an auto-ventilator so they could get oxygen going to his lungs. That started him fibrillating—"

"What's that?" Angie whispered.

"Fibrillating means the heart is vibrating fast in a disorganized way, but the muscles aren't working together to pump blood. That's when they put those pads on his chest, as you saw, and administered electric shock, trying to get the heart to stop shaking like that and do its work."

"I thought I told them he was seven," Fred said. "Didn't I? I finally remembered."

"I'm sure you did. Don't worry; the defibrillator in the ambulance is adjustable. It didn't help him, though. His heart kept failing every time they started it. That's when they took his coat and shirt all the way off and rolled him over, looking for some reason why they couldn't maintain a heartbeat. When they saw that bullet hole, they called us and told us about it. So we were prepared for the way he was when they got him here, no heartbeat and blood pressure dropping fast.

"We put him on ACLS, that's advanced cardiac life support, a set of equipment that repeated the basic cardiac life support methods that they were using, and we hooked him up to a scanner so we could watch his brain waves, which unfortunately remained flat. We injected adrenaline and got no result, so we administered atropine and then epinephrine. Those substances are powerful stimulants that would start a heart beating if it wasn't too damaged. We couldn't get a heartbeat, so we did an echocardiogram and found out his chest was full of blood. Then we brought in the portable X ray and took a picture of his chest. On the X ray we could see that the bullet had damaged his heart, and I believe we saw the bullet, lodged in the lung or perhaps against the ribs in front.

"But you understand," Dr. Pike said, "your boy had been on the ground for maybe fifteen minutes before the ambulance got to him, and on the basis of the evidence probably not breathing for a good part of that time. It took ten minutes more to get him in here. Five minutes is the normal outside limit for a brain to be deprived of oxygen. On an older patient who'd been unresponsive that long, we'd administer life support for no more than ten minutes, because we'd be certain the patient was brain-dead. But on young children we've seen some remarkable recoveries, so we kept going for ten minutes more. We never got any response at all, though, so five minutes ago we had to give up."

Fred and Angie sat still a moment, waiting for him to go on. Then Angie realized he had said "give up," and her mouth formed a little O of horror. All the color drained from her face, and she collapsed sideways against her husband, who was still staring at the doctor. He looked down, startled by the weight of his wife's body, looked up again, and cried, "What are you saying? You saying Billy's dead?"

"Yes. I'm very sorry," the doctor said. "I assure you we used all of our resources." He looked around for the aide, murmured something to her, stood up. She stood by his side while he leaned over the devastated parents, delivering another set speech that expressed quiet regret for their loss, while carefully absolving the hospital of any blame. He did everything by the book and then got ready to go, having shown this couple as much compassion as his frenetic workday allowed. His eyes changed as he turned toward the door, and I could see he was already calculating the time to urinate, get a coffee, perhaps do stretching exercises before his beeper called him to the next emergency. Behind him, Fred Sheets's face was growing pasty with shock.

I followed Dr. Pike into the hall. He was moving right along. I knew he had plenty on his mind, but I needed to slow him down so I could get a few more details. Walking quickly, resisting the urge to yell, I said firmly to his retreating back, "Dr. Pike, I need to ask you—"

"Oh . . ." He half turned sideways but kept walking. "Yes. What?"

"Well . . . you're pretty sure a gunshot killed that boy?"

"Yes. But I'm signing him off as DOA. You'll have to get cause of death from the autopsy."

"Understood. I need to see his body."

"Sure. One of the nurses will . . ." He waved his right hand vaguely.

"Where's it likely to be by now?"

"Probably still in examining room E, all the way down at the end of this hall, see? Excuse me," he said, and disappeared through a door marked "Staff Only."

I stared in frustration at the door as it swung shut behind him. Something nudged me in the back. Turning, I confronted a procession of white-clad people moving a comatose man on a gurney. The hall was full of rolling tubes, bags, and gauges that had to keep pace with the patient. A nurse at the front of the group backed up carefully, holding an IV bag on a pole. When she felt herself collide with me, she half turned and said softly, "Excuse me?" I pressed flat against the wall and sucked up, and the complex tangle of people and machines slithered past me. For a moment, as the gray face of the elderly patient rolled by, I felt almost embarrassingly healthy; I was aware of my heart pumping blood to all parts of my body, bringing life, keeping death away.

As soon as I got my space back, I called Victim's Services and described the disaster that had overtaken Fred and Angie Sheets. A female with a friendly voice said, "Hang on just a minute, will you?" Her speech had the homey quality of a woman asking me to wait while she checked on her cookies. But after the line clicked and thumped and played bursts of canned music for a while, she came back, all business, and said, "Dorothy Delaney is on her way. She'll be there in twenty minutes."

I found the aide in the pink apron, standing quietly in the waiting room, a few feet away from the couch where Fred and

Angie Sheets had been shaped by grief into a single wretched mound. I told her about Victim's Services, and she said, "I'll try to stay with them till she gets here, Lieutenant."

"Thanks." I stood over the grieving parents and repeated that Dorothy Delaney from Victim's Services was coming to help them. If they heard me, they gave no sign. "I'll be in touch with you later," I said, aware of sounding more and more inane. I made what felt like a cowardly escape into the hall, where I called the coroner.

Hampstead County still doesn't have a full-time medical examiner. The coroner is a dermatologist named Adrian Pokornoskovic, who holds an elective part-time position, which he fits in around his acne patients. The arrangement works well enough ordinarily, because Rutherford, with fewer than a hundred thousand people, is the biggest town in the county, and the crime rate in southeast Minnesota stays well below the national average. For the past couple of years, though, a growth spurt in population and increased drug traffic up the Mississippi have combined to make the coroner's life pretty lively.

The doctor was with a patient. I left a message. Then, hurrying down the long, busy hall to Examining Room E, I punched the speed-dial button for the county attorney's office. A secretary told me that Milo Nilssen, still acting county attorney till the next election, was in a meeting. Hoping to shortcut some phone tag, I gave her the address of the Sheets house, adding, "Tell him we're investigating a possible homicide there, will you? And if he can get out there in the next hour or so, I'll give him the rest of the details when I see him."

Far ahead, I saw an orderly in green scrubs wheeling a gurney out of Examining Room E. Breaking into a trot, I called after him, "Is that Billy Sheets you've got there?"

"Uh . . ." He kept walking while he looked at the toe tag. "Yeah." He was maybe nineteen, and skinny, his shoulder blades pushing sharply out the back of his shirt. His thick, lustrous black hair was elaborately cut and tousled.

"Wait," I called. "I need some things."

"Who're you?" he asked over his shoulder, still moving away from me. Breaking into a run, I passed him and swiveled to stand directly in his path, holding my shield three inches from his eyes.

"Lieutenant Jake Hines. Investigative section, Rutherford Police Department."

"Outstanding." He had five silver rings marching up the side of his left ear, and one more perched precariously in his right eyebrow. He leaned back a little, sublimely self-possessed, and scanned my ID. "Whassup?"

"First, I need to look at this boy's body. While I do that, I need you to bring me the clothes he was wearing when he got here."

"Hey, I don't do McJobs like that." His handsome face took on a Bruce Willis smirk. "I work in the morgue, I just do stiffs."

I was a few inches taller than he was. I leaned down and pulled his name tag up toward the light. "Ricardo," I said, when I had read it, "are you thinking it would be okay if you pissed me off?" I scowled directly into his face, looking as badass mean as I knew how. "Because I am the chief of detectives at the Rutherford Police Department, conducting an investigation into this boy's death, and I assure you"—I resettled my jacket, making sure he got a good view of the gun in my shoulder holster—"that unless you help me as much as you can, I am gonna bury you in shit clear up to your eyebrow ring."

"Hey, take a pill," he said, finally backing up a step. "I don't *know* where his clothes are!"

"Find out," I said, "and bring them to me." He went away muttering unhappily, but he went. I heard him grousing to a nurse inside a curtained space.

I lifted the cover and looked down at Billy Sheets, small and silent, growing cold. He had mouse-colored hair with a cowlick in front. There was a Band-Aid on the index finger of his right hand. His mouth was bruised and a little bloody from the entubation. They had closed his eyes. He had looked like his father, I thought, till an hour ago. Now his oval face and slender neck were turning to blue marble, and his features had taken on that alien stillness of the dead.

I folded the sheet at the bottom of the gurney, pulled my camera and tape recorder out of my briefcase, and told my tape recorder that shots one through four were of the body of Billy Sheets, age seven, recently deceased at Methodist Hospital. I took two frontal shots and one from each side, and covered him up.

Ricardo came back with a pile of small garments. "They said to tell you maybe some stuff got left in the ambulance. His coat and like that."

"Thank you. Now, next thing: I need to make very certain this boy's body doesn't get released to the mortuary until after an autopsy has been done." I did not want Billy Sheets embalmed by the mortuary of his parents' choice while the medical and law enforcement communities were still dickering over the time and place for his autopsy. It's been known to happen. "You hearing me clearly, Ricardo? I want you to point out to everybody who works in your section that there's a note on his ID tag here, see right here?" I held the tag in my left palm while I printed, in bold block letters, "Hampstead County Coroner will schedule autopsy." My phone rang. I punched send and said, "Hines," while I finished the tag.

"What's shakin'?"

"Hold on a second, Pokey." Rutherford cops gave the coroner his nickname so they could quit trying to remember how to say "Po-kor-no-SKO-vich." I added to my written note, "Any questions, call Jake Hines," and wrote my cell phone number after that.

"That gonna do it, you think?" Ricardo asked me, letting a little irony ooze out over his new stance of rigid attention.

"I believe it will, Ricardo, if you bring it to everybody's attention." I glared at him ferociously. "And I'm counting on you to do that, you hear what I'm saying? I'm a royal pain in the ass about the bodies in my cases, Ricardo. I turn into a mean sumbitch unless my bodies get the best of care."

"Hey, trust me," Ricardo said.

"I certainly shall," I said, holding his name tag up to the light again, copying his full name and employee number into my notebook, "unless you give me any reason to change my mind." I dropped the tag and walked away, saying into the phone, "I'm sorry to keep you waiting."

"You got sore throat?" The coroner learned his English on the run from a Soviet work camp, and he's still a little short on articles. "You sound like Jolly Green Giant."

"Not jolly. Mean as hell. Kicking butt big-time, gonna get some respect."

"Is just light deprivation, Jake. I got pills, you want some?"

"No. Listen, I'm at Methodist, we've got a DOA. A little boy. His parents say he just fell down in the yard, but the ambulance crew found a hole in his back, and the ER doc here says there's a bullet in his chest. They want to do the autopsy at the Med Sci building this afternoon, can you make that?"

"Can if I have to. Bullet still in him?"

"If there is a bullet, it's still in him. You got time to take a look at him first?"

"Sure. Methodist? Boy's name? Spell again."

"I thought maybe you could take a look at the hole in his back while it's fresh. If he's got a bullet in him, we need to find out where it came from, because there were people all around him and nobody saw him get shot. The angle of entry could be very important."

"Uh-huh. I hear ya. Be few minutes; maybe half hour." He hung up, bang, without saying good-bye.

2

WALKING back toward the admissions desk, I punched four on my speed-dial array. A hurried voice answered, "Bureau of Criminal Apprehension, this is Robin."

"Jake Hines, Robin, may I speak to Jimmy Chang?" BCA is a big brick building in south St. Paul, and Jimmy roams all over it; Robin had to hunt awhile. After a lot of clicking and Muzak Jimmy came on, and I said, "Jake Hines. We've got a DOA at Methodist Hospital. Autopsy's scheduled for this afternoon, here in Rutherford at the Medical Science Building."

"Jake—"

"I know, I know, but they say he died under their care, they have to determine cause of death."

"So why are you calling me?"

"Well, the eyewitness accounts are very confusing. The ER doc believes he died from a gunshot wound, but the mother says she was looking at him when he fell down and she never saw him get shot, and there weren't any guns around. I'm on my way to the crime scene now, but I'm afraid it's not gonna tell us much, because two dozen people trampled all over it before they got the kid in an ambulance."

"Is there a question in here someplace?"

"Well, yeah. I'm debating whether to ask you to send a van down, and you're helping me decide."

"Well, let's see. Assuming your brains came to work when you did this morning, you can probably still work a camera, right? So you can take pictures of that trampled crime scene as well as we can. If nobody saw a shot fired, I suppose you have no weapon?"

"That's right."

"But if there is a bullet, you'll get it at the autopsy this afternoon?"

"Yes."

"Clothing? Do you have the victim's clothing?"

"Yes." I saw Bo at the end of the hall, shaking hands with the ambulance crew. They turned and began to wheel their cart out through the entrance doors; I said, "Hang on a sec," and called to Bo, "Ask them if they've got any of the vic's clothing." Bo pointed to a brown paper sack behind him, and I told Jimmy, "Yes, we've got it all."

"Okay. The labs at Med Sci will do the blood and tissue work. Bring us the bullet and the clothing. You ready for the next step? Hang up the phone."

"Thanks," I said, but the line had already gone dead. Jimmy Chang has always been penurious with time, and becoming head scientist at BCA this year did nothing to improve his patience.

"Is the kid dead?" Bo held the door open with one hand, carrying his bag of clothing in the other.

"Yeah." I backed out through the open door, careful not to let the garments I was carrying touch anything. We trotted cautiously across the filthy slush outside the emergency entrance, watching for incoming traffic, which tends to be crazy. At my pickup, he stowed his bag, dug out another, and held it open while I dropped clothing into it.

"The guys on the crew were pretty sure he was dead," Bo told me while I wrote the tag. "They feel real bad. They got to the scene so fast, they were sure at first they were gonna save him. But they said he never responded to CPR."

"Mmm. I'm gonna drop you at the station, okay? You check this stuff into the evidence room, tell whoever's on duty to get these garments on drying racks right away. Then check out another car and come on out to the Sheets house."

My phone rang. Kevin Evjan said, "Jake? How's the little boy doing?"

"He didn't make it."

"Oh, damn. Well—" He made thinking noises for a few seconds, breathing hard and clearing his throat. "Well . . . what I wanted to know, are they still saying he was shot?"

"The doctor thinks he's got a bullet in his chest."

"Huh. Jeez, this is hard to figure. I can't find anybody here who saw a gun or heard a shot. Are you coming out?"

"Yup. Be there in ten minutes." I hung up and asked Bo, "What else, from the ambulance crew?"

"They said it was total confusion when they got there, everybody running around screaming. They could see right away that the kid on the ground was in bad shape, so they got a tube in him, got him on the gurney, and came in as fast as they dared. They administered several shocks, but each time he just showed a little fibrillation before he went flat-line again."

"They never saw anybody with a gun?"

"No."

"Damn strange."

"That ER doc says there's a bullet in the kid?"

"Yeah, says his chest is full of blood, heart is all messed up—"

"You see the body?"

"Yeah."

"Well, is there a hole in his back?"

"I couldn't tell. He was lying on his back, and I didn't want to touch him before the coroner got there."

"Well. If there's a bullet, you'll get it after the autopsy, won't you? When's that?"

"This afternoon, probably." I dropped him and the two bags of clothing in front of the station and drove on toward Thirteenth Avenue Southeast.

The Sheets house was a small stucco bungalow on a street of modest one-story houses. Two blue-and-white squads were parked in front of the house, and Kevin had wedged a department Ford into a tight space between them and an SUV farther south. The county attorney's tan four-door was hopelessly marooned within a knot of double-parked vehicles across the street. Parked crosswise behind all of them, blocking everybody, was a white van with a red KORN-TV logo on the side. Greg Prentiss was on the sidewalk with his video camera, panning across the crowd.

I parked the pickup in the first space I came to on the north end of the block, to minimize the chances of getting blocked, and hiked south toward the noise. The Sheetses' front yard held maybe three dozen people, in small groups, with more coming and going in the street.

Milo Nilssen hurried along the sidewalk toward me, saying, "Here you are! Tell me what we've got here, quick; the TV guy's here!"

Last summer, the incumbent county attorney flamed out in a bonfire of scandal. Milo got his job, rightly so since he'd been the workhorse assistant for several years. He had plenty of smarts and experience for the work, but his title still read "acting county attorney," and his relationship with the commissioners was still a little rocky. Short on self-confidence to begin with, these days he seemed to be on an emotional roller-coaster, caroming between arrogance and self-pity. Public appearances made him race his motor faster.

"A boy, seven years old, DOA at Methodist Hospital," I said, talking fast. "For cause of death, Milo, the safest thing is to say we're not certain yet. The doctor who treated him thinks he was shot, but the people here say nobody had a gun. We're investigating."

"You got a suspect?"

"No suspect, no weapon. So let's keep calling it unknown causes till after the autopsy."

"What else? Victim's name, parents' name?"

"Sheets. Father Fred, mother Angie, victim Billy. I gotta go now, Milo." I hurried away from him, toward the yard full of milling, chattering people. Was this our idea of crowd control? It looked like a PTA picnic.

Ray Bailey, near the front door of the house, was listening intently to an elderly man in a plaid mackinaw. A black lab on a leash stood quietly beside them. Kevin was leaning across a cedar fence on the south side of the yard, chatting with a woman in a gray sweat suit who stood on a step by the side door of the gray duplex behind her. She must have come outside without intending to stay; she wore canvas shoes with no socks, and was hugging a skimpy little cardigan sweater around herself. She needed more clothes to stand out in this weather, but she seemed willing to shiver for the fun of gazing into Kevin Evjan's handsome, friendly face. People of both sexes trust Kevin on sight; women usually tell him everything they know. Sometimes a little more than they know; I've learned to discount his investigations by about 10 percent.

Both the uniformed officers were busy in the street. Eldon Huckstadt had finished stringing a circle of crime scene tape around the front section of yard and sidewalk, and was loading the gear back in the trunk of his car. Ted Longworth was standing outside the tape line, making careful eye contact with people through the tops of his bifocals while he explained, in the professorial manner he adopts for crowds, why he could not allow them to crawl under the tape. "That is exactly right, ma'am," he was saying. "Evidence. Very important. Precisely. Yes, indeed." Besides a million dirty boot prints in the snow, there was nothing inside the taped circle but the outline of a small human figure chalked on the sidewalk.

"I'd like to run these buzzards off," Huckstadt muttered when I walked up to him, "but Kevin said he wanted to talk to everybody that came by."

"I'll see how he's doing," I said. "Maybe we can speed it up some."

I inserted myself gently between Kevin and the shivering woman and said, "Tell me which ones you haven't talked to. Bo and I will help."

He looked around the yard and said, "Bo's here? I don't see him."

"Took some evidence to the station. He'll be here in a minute."

"Okay. I haven't talked to the woman in the brown coat, or the teenager in the vest and chinos. Also, see that short couple talking to Longworth? Um . . . and the blond girl on the in-line skates. How can she use those things in the snow?"

"I don't know. Let's see . . . you keep the kid in the vest and we'll get the rest."

I walked to the gray-haired woman in the brown coat, introduced myself, and showed her my badge. Her name was Joanne Horske, she said. She gave me an address on Thirteenth Avenue.

"That's nearby, isn't it?"

"Up the block there, the yard with the swans in front. Is Billy Sheets all right?"

"No, ma'am, he died."

"Oh, no! Oh, that's terrible! Well, what . . . what was wrong with him?"

"The doctor says he might have been shot."

"Shot? You mean . . . shot with a gun?"

"He thought it looked that way, yes."

"Oh, I don't think that can be right. Nobody had a gun. Nobody around here would *ever* bring out a gun while all the kids were around. There must be some . . . Omigod, his poor mother."

"Yes. Anybody else live in your house, Mrs. Horske?"

"My husband. Wilbur. And right now Justin, our grandson. Just till my daughter gets resettled after her divorce. Which if you ask me is a mistake, but who asks me?"

"Yes, ma'am. Were you here when Billy Sheets fell down?"

"I was up there at the corner, waiting for the school bus with Justin. He hates having me walk him to the bus, he says, 'Oh, Gram, you make me look like a baby.' But I said, 'Listen, you're not getting killed while you're living with me, understand?' My God, maybe after today I'm not so sure I can say that, huh?"

"Did you see Billy Sheets fall down?"

"Not exactly. I saw him talking to some other kids in front of his house. Then I turned to see if the bus was coming, and when I turned back everybody was running around yelling, and Billy was on the ground."

"And you didn't see anyone with a gun?"

"No, of course not. Why, I'd have been yelling my head off if I saw anybody bring a gun around all these children."

"You never saw anybody point anything at him, anything like that?"

"No. We've all been standing around here asking each other what made him fall down like that. Nobody that I've talked to had any idea he might have been shot. Good heavens."

"Do you know which way he was facing when he fell down?"

"Well. Facing—turned, you mean? Let's see. They were all walking toward the corner where Justin and I were standing, I think. So I suppose he was facing toward me. But I can't be sure because I turned to look at the corner, and when I turned back he was already on the ground."

"With his head toward the house?"

"Uh . . . yes. I think so. How am I going to tell my daughter about this? She sent Justin to me because she was sure he'd be safe in Rutherford."

"We're going to try to find the person who did this, Mrs. Horske. Thanks for your help. If you think of anything else, or you hear anything around the neighborhood that you think might be helpful, will you call me?" I handed her my card, turned and saw Bo getting out of a department car across the street, walked over to him, and said, "See the short couple talking to Longworth? Find out what they know about the boy getting hurt." I turned away from him abruptly and hurried after the blond girl, who had just jumped a snowbank and was skating away on the sidewalk.

I said, "Excuse me?" She looked over her shoulder, made an expert one-eighty turn, balanced easily on her wheels, and gave me a challenging smile, saying, "Yeah?" I walked over to her, held up my badge, and said, "I just need to ask a few questions, if you've got a minute."

Her flirtatiousness faded. "You're not going to put me in front of that TV camera, are you?"

"No, ma'am. He's got nothing to do with us. He works for the TV station. I'm a cop."

"Oh. I thought you wanted to ask about my skates."

"Okay, let's do that first," I said, since it seemed to be her paramount issue. "How can you use those things in the snow?"

"Most people shovel their sidewalks. And I'm a good jumper, so I can get to the bare patches."

"Is it worth the effort?"

"It is if you're a fanatic like me." She smiled proudly. Her name was Marcy Keating, she said; she was a checker at the supermarket on the highway a few blocks south, "and still living at home, sponging off my folks," she said, with a defensive laugh.

"They live near here?"

"On the other side of the block. Our backyard joins the Sheetses', across the alley."

"Were you near here when Billy Sheets fell down?"

"No. I just heard somebody say maybe he was shot. Was he shot?"

"We don't know for sure yet."

"Wow. I just happened to skate over here, and saw everybody running around the ambulance, so I stopped. Jeez, that's terrible about Billy. Is he gonna be all right?"

"He died."

"*Died?* Oh, *no*. Oh, damn, damn, damn." She made a tiny, expert move with her feet that turned her away from me and stood with her shoulders hunched, fumbling in her pocket for a tissue. After she blew her nose she stood looking at the tops of trees for a while, sniffling, and finally blew her nose again. When she turned back, she looked flushed and damp.

"You knew him pretty well, huh?"

"Well, not really knew him, I guess. I used to talk to him, that's all. He was real interested in my skates, he wanted a pair for himself. Oh, *damn*, he was a nice little kid."

"You know his parents?"

"His mother, just to say hello to. I don't think I've ever seen the dad." She cocked an ironic eyebrow and added, "Heard him a few times."

"Heard of him? What did you—?"

"No, heard him. He makes a lot of noise coming home, some nights."

"Doing what?"

She shook her head and said, "No, hey, I'm sorry I mentioned it, they've got enough trouble." She began gliding away. I caught the sleeve of her fleece jacket and held it while I shoved one of my cards in her hand and asked her to call if she thought of anything else. She bobbed her head impatiently, and was gone as soon as I let go of her.

I looked around for my crew. Ray had just flipped his notebook shut and was shaking hands with the man in the mackinaw. Bo was handing out cards to the short couple, whose bright red watch caps bobbed in unison as they followed his every word. Kevin Evjan was talking to Milo Nilssen.

Huckstadt came over and asked me softly, "That kid okay, Jake?"

"No. He was DOA."

"Aw, shit."

"Yeah," I said. Huckstadt turned his face away. It's hard when somebody dies after you've given first aid. Little kids are the worst. After a few seconds I asked him, "You see anybody else here we haven't talked to?"

"Uh . . . " He shook himself and looked around. "Lessee. The young guy in the leather jacket? No, Kevin talked to him before. Nope, looks like you got 'em all."

"Guess I'll start on you then."

"Oh? What?"

"The outline on the ground, is that pretty exact, you think? Or sort of an average?"

"That's where he was when I got here."

"You were first on the scene?"

"A couple minutes ahead of Longworth, yeah."

"Nobody told you he'd been shot?"

"No. Is that true, then? What Kevin said, that the ambulance crew found a hole in his back?"

"So they say. And the ER doc says there's a bullet in his chest. That's not for publication till after the autopsy, though."

"Boy, a gunshot is hard to believe."

"How so?"

"Well, there wasn't any blood. And everybody around him kept saying, 'What's wrong with him?' They all seemed completely puzzled about why he fell down."

"Seems odd, for sure." Ray and Bo walked up to us then and stood listening. I asked Huckstadt, "Is that how he was lying when you got here? His head toward the house?"

"Yeah. And they all said they hadn't moved him, nobody touched him but his dad."

"Was he faceup or facedown?"

"On his back. Faceup."

Ray said, "But the man I just talked to there, see him? In the plaid coat, walking away? Lyle Eickhoff. Pretty sharp old dude. Lives in the corner house with all the birdhouses on the fence posts. He was walking his dog past here when the boy fell down. He says the kid fell facedown. Then the father came out of the house, Lyle says, and turned him over, to give him mouth-to-mouth."

"Huh. Well, that could be," Huckstadt said. "All's I know is, when I got here he was on his back."

"So. And there's no blood there? Where he was lying?"

"Take a look. I never could see any."

I raised the tape, stepped under, and went over every inch of the ground around the chalked figure, first just looking, then taking pictures. Eldon was right; there wasn't any blood on the sidewalk.

Greg Prentiss came up to the tape line to take a picture of me taking pictures. When he turned his camera off, he asked, "How about a little interview here, Jake?"

"Not encouraged at my pay grade," I said. "Check with the acting county attorney, he's here someplace. There." I pointed. "You know him? Milo Nilssen? Time you did, then. Come on."

By the fence, Milo stood peering around the yard, looking jumpy and dissatisfied as he talked to Kevin. I introduced Greg, who asked for an on-camera interview.

"Of course," Milo said. "Where do you want me? In front of the house? Or maybe by the tape line." When Milo was assistant CA, he used to suffer spasms of embarrassment over his boss's showboating ways. Now that election day loomed for him, I could see he was rethinking media exposure.

"Will you stick around," he asked me, "in case there's something I'm not clear on?"

"It's Tuesday, Milo," I said, but he glared at me so indignantly I gave him a conciliatory wink and shrug, and stood by quietly while they lined up the shot. Milo was antsy at first; he lapsed into his anxiety sequence, smoothing his mustache and shooting his cuffs. But he caught himself before he had looked at his watch or tucked in his tie, and by the time the camera was rolling, he was focused and steady. He gave a quick overview of the incident, outlined the likely course of the investigation, and finished strong with condolences to the family and an assurance of prompt action. It was boilerplate bullshit, but he made it sound pretty credible.

I gave him a quick thumbs-up and hurried back inside the tape line. Kevin came back with me and stood watching while I took some final shots of the chalked outline, saying "Man oh *man*, this is one confusing accident. If it is an accident."

"Yeah. That's the first thing we gotta decide, I guess."

"We gonna walk through it now?"

I considered. "Too many people still hanging around, I think. Let's go back to the station first and pool information."

"Okay. But then I'd like to come back out here and draw a picture."

"You're right, some drawings would be helpful. Measure off some distances, get some elevations. We'll have to do that, soon as we can. I think we oughta get some warrants signed, too."

"For what?"

"The Sheets house, for starters."

"You're not thinking—" He looked at me. "Oh, you are. Somebody told you about the father's drinking, huh? And the loud arguments?"

"Is that what you got from the lady in the sweater? The girl on skates hinted at it and then backed off."

A radio squawked in one of the squads; Longworth answered, turned in the open door, and yelled, "Jake?" I walked over, and he said, "Dispatch wants to know, how much longer here?"

"See if they can spare one of you for another hour."

He spoke into his mike, and then Schultzy's voice, distorted by the radio, said, "Eldon can stay, but we need you downtown for a big fender-bender."

"Copy," Longworth said.

"Go ahead, then," I said. And suddenly, as if I had picked up a bullhorn and yelled, "Clear the street!" everybody started to leave. There was a big racket of slamming doors, roaring motors, and spinning wheels. Sprays of dirty ice flew across everybody who forgot to duck. Half a dozen cars untangled themselves from the knot around Milo's car, with a lot of backing and skidding and foul-smelling exhaust.

Longworth's blue-and-white pulled out after the first group of cars, with the TV truck right behind him. Milo spun his wheels at the curb for some time and then waltzed and shimmied northward toward me, missed my rear bumper by inches, and went on downtown.

Kevin and Ray maneuvered their department car into southbound traffic, and Bo followed, with me right behind him. I eased back to leave an extra car's length between us after I felt how slippery the street had become. Turning the corner, I looked back and saw the short couple in their cheery red caps, still standing by Huckstadt, who was suddenly standing guard over an almost empty street.

Driving one-handed, I dug my phone out of my briefcase and punched the speed-dial button for BCA.

"What now?" Jimmy Chang said, when they got him on the phone.

"This case is beginning to turn entirely on the bullet and the track of the bullet wound. Any chance you could get a photographer down here for the autopsy?"

"Just any photographer? You're not asking for Trudy Hanson?" My significant other is the top photographer at BCA, as well as one of two acknowledged fingerprint experts. Her services are much in demand.

"I would if I could, but she's not on van duty this week, is she?"

"No. I might spare one of the other photographers. What time?"

"Two o'clock. And as long as a photographer's coming," I said, overreaching shamelessly, "could you send Ted Zumwalt along? It would help us a lot if he'd make some sketches of the crime scene. We need to figure out where the shot came from."

"What have you got there, Jake?"

"A little kid that fell down in front of his house. People who were all around him said they had no idea what was wrong with him, but then on the way to the hospital the ambulance crew found a hole in his back, and when they got him to the ER the doc there said he was DOA from a gunshot."

"So you want a photographer at the autopsy, and you need Ted to make sketches of the track of the bullet through the body and the position of the body when you found it. Actually Ted can do both those jobs—there's no need to send two people."

"Oh? Ted's a photographer now?"

"Yes. Trudy taught him. You know, Jake, if he can get good sketches and you can pinpoint the position of the body when it was shot, he can use our laser trajectory pointer to help you find the source of the bullet."

"Really? Is your laser trajectory pointer any better than the ones the kids keep getting kicked out of school for?"

"Yes. You'll see."

"Will we need a mannequin? You got any kid-size ones?"

"No. It works better with a live model anyway. Get somebody of similar height and weight."

"How would I do that without spooking hell out of a kid?"

"Make it a game. Children love violent games."

"Swell." I crammed my phone back into my briefcase while I concentrated on the tricky traffic east of Government Center. I parked in the outdoor lot beside Kevin and Ray, and Bo pulled in beside me.

"In the meeting room, in ten minutes," I said as we all pounded up the front stairway together. As the others turned right down the hall, I went left, held my key card up to the proximity reader by the heavy door next to the chief's office, and stepped into the electric atmosphere of the dispatch center.

Four intensely focused people in headsets faced each other in a circular arrangement of workstations. Marlys Schultz was in the workstation nearest the door. I stood by her shoulder while she talked, listened, typed rapid amendments to glowing pages of data on her screen, and finally said, "Copy." Without taking her eyes off the screen, she said, "Hey, Jake."

"Schultzy, howsgoin'?"

"Pretty good, now. Sure was a barn burner for a while here this morning." She hit something that sent the stuff on her screen away to information heaven, spared a second to glance up at me, and said, "You need something?"

"I have a somewhat unusual request. Would you let me borrow your daughter for a while this afternoon?"

She snorted. "God, take two or three of 'em, why dontcha? Keep 'em overnight, maybe I can get the kitchen floor clean."

"I only need one," I said. "About the size of Jessica." She was a couple of years younger than Billy Sheets, but he had been small for his age, and Jessica already showed signs of inheriting her mother's heroic proportions. "You think she'd be willing to come play with me for an hour or so?"

"You kidding? You're her hero; she'd love it." I got acquainted with Schultzy's youngest child last summer, when she was kidnapped, sort of by accident. She was unharmed when we got her back, but screaming at a pitch that made us pity the felon who took her.

"Good," I said. "What's her schedule?"

"I pick her up from kindergarten at three-thirty. What do you want her to do?"

"I want her to pose for me." I explained about the laser pointer.

"I guess it's okay," she said. "She doesn't have to know she's standing in for a victim, does she?"

"No. Uh . . . she hasn't ever seen crime scene tape, has she?"

"I guess not. But is this the yard where the kid got shot this morning? What if one of the neighbors—?"

"You're right. I just realized this is a terrible idea, forget it." I turned to leave, turned back, and said, "You know what, though, I've got a better idea. Is Winnie working today?"

"Yeah." She laughed. "What are you thinking? Winnie's not *that* small."

"You know anybody in the department any smaller?"

"No."

"Find her, will you? And put the call through to my office."

The phone was ringing by the time I got to my desk; I picked it up and said, "Winnie?" After a losing struggle with Vietnamese pronunciation, the chief introduced Amy Nguyen to the department last year as "Amy Win," and she quickly got nicknamed Winnie.

"Yes, Jake?"

"I have a job that's gonna take maybe an hour this afternoon. If I square it with Russ, will you come and help me with it?"

"Sure. Where do you want me?" I gave her the address.

"Anything I need to bring?"

"Nope. Just yourself." She is a distance runner who weighs maybe ninety-five pounds soaking wet. "We'll show you what to do when you get there."

"You got it." Like me, Winnie grew up in Minnesota and sounds like everybody else in the department, so people get very surprised by her appearance if they've talked to her first on the phone. Even in uniform, she looks like Miss Saigon; off duty, she is an almond-eyed beauty of the Asian persuasion.

I stopped at Lou French's open door. "Bring a recorder and a fresh tape to the meeting room. Are Darrell and Rosie back yet?" His worried face stopped me. "What's wrong?"

"Darrell and Rosie are still at Central School, and so is the chief," he said. "One of the kids that started that fight was P. K. McCafferty. And the boy he hit first just went to the hospital."

3

I don't have all the details yet," Lou said. We were all at the oval table, rattling coffee cups, pulling notes out of briefcases. "Rosie phoned first and said, 'This is bad. The chief's son is in trouble up to his butt. Do I have to tell him, or will you?' and I said, 'Hey, it's your incident, be my guest,' and switched her call to the chief's office. I heard him go storming down the stairs right after that. Then a few minutes ago Darrell called me. Said one boy was on his way to the hospital, and the school parking lot was wall-to-wall cops and media types. Do you love this? Apparently the little bastards broke out tire irons and lug wrenches and went after each other's cars."

"Better than their heads, I suppose," Ray said.

"Ah, testosterone," Kevin said, "there's nothing like it. Sometimes I miss being sixteen, don't you, Jake?"

"No." When I think about it, which I try not to, I can hardly believe I survived growing up. "Listen, guys. I'm sorry to hear this about P. K., but if the chief is up there, he'll decide how to deal with it. Let's stay focused on what we've got in front of us here. Lou, you ready to roll that tape?"

"Just about. There." He pressed record. "Go ahead."

I set the mike up on its support leg in the middle of the table, pointed its receiver toward me, and said, "This is an informal meeting to discuss the investigation into the death of Billy Sheets, age seven. This tape is for our own use. I'm going to date and time it for convenience, then we're all going to report everything we can remember about the death scene we just examined and the bystanders we interviewed." I put in the day, date, and time—ten-forty-five—and added, "Kevin, you headed the team at the house, immediately after the shooting—you go first," and turned the mike toward him.

"The victim was gone by the time we arrived," Kevin said, "but just about everybody else in the neighborhood was in the yard, looked like. We had a helluva time clearing 'em out of the place where the kid fell down, and even after we got it taped, people kept ducking under to get a better look. So if there ever was any footprint evidence there, it's completely obliterated. And there's nothing else to see! We drew the outline on the sidewalk, working from eyewitness accounts. Aside from that, there's nothing there to look at but messy snow. No bloodstains, no bullet, no gun, and no other weapon."

"Did you find anybody who saw the boy get shot?"

"No. Ray and I started taking statements right away, but nobody knew anything. They were all there to find out what *we* knew. Every time I asked, 'Did Billy get shot?' or, 'Did you see anyone shooting?' the person I was talking to would say, 'Shot? Oh, no, he wasn't shot.'" Heads were nodding all around the table; we'd all had the same experience.

He flipped through his notebook. "I can go through these one by one if you like, but they all read that same way, 'Oh no, he wasn't shot'; 'Oh, for Christ's sake; shot, was he shot?'; 'Nobody got shot, there wasn't a gun anywhere in sight.'"

"Okay. So you got nothing?"

"Well, not quite. I started asking background questions like, Do you know the parents, Is this a close family, Does Billy get along well with the other kids in the neighborhood?"

"And?"

"Well, everybody knows Billy and likes him—"

"Knew," I said.

"Yeah. Shit. Knew. He seems to have been an extremely likable kid, friendly to everybody—an unusually good talker, musta been, because all the *grown-ups* knew him, not just the kids."

"What about his parents?"

"Mom is shy but nice, the neighbors don't know her well but

opinions are generally favorable. Several people volunteered that she was affectionate with the boy, took good care of him. Most people say they don't know the father at all; he works nights and they rarely see him. But the lady next door told me he drinks a lot; she sees him sitting at the kitchen table drinking beer before he goes to work, and every so often he comes home drunk at two or three in the morning and makes a lot of noise."

"That's what the girl on skates said." I looked at my notes. " 'He makes a lot of noise coming home, some nights,' she said. She didn't say anything about fighting or abuse, though. Did you hear anything like that?"

"Neighbors weren't sure. Or they didn't want to say. Noise, was all I got."

"Okay. Ray, you were the other detective at the scene, did you get anything else?"

"Same stuff about the shooting," Ray said. "Nobody saw it, nobody heard it." His lank dark hair hung over his forehead as he reviewed his notes.

"Everybody you asked seemed believable?"

"Yes. Confused, but straightforward. And completely bummed out by the idea that anybody would shoot off a gun on their block. It's a peaceful neighborhood where people know each other. Nobody heard a gunshot." He rapped his skinny, freckled knuckles on the table to emphasize each word, "*Nobody heard that gunshot,* that's what I think we ought to keep thinking about."

"Okay, I'm thinking about it. Have you got any suggestions?"

"Well, a silencer? Seems completely out of place in that neighborhood. So—a shot from quite a distance? Maybe we're not talking about a handgun."

"Yeah. Well. The autopsy's gonna give us more information on the type of weapon—the autopsy's the key to everything right now. We get that bullet, and a description of the wound, BCA will tell us what size gun we're looking for. Meantime, anything more about the neighborhood? Anybody talk about troublemakers, grudges?"

"Lyle Eickhoff mentioned one thing."

"Lyle Eickhoff, that's the man with the dog?"

"Yeah. Which he's keeping an eye on lately, he says, because dogs have been disappearing from the neighborhood east of there within the last couple of weeks."

"Huh. Are missing dogs relevant?"

"I don't see how, but Eickhoff kept coming back to it. Says he's always had a dog, knows a lot about dogs, says dogs that have lived in the same house for years don't just suddenly leave. But you're right, I don't see any connection. Let's see what else. Oh, he started to say something about Billy Sheets's father, too, but then he kind of backed off."

"What did he say?"

Ray followed a line in his notes with a bony finger. "He said, 'Evidently he doesn't always come straight home from work.' But when I asked him what he meant by that, he didn't want to talk about it any more."

"Okay. Bo, will you repeat what you told me before about the ambulance crew? And then tell us about your interview at the scene."

Bo reviewed the ambulance pickup and ride, quoting the crew several times from what looked like minimal notes. Poised and circumspect, Bo is an excellent interviewer who listens well and notices everything. I've heard him repeat a conversation almost word for word, from memory, days later. When he finished the report from the crew, he flipped forward a page in his book and said, "At the Sheets house I interviewed Mr. and Mrs. O'Connell."

"Jim and Kay," Kevin said, nodding and chuckling. "The short couple with the matching red caps."

"What?" Bo raised his cool blue stare. "Oh, yeah, red caps."

"And red mittens. Weren't they great? I mean, everything *matching*. Even their size."

"Yes," Bo said. He stared at Kevin quizzically through two heartbeats, till Kevin's smile faded and he looked down at his hands. Bo and Kevin march to very different drummers. I value them both, but I never team them up.

Bo turned back to his notebook. "Mr. and Mrs. O'Connell have been married forty-seven years, have eight children. Raised them all in the house they presently occupy on Twenty-fourth Street, four bedrooms, two baths. It's three doors north of the Sheets house. Sheetses rent, O'Connells own their house." He cocked an eyebrow. "O'Connells know the neighborhood *well*." He turned a page. "And Jim O'Connell knows Fred Sheets pretty well, too; he's talked to him several times, mostly about guns and hunting. They both own .22 rifles, go after small game like squirrels in the fall. Sheets has several other guns, Mr. O'Connell says, including a revolver he uses for target practice at a range." Scanning, he added, "Billy Sheets was nice to the O'Connells' dog." He turned another page and said, "Kay thinks she saw somebody making a video of the kids waiting for the bus, just before Billy got shot."

"What?" We all sat forward. "Who? Does she know who it was?"

"No. She said as they were walking through the noisy crowd of kids on the sidewalk, she turned to her husband to say that they should find another way to walk in the morning, to stay out of this crowd by the bus stop. As she was turning back, she thought she saw someone holding a video camera. Jim didn't see it."

"Well, shit," I said, "a *video*." We all stared at him. "That could be a picture of the shooting. She wasn't sure, though, huh? You couldn't pin her down about it?"

"No. It was just an impression she remembered after we started talking."

"Wow. Soon as we're done here, Bo, I want you to go back out there and talk to her again. Get her to go back over the memory, see what else she can dredge up. She wouldn't just *make up* a camera, would she? She must have seen it."

"Uh-huh."

"What, you don't believe she really saw it?"

"Well . . . she seemed pretty sure when she first remembered it, but the more times I asked her about it, and her husband kept saying, 'Well, Kay, I certainly didn't see any camera,' the more uncertain she got. After a while she said she must have seen somebody's purse and mistaken it for a camera."

"Somebody's purse? A purse doesn't look like a camera. I think you better go over it with her again."

"If you say so."

"If Mrs. O'Connell can't remember anything more," I said, watching him carefully, "maybe you could go door-to-door until you find somebody else who saw it. Or find the person who had it there."

He recrossed his legs, cleared his throat, and said, "All right."

Sometimes the only way to manage Bo Dooley is to outquiet him. He had a bug up his ass about this camera search—he didn't want to do it—but I wanted it, and I wasn't going to back off. I stared at him soberly for a few seconds longer, and then picked up my notes.

"Lessee," I said, "I guess I'm next." I went over my conversations with Marcy Keating and Joanne Horske, both of whom echoed the surprise of the rest of the neighbors about the gunshot. But in reviewing my notes, I found one thing nobody else had mentioned. Mrs. Horske said that Billy Sheets had been walking toward her when he fell.

"She did, huh?" Ray shuffled back through his notes. "Lyle Eickhoff thought he was turned toward his house when he fell."

I looked around. "Anybody else got anything on that?"

Nobody had.

"If Mrs. Horske is right," I said, "that Billy was walking toward the bus stop when he fell, then the gunshot had to come from one of the houses behind him. His own house or one of the near neighbors."

"Jesus," Kevin said.

"But it doesn't seem like it could have," Ray said, "because nobody heard it."

"There was a lot of noise, though," Kevin said.

"A gunshot is different," Ray said. "You'd hear it over voices."

"And it doesn't seem to fit with the way Huckstadt found him lying," I said. "If he got shot in the back while he was walking toward the street, he'd fall that way, wouldn't he? With his head toward the street?"

"Uh . . . yeah," Ray said. "I guess."

We all looked at each other till I said, "I guess we're just spinning our wheels till we see the autopsy results."

"Which is when?" Kevin dragged out his big assignment calendar, scribbled all over and hung with Post-its.

"Two o'clock this afternoon. I'll have to be there. What time is it? Eleven-thirty-five. Let's talk about afternoon jobs."

"I think we ought to go back out to the Sheets house and walk through all this, start writing down the sequence of events and drawing pictures," Kevin said.

"Exactly. And BCA's sending Ted Zumwalt down to help us with that. And to take pictures of the autopsy."

"Oh, yeah? You couldn't get Trudy, huh?"

"She's not on call this week. When we finish the autopsy, we'll take Ted to the Sheets house and go through the incident, one step at a time. By then we'll have a good picture of the entrance wound, if we're lucky. The artist and the doctors should be able to help us estimate the angle of entry. They might even give us a fair estimate of the distance of the shooter."

Kevin said, "That'll be three-thirty, quarter to four? So I guess we can all work on pending cases in the meantime?"

"No. I want you to go back out to the block around the Sheets house. Talk to the neighbors some more. Try for names and ages of the people around Billy when he fell down. Talk to the adults first and then, as the kids come home from school, talk to some of them. See if you can get a composite picture of what happened.

"Ray, go down to the county assessor's office, get a record of the owners of every building on both sides of that street. Maybe even, let's see, the houses behind the Sheets house, across the alley on Twenty-third Street, and the east side of the other block, the houses on Twenty-fifth Street."

He looked up from his notebook. "What am I looking for?"

"Buildings within gunshot."

"But what kind of a gunshot?"

"I don't know yet! Use your imagination, consider everything from small handguns to a hunting rifle." His expression grew even gloomier than usual. "Start with the nearest houses and work outward. Find out which houses are occupied by their owners. Then start getting the names of the tenants in the rented ones. Build me a picture of the neighborhood."

A burst of talk erupted in the hall. I opened the meeting room door and saw Rosie and Darrell with a clutch of support staffers, Mary and Rae and Mabel, crowded around them asking questions.

"Come quick," I said. "We need you in here." They pulled away from their attentive audience and came toward me, tousled and still red-cheeked from standing out in the cold. We cleared spaces at the cluttered table, and they thumped down briefcases heavy with notes.

"There isn't much time before lunch," I said, "but give us a quick review of where it stands."

"The chief is still up there," Darrell said, "sorting it out."

"They're holding P. K. and three other boys in four separate rooms near the principal's office," Rosie said, "and there's a bunch of parents in the library, yelling for blood. The chief and the principal and Mr. Munger are trotting back and forth, negotiating."

"Dan Munger?" Lou said. "The hockey coach? Why him?"

"It seems to be mostly hockey players involved. The first and second teams."

"Looks like some of those practice games got pretty physical," Darrell said. "I guess the rivalry for spots on the first team got a little out of hand."

"Which I can well see how it might," Rosie said, "with that Munger guy in charge."

"Come on, Rosie," Darrell said, "he's just doing his job."

"Boy, and then some. Talk about a take-no-prisoners coaching style—"

"He wins games," Darrell said, "isn't that what it's all about?"

"Is it? I thought it was about teaching teamwork and responsibility."

I rapped on the table twice. "Finish this argument on your own time! What started it?"

Rosie shrugged hugely and said, "Like you said, Jake, it depends who you ask. But most of the kids agree that the captain of the first team, his name is . . . uh"—she flipped through her notes with a pencil eraser—"here it is, Jason Hadley. He said something insulting to P. K. McCafferty."

"What did he say?"

She smiled grimly. "It must have been monumentally obscene. P. K. won't repeat it."

"I see. So, Hadley said this thing, and P. K. punched him?"

"I wish. He coldcocked him with his backpack."

"That's a weapon?"

"Well, yeah, when it's full of books. Hadley just went to the hospital, they think maybe he's got a concussion."

"Okay. What got all the other guys into it?"

"Well, Hadley's got a sidekick who's a real mouth, his name I have no trouble remembering: Brian Coe. He started yelling, 'Get McCafferty!' and he came at P. K. with one of those club things that you lock on a steering wheel. To stop him, a couple of other second-teamers jumped on Coe and changed his hairdo from a ponytail to a partial crew cut. After that I guess the fight just kept spreading."

"The parking lot is full of broken glass," Darrell said, "and angry fathers."

"Yelling at their sons." Rosie shuddered. "Calling them awful things like Shit-for-brains and Asshole. And the weird thing is, the sons are yelling right back. Nobody's giving an inch today. I never saw so much hostility."

"It's a good thing there were no firearms handy," Darrell said. "This coulda got ugly."

"It's ugly now," Rosie said. "With guns, it would have been World War III."

"Okay. Are you done up there? Or do you have to go back?"

"One of us does, probably," Darrell said. "When we compared names with the coach, he said there were a couple of boys on the second team that we missed. So after lunch I guess we'll have to go get their statements."

"Can Darrell do it?" Rosie asked me. "I'm supposed to put in a couple of hours in the records room with Stacy this afternoon. Unless you want me to skip it."

"Uh . . . how important is it?"

"Well. We're testing our interfaces with the national databases, MINCIS and NCIC and so on. But if you want me to wait—"

"If I give you some names, could you do a couple of searches for me? Or won't you have time for that?"

"Oh, we'd love to have some real-time searches to try."

"Good. See if you can find anything on Fred Sheets"—I gave her his full name and address— "like registered firearms, DUI, domestic complaints. Why don't you check the credit bureau, too, for money trouble: bankruptcy, garnished wages, any of that." On a sudden impulse, I added, "Say, and as long as you're searching, take a look in Al Stearns's service jacket, will you? I'm supposed to organize his retirement party, and I don't know anything about him."

"What are you looking for?"

"Oh, you know, unusual collars, interesting cases he took part in, amusing incidents . . ."

"Amusing incidents about Al Stearns? That sounds like one of those very short books."

"Yeah, well—" I looked at my watch. "Damn, it's ten past twelve. Okay, Ray, Kevin, Rosie, Darrell, you've all got your afternoon assignments. Kevin and Ray, I'll meet you at the Sheets house right after the autopsy. Lou, you're still home base. Be sure you tell Lulu where we all are so she can tell the chief if he asks. Are the calls piling up?"

"Three or four break-ins. One domestic disturbance."

"Time-stamp everything, do as much as you can on the phone. We'll get to the on-site inspections as soon as we can, in the order received. Bo—" I turned and stared at him.

He raised his square, capable hands, palms toward me in an I-surrender stance. "I know," he said. "Find that fucking camera."

A fifteen-knot breeze fresh from the Arctic tormented my neck while I paced in short circles in front of the medical sciences building, protecting a parking space I really had no right to hold. My watch, for the fourth time in thirty seconds, told me it was six minutes to two. I decided to give Zumwalt one more minute before I bagged it and went inside. Then I saw the big sedan marked "Bureau of Criminal Apprehension," with its blinkers on, waiting to turn across hell-bent First Avenue traffic. When it found a break and headed toward me, I stepped out and pointed. Ted Zumwalt pulled into the space, set the brake, and slid out the door in one motion.

"Excellent service, my good man," he said. "I dare say you thought I had died." Ted affects a magisterial manner somewhere between Mark Twain and Major Winchester. I guess he's trying to compensate for looking five years younger than his age, which is twenty-two.

"Looks like you hit the noonday rush."

"Which segues directly into the afternoon rush, right? Highway Fifty-two, Minnesota's mosh pit for road warriors." He slid the side door open, leaned into the crowded space, and began pulling out gear.

I said what I always seem to say to the rear ends of BCA personnel when they arrive. "Can I help?"

"Yes. Here." He hung a half-dozen Dacron bags on me and scooped up another load for himself. We staggered through the big front door, grunting.

"Stupid easel," Ted muttered, as he banged against the doorjamb. We thumped down the hall to a door marked 4-A. I opened it tentatively and stuck my head in. Two shrouded figures stood by a high steel table in a punishingly bright, clean room. Light from big ceiling fluorescents bounced off scrubbed surfaces of metal and tile. The room looked hot but felt chilly, at least ten degrees cooler than the hall outside.

Pokey's voice said, "Well, by cracky, ain't this mad cool? Jake Hines gonna come to our autopsy." Pokey gets his slang from three generations of patients, and doesn't seem to give a rip what's in or out. His appearance this afternoon balanced on some improbable line between spooky and hilarious; he was swathed in a rustling plastic gown several sizes too large, wearing plastic gloves and booties, and a wanna-be shower cap.

"Bags okay right there," Pokey said. "You both got gloves? Don't need aprons, we'll do all the dirty work." He turned and gestured grandly toward a tiny mahogany-colored person, equally plastic-wrapped, across the table from him. "Meet Dr. Mehta. Is chief of pathology for Methodist Hospital, very big cheese." Mehta's smile was a dazzling flash of white in his dark face.

"Dr. Mehta," I said, "this is Ted Zumwalt. Pokey, you remember Ted?"

"A very small cheese from the Bureau of Criminal Apprehension," Ted said. "My pleasure, doctors."

"Good afternoon to you both," Mehta said. "Please let me know if we can do anything to assist you." His accent was upper-crust Brit boarding school overlaid on the dialect of his native province of India; it came out "if vee can do anyteeng to ass-eest you." I had to concentrate hard to keep his singsong falsetto from sliding into elegant-sounding gibberish. In response to the stately courtesy and cheerfulness of his manner, I found myself involuntarily nodding and smiling.

"Well, okay to start?" Pokey asked him. Dr. Mehta nodded and smiled brightly. I smiled and nodded back, like a toy duck over a water dish. He touched a wall switch with his elbow. A red light came on below a microphone that was attached to the upright of the tray table beside him. Dr. Mehta spoke his name, the day's date, and the time, and then graciously asked each of us to enter our own name and function. I began to pity the unsuspecting transcription clerk who would soon hit the start button on this tape, hear all these accents, and then undertake the spelling of Rajeej Mehta, Theophilus Zumwalt, and Adrian Pokornoskovic.

"Deceased is William Sheets, male, age seven, brought to

Methodist Hospital at eight-thirty-seven this morning suffering from cardiac arrest and apnea. Patient was unresponsive to . . . " Mehta, reading from ER notes, reviewed the many shocks and stimulants to which Billy Sheets had been subjected and listed the time at which he had been declared dead, 8:57A.M.

They weighed and measured, and reported that the deceased was forty-six inches long and weighed fifty-nine pounds. He had light brown hair and blue eyes, and showed no sign of previous injuries except the tiny cut on his finger that had been covered by a Band-Aid this morning. The temperature of the body was now eighty-four degrees.

"Rigor mortis is well started in neck and jaw. Lividity" —Mehta lifted the child's right shoulder, pushed a delicate finger against the skin of the back, released, watched a moment—"almost fixed." He looked up at Pokey. "Did you tell me you have all the X rays you need?"

"Think so. Got the technician at Methodist to take two sets for me. Thought we better get lateral views while arms were still soft, easier to move around, huh? But we can take more, if these don't show everything. You wanna look, Jake? See if I got what you need here? Ted, you wanna take some pictures while we're looking, yah? You need any help?"

"Not with photos," Ted said, blazing away with his flash. "I might need to slow you down a bit if Jake decides he wants sketches."

"Not here," I said. "At the crime scene. You got the X rays, Pokey?"

"Betcha my booties," Pokey said, carrying the big brown envelope full of films toward the view box on the end wall. He slid the crackling sheets into the clips and turned on the light.

"Here's anterior view." He pointed. "Left ventricle sure looks messed up, don't it? White spot here could be bullet, huh? Probably is. Here's posterior. Clean hole punched through trapezius and scapula, see? Looks like bullet mighta tumbled then, huh?"

"Yes," Mehta said. "All this messiness in the thoracic cavity, the uneven spirals of tissue trailing downward, probably shreds of pericardium here—"

"Right. Now, lateral views. Left side oughta be best. Yah! See this, Jake?"

"Are these bone fragments? Trailing downward from the entry wound?"

"Yup. Shot came from above, looks like," Pokey said. He cocked an eye at Mehta. "You agree?"

"Well . . . " Mehta shrugged. "The hows and whys are your bailiwick, of course. The hospital's only interest is in establishing cause of death. But . . . I did my residency in an ER in Chicago, where I treated a good many gunshot wounds. And I think I could confidently predict that if the bullet entered at an angle, we should see an eccentric abrasion ring."

"Oh, yah?" Pokey said. "Let's go see." They waited while Ted finished his first set of shots. When he stepped back, they moved to opposite ends of the table. Mehta murmured something, and with one adroit move they rolled the small body facedown. High on the left side of the child's back was a surprisingly small hole, half the size of a dime.

"No soot around the wound," I said, "no powder burns."

"No," Pokey said, "but he was wearing coat, huh? And shirt? You got 'em, Jake?"

"On drying racks, at the station. I'd like to send them up with you, Ted."

"And we'll be testing for what? Soot, powder burns?"

"Yup. Coat oughta show soot or burns, if this was contact shot." Pokey squinted, thinking. "If not—if this ain't contact shot, Jake, you wanna think about—look here—no stippling at all around entry wound."

"So then I also rule out a shot from within the next— what—six to ten inches?"

"Yah."

Mehta picked up a small metal ruler and measured the entry wound. "More than four millimeters," he said, "but not quite five."

"So—maybe a .22?" I looked from one to another of them, and almost in unison they did the famous medical shrug.

"Could be." Pokey bent down and stared. "Abrasion ring kinda lopsided, huh?"

"Eccentric," Mehta said.

"What's word you used?"

"Eccentric." He beamed at Pokey in sudden camaraderie and said, "English is a difficult second language, is it not?"

"Better believe it," Pokey said, and repeated softly, "Eccentric."

"Show me," I said. "What's eccentric about it?"

Mehta said, "You see the red skin around the entry wound?"

"Like it was chafed, kind of."

"Exactly. The bullet stresses it, rubs it raw." He leaned back while Ted took several shots. When he moved back in, he said, "But then, do you see how the abrasion stretches out here, on the upper side of the hole? And on the lower side of the wound, the bruising is extended also, and the skin is somewhat . . . heaped up. If the bullet had entered straight, there would be an even abrasion ring all around. This bullet entered at an angle, from above, about like this." Mehta held his finger at a sixty-degree slant above the boy's back.

"Can you hold it there while I measure, Doc?" Ted asked him, digging a protractor out of a box.

"Certainly. I am only approximating, of course."

"After you measure the angle of his finger," I said, "let's compare it to the angle on the X ray between the spine and the downward track of those bone fragments. We can average the two and get a likely trajectory."

While we did that, the doctors turned the body onto its back again, and Dr. Mehta made the big Y incision that opened it up from breastbone to genitals. They drained the blood out of the chest cavity into a glass jar and measured it, took blood and tissue samples for testing, and dried the area with paper towels.

"Like to find that bullet first," Pokey said, when they were ready to go again. He walked back to the view box and studied the anterior view again. "Could be in the ribs, huh?"

Mehta stood beside him, peering up. "Really, it looks more like the inferior lobe of the left lung, to me," he said, "but let's see." He went back to the autopsy table, picked up a long-handled device like a tree pruner, and cut through the ribs on both sides of the chest cavity. He lifted out the breast plate and laid it inside up. The doctors leaned over it, studying it closely, then looked at each other and shook their heads. Dr. Mehta set the breast plate aside.

He lifted the lower half of the left lung in the palm of his left hand, poking gently at the bottom lobe with the fingers of his right hand. Suddenly his fingers grew still; he raised all but the middle one and said, "Right here."

Pokey did something I couldn't see, and suddenly the lung lay upside down in a dish. He leaned, squinted, and said, "Ee . . . might be entry wound there? Lessee." He probed carefully with forceps, extracted something gently, and slid it into a clear plastic envelope. We all leaned in to look.

"Damn, you found it," I said. "Flattened a little, but not bad."

"Rifling still shows pretty good, huh?" Pokey said.

"Yeah. Traditional rifling. Right-hand twist. Nothing fancy. Looks like a .22, huh? Whaddya think, Ted?"

"I know exactly zero about firearms," Ted said. "But our ballistics guys will tell you. Let me get a picture."

"I brought along some evidence forms," I said. "I can sign for it now, right? So Ted can take it back with him this afternoon?"

"Yes, all right," Dr. Mehta said. "Now. You people have your bullet, that is very good. Now I must demonstrate that the bullet killed our patient."

"Ain't gonna be too hard," Pokey said. "Looka that left ventricle."

The two doctors began to pepper each other with long, Latin-sounding words. After they inspected the undamaged organs and the stomach contents, Mehta bent toward the mike to detail the torn pericardium, the shredded arteries and veins that the tumbling bullet had left behind, and to describe precisely the damage to the poor little lemon-sized heart. When he felt he had enough evidence, he began summing up. "Loss of blood and shock were the mechanism of his death," he said. "The cause of death was gunshot through the heart; the manner of his death was homicide. These findings are of course subject to the results of ongoing blood and tissue examinations."

Ted Zumwalt shot one final round of pictures, the doctors exchanged a few professional courtesies, and suddenly we were packing up.

"So now," Ted said, as we loaded his gear back in the van, "I follow you to the victim's house, I suppose? Or are you going to tell me first what you want me to do there?"

"Easier to show you out there. Wait, though"—I handed him the tagged paper sack with the bullet in it—"you want this up front with you?"

"In the clip." He signed for it and then hung it neatly from a clipboard screwed to the inside of the passenger-side door. "This contraption came into being a few months ago, after I laid some tissue samples on the front seat so I could keep my eye on them. Braked for traffic and they slid off, sped up and they rolled under the seat. Jimmy found them a week later. Zounds, he was irate."

"Okay. We'll be turning right out of here and left at the next light—"

"Right and then left, then right and another left. I hear you," he said, but he followed close behind me out the driveway and tailgated all the way to Thirteenth Avenue.

"It's lucky he's a good artist," Trudy told me once, "because in some other ways, Ted Zumwalt is kind of a ditz."

"Like what?"

"Well, for one thing, I think he could get lost in his own driveway."

4

A department car was parked in front of the Sheets house. I motioned Ted into the space behind it, backed up, parked in front of the swan lady's house, and walked back to the van.

"I don't see Kevin," I said, climbing in beside Ted. "He must be still canvassing the neighborhood. While we're waiting for him, let me fill you in." I described the calamity that had taken place in the yard that morning—the child who fell down, the shocked and puzzled neighbors, the mother who insisted her son was never shot.

"These people aren't lying. They're trying to help, they want to tell us what happened." I stared at the tape around the chalked figure on the sidewalk. "But they have this clear perception that the boy was not shot. There was no gun, he wasn't shot, they keep insisting." I stared at the Sheets house, ominously dark and silent, while I told him, "But you and I just watched two doctors take that bullet out of his lung."

"Mmm-hmm," Ted said. "Quite a conundrum." He tapped his lip a minute and said, "Why don't I go ahead with some preliminary sketches of the yard, maybe an elevation of the house? Will you do some measurements for me?"

"Of course. Anything to speed things along."

Ted got out his easel, attached a pad of drawing paper, and drew a picture on paper of the outline that had been drawn in chalk on the sidewalk. He was equipped for working in the cold, I saw; he had wool knit gloves with the ends of the fingers cut off, and a watch cap that covered most of his head without getting in the way of his glasses. As he worked, he told me what information he needed. I trotted around him with the tape, calling out the distances from the chalked figure to the street, to the front door of the Sheets house, to the neighbors' fences.

Then Ted picked up his easel, I carried the rest of his gear, and we walked across the street and set up on the sidewalk opposite. He began to draw a front elevation of the house. I went back and measured the height of the house and the height of the curb.

"I can measure the slope of the lawn," he said. "This is somewhat crude, but—" He went back to his van and came back with a tripod, screwed a surveyor's transit on top of it, and sighted on the bottom step of Billy Sheets's house. "There," he said, scribbling figures, "I can do the lateral view from these figures. I mean, my software can, if the computer gods are smiling."

While he sketched, I crossed the street again and walked to the south end of the block, where I began writing down house numbers, jotting brief descriptions, and taking pictures. Between the corner and the Sheets house there were only two houses: a tan stucco bungalow much like the Sheets house on the corner, and next door to it the gray duplex with aluminum siding where the fast-talking neighbor had stood shivering in her sweater. I noted the number of the Sheets house and went on up the block, writing descriptions like "white prebuilt w/red door" and "pink stucco w/stone chimney," and taking a picture of each one.

At the north end of the block I crossed the street and continued the procedure, working my way back down to Ted. He was still sketching and didn't need any help, so I went on to the corner, where I took a picture of the last house and wrote, "two-story plus attic w/hedge, peeling paint." Then, looking for ideas, I turned the corner and walked east a few feet, to the school bus stop on Nineteenth Street.

The stop had no shelter; it was just a yellow-painted area on the curb, with a sign above it. Standing under the sign, I looked across Nineteenth Street. The other side of the street was lined with one- and two-story houses like all the others in the neighborhood. Some had attached garages, and one or two had sheds in their backyards. I turned right ninety degrees. I could see the tan stucco house on the corner, and a sliver of the gray duplex next to Sheetses' house. Because of the hedge around the yard next to me, I couldn't see Billy Sheets's house or yard until I got back to the corner.

Ted beckoned, and I walked back to him.

"This is done. What's next?"

"Well, let's see; here comes everybody, I guess." Kevin had come out of the house with swans, just as Winnie pulled her blue-and-white around the corner and stopped in front of us. She slid the passenger-side window down and asked, "Okay to park here?"

"Sure. Thanks for coming, Winnie. This is Ted Zumwalt, from BCA."

Ted bowed very slightly from the waist and said, "Enchanted."

Winnie, watching him carefully, said, "How do you do?"

I asked Ted, "You got the pointer?"

"In the van. We'll want the protractor, too, won't we? And the fogger?"

"You're the expert, bring what you want. To the yard over there. Winnie, I'll show you what we need to do." While Ted stowed his sketching gear, we crossed the street to the Sheets yard and ducked under the tape.

Kevin came in behind us, smiling, saying, "Hey, Winnie, you gonna help us figure this mess out?" Kevin, like most of the men in the department, still considers Winnie some kind of delightful joke. She's been eight months on the street, and she pulls her own weight, refusing to play the perky doll. But she's exceptionally small and pretty, so they find it hard to take her seriously. I've known she was a no-foolishness cop since the day, early in her career, when she put a bullet through a man who was about to kill me.

"Listen, do you need me right away?" Kevin asked me. "I

gotta couple more houses to talk to, and it looks like they're home right now."

"Go," I said. He flashed Winnie another big smile and a thumbs-up as he strode past her. She gave him the palest ghost of a polite smile.

"This is where that little boy was shot this morning, huh?" Winnie looked at the house uneasily. "Are his folks in there?"

"No. I checked with Victim's Services, they've gone out to Byron to stay with her mother for a couple of days. They might never come back here, they said."

She muttered something.

"What?"

She cleared her throat. "Terrible."

"Yes. Worst part of being a cop, when kids get hurt." I pulled out my notebook and flipped through pages.

"You're used to it, huh?" She shuffled her feet and looked at me sideways. Like all new cops, Winnie had learned to deal intellectually with the confusing guilt and shame that hangs around the scene of a tragedy, but was still struggling with the emotional freight.

"No. I hate it every time. Only way I can stand it is to just keep doing my job."

"Oh, right." She straightened inside her perfect jacket and stood looking even neater than before. "What do you want me to do?"

"I want you to be a stand-in for the little boy." I explained as much as I knew about the laser pointer.

Ted ducked under the tape, carrying several bags as usual, and said, "Is that what you're going to do? Jimmy said try to find a kid about the same size."

"I thought about that, but I decided against it."

"I should hope so," Winnie said.

"Why?" Ted said. "It would work better if—" His eye fell on the chalked outline on the sidewalk. "Oh." He met Winnie's eyes, nodded, and said, "Right."

"Billy Sheets was"—I flipped through my notebook—"forty-six inches tall." I unclipped a metal tape measure from my belt and said, "May I?" Winnie stood obediently; she was five feet one in her boots. I measured her from the knees down. "Nineteen inches. If you kneel down, you'll be four inches short. What have we got—"

Ted said, "Wait," and ran and got a seat cushion from his van.

"Looks close," I said. "Face the street."

Winnie knelt on the cushion. I measured. "Can you sink about an inch?" She sank. I measured again and said, "Perfect. Okay, where's the, uh . . ."

"Laser trajectory pointer," Ted said, taking a small device like a pencil out of a case. I pointed to a spot on Winnie's left shoulder, and he placed the blunt end of the pointer there. "I'll hold it," I said, "while you get that protractor. We decided on sixty-five degrees, right?"

"Exactly." He set the angle, and I leaned the pointer against it. "Now, hold it there," he said, shaking an aerosol can in his left hand.

"What's that?"

"Photographic fog." He turned on the laser light. Nothing happened, that I could see. Then he sprayed the area in front of the pointer. A beam of light appeared in the fog. Following the path upward, he sprayed some more. The beam kept appearing in the fog, with the far end pointing over the roof of the Sheets house.

"Well, so much for that," I said. "Rotate about ten degrees right, will you, Winnie? A little more. Try that, Ted." I held the pointer while Ted turned it on and sprayed again. The beam sailed over the roof of the neighbor's house. We tried it again with the duplex on the other side, and the stucco house on the corner.

"The corner house, possibly," Ted said, "if you stood on the chimney."

"Might be a little conspicuous. Turn all the way around," I told Winnie. We posed her facing the Sheets house and set the pointer again. Ted sprayed fog as far along the beam as he could reach. Plainly, the trajectory was headed over the roof of the house across the street. We tried the houses on either side and got the same result.

"Let's try that big two-story house on the corner," I said.

"Behind the hedge over there?"

"Yes. Turn right about twenty degrees," I told Winnie. "That's a little too far. Back about—yeah." I measured again, asked her to sink an inch, and set the pointer again. Ted turned it on and sprayed, and said, "Bingo."

I squinted along the beam. "On the attic, you think?"

"Yes. Let me see if I can—" Ted pulled a little set of birder's binoculars out of a leather case on his belt and peered through them. "There. Take a look." He handed the glasses to me. "See the dot? Here. I can hold the pointer."

I fiddled with the focus for a few seconds. A red dot was dancing on the frame of the attic window. "Okay, I see it."

Ted smiled smugly. "Deucedly clever device, eh, Watson?"

"I love it. Let's do it again. Check everything, huh? An angle of sixty-five degrees from the height of Billy Sheets's shoulder" —we checked the angle, I held the pointer—"and there's nothing in the way, is there? No tree limbs or—"

"If there was," Ted said, "you wouldn't see the dot."

"Okay, that house is a definite possible. Look around, do you see any other candidates?"

"Uhhh . . . " Ted looked around, walked to the bottom of the yard and looked again, walked into the middle of the street, and finally said, "I don't think so."

Winnie jerked on my pants leg and said, "Jake?"

"What?"

"Okay if I turn around?"

"Sure. You got a cramp in your legs or something?"

"No. But when I was facing toward the street I thought I saw something . . . yeah. Stoop down here by me a minute."

I squatted by her side, and she pointed. "See the brick house on Nineteenth Street, a couple of doors east of the intersection?"

"Uh-huh. It's too low."

"The house is. But what about the shed in the backyard?"

"That thing that looks like a toy barn?"

"Okay, barn. It seems to have a sort of attic, doesn't it? With a window?"

"Well . . . yeah, it does. Ted? Come back here and look at what Winnie found."

He knelt by her and looked where she pointed. Then he turned, smiled directly into her eyes, and said, "Oh, excellent work." He turned back and looked at it some more and said, "But it's too far away, isn't it?"

"Not for a rifle," I said. "Let's try it."

We posed her facing the Sheets house again, rotated her till her shoulder faced the front of the little barn. I measured her height again and asked her to sink an inch. Her muscles had memorized the distance; she sank exactly one obedient inch on the first try. We set the pointer at sixty-five degrees, turned it on, sprayed the beam, and squinted along it.

"Looking good," I said.

Ted sighted through his binocs and said, "Right on the window frame." He handed the glasses to me. "We owe you a big one, Officer Nguyen."

I looked and said, "Yes, indeed. Good job, Winnie."

Kevin came out of a house up the street and walked toward us, looking at the sky, asking, as he stepped in the yard, "You guys realize it's gonna be dark in about ten minutes?" I turned and saw a thin streak of red sunset between the horizon and the overhanging clouds.

"What do you think, Jake?" Ted said. "Are we done here?"

"Best we can do for now, I guess." He started zipping equipment into bags. "Winnie, thanks for your help," I said, helping her up. She stood stiffly on half-frozen knees.

Kevin beamed down at her and said, "Hey, Winnie, from now on we'll call you whenever we get stuck, huh?"

She shrugged ambiguously and turned to go. Ted straightened up from the bag he was closing, leaned across the jumble of equipment at his feet, and grabbed her hand. "Winnie," he said, seriously, "it has been a pleasure to work with you."

She met his eyes, smiled sweetly, and said, "For me, too."

Ted let her hand go finally and she walked tidily across the street.

"Cops are not supposed to be that cute," Kevin said, watching her climb into her squad. "There should be a rule."

"She seems very intelligent," Ted said.

"So am I," Kevin said, "but I don't see you holding my hand."

I know the chief dismisses SAD as a piece of medical quackery, but personally I think there's something to it. February's always felt like the spookiest, most ominous month of the year to me, and the late-afternoon hours in February are the toughest. By four o'clock, fatigue is already a brown taste at the back of my throat, and thinking about the work that's left to do before bedtime makes my bones ache with exhaustion. I feel like it's been cold for two or three years, and spring is still so far off I'm not sure I believe in it. Old grievances and bitter regrets creep along the streets in the lengthening shadows and pounce on me like predatory beasts. So far I've never been suicidal, but I've dodged around the wintry edges of depression long enough to know that if I ever do off myself, it will be in late February, right around sundown.

Of course, you don't survive thirty-three years north of the forty-third parallel without finding some remedies for late-winter funk. Everybody knows that laughter helps; cops' jokes always get raunchier during long cold spells. Warm, savory food is also a good antidote to a cold snap, and a few drams of a favorite alcoholic beverage melts my permafrost even further. This winter I've been perfecting what I think of as Jake's Special Combo: I spend my evenings enjoying good food and drink, with talk and jollies and erotic treats, in the company of Trudy Hanson, my live-in lover since last October.

To get this smart, handsome woman into my daily life, I agreed to a nightly forty-mile commute to Mirium, a small town halfway between my job in Rutherford and her job at the Bureau of Criminal Apprehension in St. Paul. To keep her contented in the country, I cheerfully took on more than my share of the household chores in the aged farmhouse we rented together.

This was my week to tend the supplies, so as I watched my homebound headlights cut through the chilly darkness, I reviewed the evening's options. There was beer in the refrigerator, and a bottle of cabernet on the pantry shelf if we wanted it with dinner. I'd put a couple of chops in the meat keeper to thaw, but if that didn't please her, there was plenty of pasta in the cupboard, fresh eggs and cheese, and greens for a salad.

Everything was in place for a heartwarming evening, except I hadn't had time to address the problem left over from morning, when my beloved had quit talking to me and started throwing my boots around. The workday had erupted so suddenly into a spasm of chores that I had not thought about Trudy's outburst since I mentioned it to Frank. Now, driving home, I reviewed that first morning hour after the alarm rang and I got up.

As soon as I was dressed, I had gone outside and started both our vehicles, as I have done every weekday morning since winter got serious. I scraped the frost off her windshield and rear window, and set the heater to defrost. I brought an armload of wood to the box on the porch, to have it ready for the comfort of a fire in the wood stove in the evening. Then I brushed the chips off my jacket, stepped inside, took off my snowy boots on the doormat, hopped in my sock feet to the kitchen table, and poured cereal into a bowl.

Trudy was braiding her hair in front of the mirror by the sink. It seemed to me she had been a little touchy for the last couple of days, and I was looking for a way to cheer her up.

"What do you think?" I asked her. "You want to go ice fishing next weekend?"

"Ice fishing? Are you serious?"

"Sure. It's Winter Fest weekend at Lake City. Should be lots of fun."

"A bunch of crazies getting drunk while they freeze to death on the river? What's fun about that?"

"They don't all get drunk. Getting drunk is optional. And you don't get cold, there's too much to do."

"You keep warm by watching a hole in the ice?"

"No, no, no. You set up your tip-ups with hooks and min-nows, and then you and your neighbors take turns watching. The rest of the time you go play golf—"

"Golf?"

"On the ice. With golf clubs and tennis balls. It's a hoot. And you dance to old-time music by the Six Fat Dutchmen, and win prizes for the fish you catch. It's all in the paper, didn't you read it? Where's last night's paper?"

"I threw it out."

"Is it on the recycling pile?" I got up to look.

"No, I wrapped the garbage in it."

"Oh." I sat back down. "Damn."

"Look"—she slammed down her brush and began wrapping rubber bands around the ends of her braids, making harsh, snapping sounds that set my teeth on edge— "somebody has to wrap the garbage every day, or the house will stink."

"I know, I know. I just said 'damn,' Trudy, it's not a hanging offense, is it?" We're a quarter of a mile too far out of town to get garbage pickup from the town of Mirium, so Trudy wraps each day's organic leftovers as carefully as Christmas treats and stores them in a tightly covered metal can that I haul to the dump once a week. No garbage pickup was the second in a se-ries of unpleasant surprises we got after we moved here, right after low electric power and before bad insulation.

"You think I do it for the fun of it?" The anger, anxiety, what-ever it was that had been building inside her lately, found a focus, and she turned on me, eyes blazing. "You want the job?" The rubber band she was winding around her hair broke and flew away across the kitchen. "Damn!" It was an okay word when she used it, apparently. She whirled to reach for another rubber band on the shelf above the sink, and fell over my boots.

"Oh, damn, damn, *damn!*" she yelled. In one lithe, well-co-ordinated maneuver, as efficiently as only Trudy could do it, she pulled herself up by the door handle, opened the kitchen door, stooped, and threw my boots into the yard.

It was such a wildly irrational thing to do that it stupefied me into silence. I sat watching with my mouth open as she pulled her coat on, snatched up her purse, and flung herself outside. Naturally, I thought she was going to retrieve my boots. When she got back with them, I thought, I was going to sit her down firmly at the table and insist she tell me what was bothering her. Whatever it was, we would fix it together.

I listened unbelieving as her car door slammed and the motor roared to life. There was a slither, and then a crackle, as her tires threw a lot of muddy gravel up against the house. Without another word or signal of any kind, she gunned her way out of the yard.

I stared at my sock feet a minute and said, "Well, shit." I went and found the loafers I wear at work. Wearing them, I walked out into the dirty snow in the front yard and found my boots. I shook the snow out of them, came back in the kitchen and cleaned my loafers on the doormat, took them off and slid into my cold boots, put the loafers in a carrying sack, and went to work.

The day since then had brought so much trouble to so many people in Rutherford that I'd forgotten Trudy's tantrum till I was in the car, alone, headed home. Then I thought, What the hell was that all about? Normally, Trudy is a happy, energetic woman. Getting through an unusually cold winter in an old farmhouse had been taxing, but we were both raised in Minnesota, and we'd been handling it. So why had she suddenly lost it like that? Approaching the turnoff, I made up my mind again to find out what was bothering her, and fix it.

The lights were on in the kitchen. I shifted into low and powered past Trudy's little Geo to the shed in back, got out, opened the tarp I had rigged over the narrow space, and drove in. I started the tiny propane space heater, came out, and fastened the tarp securely behind the pickup. Now my truck would start for sure in the morning, and if Trudy needed a jump, I had the heavy-duty battery and the cables to handle it.

I walked toward the lighted window, planning my opening sentence. As I stepped up on the porch, a dark awkward shape rose out of the shadows behind the swing.

"Aw, Darby, are you an orphan again?" Darby was a racing greyhound well past his peak speed, with a starved-looking body curved above long, incredibly thin legs. He was maybe not the ugliest dog in the world, but he had to be considered a contender. He belonged, sort of, to the musicians who lived in the double-wide on the other side of our pasture. They were good to him, when they were home, but their lives were, to put it mildly, unstructured. Whenever his regular board and room got a little sparse, Darby had learned to pad it out by visiting around the neighborhood. Since he was totally nonthreatening and his appearance gave new meaning to the term hangdog, he was a pretty successful panhandler in our part of town. For some reason, lately he liked to hang out on our porch.

I laid my hand along the top of his narrow, bony head, and he made a whispery sound, like the ghost of a sigh. "Are you thirsty? Where's your dish?" While I was looking around the dark porch, the door opened, and Trudy stood there in the light.

"Please don't feed him, Jake," she said. "I really don't want him hanging around here."

"I was just going to give him some water. Where's his dish?"

"Well, that's the other thing. I don't like having a dog drinking out of the same dishes we use."

"I took the one with the crack that you were going to throw away," I said. "You don't begrudge him a drink of water, do you?"

"I don't begrudge him anything. But if you'd quit giving him food and water, he'd stop coming around."

"Why should he stop coming around? What harm can it do to have an old dog lie on our porch sometimes if he wants to?"

"He's always scaring me. He comes up behind me with that sneaky look. I think there's something wrong with him; he looks like a freak."

"Aw." I watched the incredibly thin, shy dog assume his favorite position, facing away from the door and staring down his ludicrously long nose to a point just beyond the porch step. "I bet to another greyhound Darby looks pretty cool."

"Yeah, yeah. Will you come in? I need to talk to you."

I stepped inside and said, "What did you do with his dish?"

She banged down the pot she was holding and yelled, "Are you going deaf? Haven't you heard a word I said?"

"Trudy, what the hell's the matter with you lately?" I forgot all my careful plans about diplomacy. "You threw my boots out the door this morning! What was the point of that? And now you begrudge a drink of water to the neighbor's dog? Have you been taken over by aliens or what?"

"Fine then," she said, pulling the dish out of the sink where it was soaking and slamming it down, wet, on the drain board in front of me. "If every stray that comes along means more to you than I do, just go ahead! Let's hang out a sign that says, 'Open House for Losers.' "

I wiped off the drops of soapy water she had splashed on my face, rinsed the dish, and filled it to an inch below the brim. I took it out and set it down in front of the dog. Then, without pausing, I walked back across the yard to the shed and got out my pickup, turned it in the crackling snow of the yard, and drove out through the gate and across the highway into Mirium.

It was only two blocks to Mac's Bar. I parked by the steps and walked up into the warm, brightly lighted building, where I took off my coat and ordered a beer.

"Trudy's working late tonight, huh?" Ozzie Sullivan said. He moonlights at Mac's a couple of nights a week to help his farm make, as he puts it, a half-assed living.

"Mmm. Lemme have a bag of those cheese things, will you?" I ate the salty snack while I finished the first beer very fast and ordered another. A couple of guys I knew slightly from the lumberyard came in and sat near me at the bar, and we started one of those rambling sports conversations that began with the game between Duke and North Carolina and went on to the Daytona 500. They ordered another round for themselves and bought me one, and we talked about the PGA tour, speculating whether Tiger Woods would ever beat Ben Hogan's winning streak, and soon we were all empty again and I bought them one.

I had intended, when I crossed the highway, to go home as soon as I cooled off, get straight with Trudy somehow, and help her fix dinner. It was still not too late to do that, and I kept formulating the opening sentence of the reasonable conversation that I knew was going to put everything back to rights between us. But every time, before I got to the end of the sentence I got angry again, so when the guys from the lumberyard went home to supper I had one more beer with a double shot of Jack Daniel's, and when I left Mac's Bar I did not go home but drove the other way, a block and a half up the street to Leonards Cafe.

Mrs. Leonard said the Tuesday-night special was meat loaf with home fries, but she could always grill me a steak if I'd rather have that. I said I'd have a beer first and think about it. After I finished the beer, I ordered the special and drank another beer with my meal. Mrs. Leonard came by as I was finishing and said coffee went with the meal, but I told her I'd have one more beer instead. I leaned comfortably in the corner of my booth while I drank it, watching the neon sign in the window slide into a red blur.

I was not too mellow to notice that Mrs. Leonard and the waitress were watching me out of the corners of their eyes, so I paid my bill then and walked carefully to my pickup. I decided to go on up the highway a mile or so and see what was going on at the topless bar. But I killed the motor on the first two tries to get into first gear, so I decided it was easier to just go back to Mac's. I drove the block and a half along the empty street with great concentration.

The jukebox was playing inside the bar, and two couples were slow dancing on the tiny floor in front of it. Ozzie Sullivan had gone home, and the owner was behind the bar with a clean white apron the size of a bedsheet across his belly.

"Hey, Mac," I said.

"Whaddya say, Jake?" I bought a beer at the bar, carried it carefully to a booth by the window, and sat watching the boys and girls dancing slowly with their bodies pressed against each other. They were all dressed alike in jeans and sweatshirts, but it was easy to see that there was no gender confusion in their minds at all. I decided I would ask the blond girl to dance. In a minute. First I would have another beer. I ordered it and watched the streetlights merge and separate and merge again while Mac brought the beer and I paid him and took the first couple of sips. Then Mac was poking my arm and telling me that it was time to go home, and I realized I had fallen asleep sitting up.

"Lemme have your keys," he said. "Fergie's gonna drive you home, and I'll have one of my boys bring your pickup over later." I tried to tell him that I never let anybody drive my pickup, but my tongue was stuck to the roof of my mouth, and the words did not come out clearly at all. Mac stood there waiting, as big as a barn and not angry but not amused either, and finally I dropped my keys in his ham-sized hand. He tucked the other hand firmly under my elbow and walked me to the door, where a quiet man in bib overalls and a denim jacket was waiting for me.

"I can drive all right," I tried to say. Even to me it sounded garbled.

"Sure," Fergie said, "but I'll do it." He helped me into his car and drove me to the door of my house. At least I suppose that's what happened, because I woke up at five-thirty Wednesday morning on my kitchen floor. I was not sure if I was dying from intense headache, a bursting bladder, or hypothermia, but clearly this level of pain must mean the end was near. I understood almost at once, though, that before it expired my body was going to perform a couple of other functions, so I got on my feet somehow and staggered to the bathroom. I stayed there for some time. When I came out, whimpering with misery, I was just alert enough to see the handwritten note in the middle of the kitchen table.

"Jake," it said in large block letters, "I'm too mad to talk to you now. I thought we understood each other, but it looks like I was wrong. I've gone—" She had written, "to town," then crossed it out and substituted, "somewhere, to think things over." It was signed, "Trudy," as if she thought I might not be able to remember who was missing from our bed.

Underneath, in smaller letters, she had added a surreal postscript. "Please don't call me at work," it said. "I'll let you know when—." The last word was crossed out, and she finished, in smaller and smaller letters as she ran out of space on the paper, "if there's anything to talk about."

5

I N the small meeting room at 8:05, my crew tactfully pretended not to notice that their lieutenant was wearing shades and having trouble holding a cup of coffee. I sat down carefully, trying not to slosh the two glasses of antacid I had just swallowed, and croaked, "Let's review yesterday."

They pawed through their notes, making sharp rustling noises that hurt my brain. I had plenty of notes of my own, but they were hard to read through my dark glasses, so I ignored them and jumped ruthlessly on the most vulnerable person in the room.

"Darrell, did you write a report on those two students you went back to interview yesterday? I don't seem to have it."

"I never got to talk to them. Time I got back to the school, the principal had them in his office."

"Why?"

"I don't know. The secretary said they were discussing, um"—he read from his notes—" 'issues unrelated to this morning's incident.' She said I could 'perhaps speak to them at a later time.' She talks like that, like a telephone answering tape."

"So what did you do yesterday afternoon?"

"Came back here, typed up all my notes, and worked on the two oldest break-ins offa Lou's report pile."

"All right. Good," I managed to say, grudgingly. "Bo, what about the camera, you find that?"

"No."

"Just no? Did you talk to Mrs. O'Connell again?"

"And Mr. O'Connell. Plus all the neighbors, and Huckstadt and

Longworth. Also both the paramedics who were on the ambulance."

"And?"

"And nobody ever saw a camera but Kay O'Connell. And now she thinks she must have been mistaken."

"So far we're two for two here," I said, casting a baleful eye on Bo Dooley. He stared coldly back. He's been on vice detail for ten years, so he doesn't scare easy. "Rosie, did you find anything on Fred Sheets in your search?"

"One complaint of a domestic disturbance in Red Wing, three years ago. It's in your reports there," she suggested gently. I pawed hopelessly through my stack of papers. She leaned across the table, plucked it neatly out of the pile, and laid it in front of me.

I pushed my dark glasses up an inch and peered underneath. "Arrested but not charged," I read. "That's all?"

"Yup. It was a neighbor's call, report of a loud fight next door. Sheets was drunk, they put him in the tank overnight. The wife wouldn't press charges, so the neighbor backed off too, and he was released the next day."

"What about guns?"

"No permits to carry. No bankruptcies, no bad credit report. Not even a parking ticket, actually. Sorry."

"Well. At least we're consistent so far, a strikeout every time." I closed my eyes as a wave of nausea washed over me. I tried to remember if I'd ever seen statistics on the number of annual deaths from hangover. If I was going to increase the number by one, I wished I could get it over with before lunch.

"I didn't find much on Stearns, either," Rosie said.

"Why am I not surprised?"

"I've been thinking about that," Kevin said. "I used to moonlight some at the *Times-Courier* while I was a street cop. I know my way around their files pretty well. Would you like to have me take a look at their archives? See if he ever rescued any cute kids off rooftops or whatever?"

"Yeah, that'd be good. When you get to it. Now. You spent yesterday afternoon collecting information on the residents of the neighborhood around the Sheets house, right? You and Ray. What—"

"We've just been comparing," Kevin said, "and what we'd like to do, Jake, is take the morning to draw a map of the block and put all our information on there. Then we can give you the whole picture at once."

"That's fine. And here—" I handed him the tape and Polaroid pictures I had made while I was waiting for Ted. "If you run this tape, you'll have the info you need to tack these pictures onto your chart in the right places. We'll go over all of it together when you're—"

My cell phone rang. "Chief wants to talk to you," Lulu Breske said, and hung up. Lulu is the boss's turbocharged secretary. He calls her "my good right arm." The rest of us have less attractive nicknames for her, but we keep them to ourselves, because Lulu has ironclad job security and knows how to hold a grudge.

"I have to go," I said. "Lou, you're still following up on the break-ins from yesterday, right?"

"And two car heists and a domestic complaint that came in after I talked to you. Yes."

"Good man. Darrell, keep taking cases from Lou as fast as you can get to them. Bo, you might as well go back to vice, for the present. Rosie, will you prepare requests for search warrants for—" Leaning over my notes, I read aloud the addresses of the two houses where we had seen the red dot from the laser pointer. When I straightened up, the earth gave a disgusting lurch, and I grabbed the edge of the table.

"—and find a judge to sign them this morning." Fighting vertigo, I looked around and found them all staring at me. "What? Somebody shot that kid! We can't stand on ceremony, we gotta find that gun!"

"We're not arguing," Kevin said, "but are you sick, Jake?"

"I have a headache. Which is going to be much worse in about a minute, because I gotta go see the chief."

"My son is grounded," Frank said, "for the rest of his natural life plus two years."

"You sure you're hanging the right man? It sounds to me like he was baited."

"He was. Does that make it okay to brain the guy?" He was banging things around on his desk, venting his outrage on pencils and printouts. His face looked puffy and red; yesterday had not done his blood pressure any good at all. "Let's not waste any more time talking about it, I'm taking care of it," he said, and flung a pile of papers into the wastebasket. It fell over, and he set it up again with a tinny clang that made me clench my teeth in pain. "I want you to bring me up to date on the other call that came in at the same time, the boy that died. Was that an accident or what?"

"Homicide. He was shot."

"Hell you say. That's what came out of the autopsy? How come we were reporting cause of death as unknown on last night's news?"

"I asked Milo to say that. We had conflicting evidence. This is a damn strange shooting, Frank. None of the eyewitnesses saw a gun or heard a shot. Nobody around him had any idea why he fell down."

"But the doctors are sure, huh?"

"His heart was torn open, his chest was full of blood. We found the bullet in his lung at the autopsy."

"You send it to BCA?"

"Yesterday. And the clothes he was wearing." I told him about the interviews we had conducted and the background check on the father. "I felt we had to consider family—"

"Always."

"Right, and in some ways the father looks good for this— we've got reports of drinking and loud scenes late at night. Possible abuse—well, fighting anyway. But unless *everybody's* lying, he was in his house, asleep in bed, when the shooting took place. Also, the angle of entry of the bullet indicates it couldn't have come from the Sheets house." I described the sketches Ted had done at the scene, and the work we had done with the laser pointer. "Kevin and Ray are mapping the neighborhood now. As soon as they're finished, I think we'll go back out there for another look. So far, we've got two houses that appear to be possible sources of the shot."

"You got warrants for 'em if you need 'em?"

"Rosie's working on them now. I asked her to write up one for the Sheets house, too; I'm not ready to eliminate him as a suspect yet."

"How much do you want me to tell the media?"

"Well . . . we can confirm homicide. By gunshot. But no suspects as yet. BCA is assisting in the investigation."

"Anything on the weapon?"

"Not yet. Frank?"

"Mmm?"

"I'm sorry to go back to this, but . . . you know how, after all the school shootings that have been happening around the country, somebody always says, 'I guess in retrospect we should have seen that blah blah blah'?"

"Yeah?" His face got a little redder.

"Well . . . shouldn't we find out what's causing all the hostility at Central School?"

"Oh, Jake, it's not very hard to see that the rivalry for places on the hockey team got too intense. They forgot they're all on the same team, started treating each other like enemies. Maybe some of the parents put a little too much pressure on. . . ." He kicked his desk and stared into the corner awhile. "I'll take my share of blame for that, I guess. My wife will see to that."

"Uh-huh. Rosie thinks the coach got a little overzealous, too."

"The principal's considering that. They're reviewing training procedures. We'll sort out the parts adults have to take the blame for, and I guess there'll be plenty to go around. But the boys have to take responsibility for what they did to each other."

"Any of the injuries serious?"

"No. The worst was to Jason Hadley, the kid P. K. hit with his backpack. At the time he complained that his head hurt bad, but this morning he's being released from the hospital with a clean bill of health. Otherwise it's mostly shiners and scratches. They beat the shit out of half a dozen cars too, did you hear that?"

"Yes. Insurance companies will fix blame for that, huh?"

"If they can, and I guess they always can. I'm prepared to take a major hit on my liability policy."

"Is P. K. in school this morning?"

"Oh, yes, indeed. He's off the team—he got his wish there —but he's in class. I thought for a while he might get suspended from school, too, but then when it turned out the whole hockey team was in the fight, they kind of backed off of that."

"Anybody else getting booted off the team?"

"Maybe Brian Coe. The coach is negotiating for him, trying to cut him a little slack since he's their star goalie, but Coach Munger is not the principal's favorite teacher right now."

"Uh-huh. Frank?"

"What?" He looked at me sharply. "Are you sick, Jake?"

"No," I lied. I took a deep breath. "Somebody has to say this to you." He sat watching me impatiently, dangerously near the boiling point and itching to vent his anger on somebody. I chose my words very carefully, thinking, The truth and nothing but the truth, it better work now. "You've done all you can as a parent, and now you ought to back off and let the department handle the rest of the case."

"What case? There isn't any case, it's just—" He stopped and fixed me in his pale blue bug-eyed stare. I waited. My stomach was doing this awful churning thing; I desperately wanted to get out of this office before I barfed on my superior's desk. But I owed Frank McCafferty big-time, and I knew nobody else around the department was going to take on the boss.

He set his coffee cup down on his desk, thunk, and got up and walked over to his big window. He stood there with his back to me, jingling the keys in his pockets, clearing his throat. Lulu's printer hummed in the outer office, and the soda machine in the hall delivered two cans of refreshing chemicals, tinkle-thump-thump, tinkle-thump-thump. Finally Frank turned halfway around and said, "I guess I was too close to see it."

"Uh-huh."

He jingled for a while longer, cleared his throat again, and came back to his desk.

"All right," he said, "who've you got that can follow up then?"

"Comes time to swallow a frog," Lou French said to me once, "Frank does it as good as anybody."

"I was thinking maybe Rosie," I said, "since she's already in on it."

"Ah. Yes. Rosie would be good." He picked up a stack of papers and knocked them against the desk, and when the bottoms were all even, he set them down again and said, "All right, then! I'll call back all the media people who've been calling me about the Sheets case, and you're gonna keep looking around the Sheets house for the source of that gunshot, and Rosie can finish up with the interviews at school. That where we stand?"

"Right."

"Okay. I've got meetings most of the day, so leave me a note if you get anything new, huh? Because other people will start calling me now—you know everybody's gonna call me as soon as we confirm the boy was shot."

"I know. You'll get everything as fast as we get it." I got out of Frank's office then and stood in the hall, taking deep breaths and counting backward from ninety-one by sevens to settle my stomach. I would be all right, I thought, if the floor would just stop rocking. Then somebody behind me said, "Hey, Jake, you havin' a vision?"

"Well, hi, Andy." Andy Pitman was standing there with his uniform all crooked, looking, as usual, like a messy freckled rube. I wasn't feeling at all cordial, but Andy's not given to casual visits, so I made myself smile and ask him, "How's it going with you?"

"Aw, just finer'n frog hair," he said, grinning all over his doughy, mottled face.

"You're a hard guy to track, you know that? For a while there last fall we saw you in here every day, and now you're practically a stranger."

"I know. Been pretty quiet in my section lately," he said, doing his best to look modest. Last September, when Andy Pitman volunteered to be the POP cop in the Horton Tuck neighborhood, some of his peers privately bet he was going to get his head handed to him on a plate. Problem Oriented Policing follows the old paradigm of the neighborhood cop: one man in blue, walking the beat and talking to people. The idea had been around awhile and proved its merit in half a dozen other sectors in Rutherford before Andy signed on. But we all thought the odds against its success climbed steeply around Horton Tuck, the raunchy low-cost housing unit that the guys in the squads had long ago nicknamed Snort'n' Fuck.

"We shoulda done one of them interventions first," Vince Greeley said, "took my ERU guys in there and kicked some major butt, cleared out a lot of hookers and crack dealers and softened the place up some before we put poor Andy out there alone."

Frank didn't want to do that. He had set up the Emergency Response Unit and put Vince in charge of it, and put the arm on the business community for the extra money to equip it, and he loved the awesome conditioning Vince's troop put themselves through and the relentless way they went through doors and windows when he asked them to. "But you gotta be careful with all that power," he told me. "We don't want to turn it into an Emergency Creation Unit."

So he asked Andy Pitman to have a go at the Horton Tuck section without any opening salvos from ERU. He told Andy to call for backup whenever he needed it, and feel free to dump the assignment if he judged it hopeless. "Andy's a lot smarter than he looks," Frank said. "I'd like to see what he can do."

The first three months were dicey. Andy walked off thirty pounds and made so many arrests my team took to calling him Andy Pit Bull. He became a well-known client at Methodist ER, but none of his injuries were disabling, and he always went right back to work. His luck turned when, late in November, he followed a bad smell down the stairs at Horton Tuck Building Three and found a couple of dead-smelling guys messing with chemicals. He called Bo Dooley, who knew a meth lab when he saw one, and together they put away the entrepreneurs who had been creating much of the urgent need for cash around Horton Tuck.

"Believe it or not, Jake," Andy said now, smiling and stretching, "these days I even got time to help people look for lost dogs."

"Wow. Pitman rules." I moved toward my office, where the message light was blinking on my phone. My headache urgently demanded another glass of water. Andy seemed to be following me, though.

"I didn't think much about the first one," he said, behind me.

The first what? I was having trouble following his drift. And I needed to find Rosie and make several phone calls, and I really had to drink some water.

"—but when three people from my section said their dog was lost, I decided something funny was going on."

Why the holy flaming shit, I thought, looking longingly at my water bottle, does everybody I meet lately want to talk to me about dogs?

Then an odd thing happened. Today's lost-dog story moved into my mind and lined up alongside yesterday's lost-dog story, and I seemed to see this row of lost dogs pointing at something I had overlooked. I wondered if Andy Pitman heard the little click when I saw that his POP section around Horton Tuck lay due east of Billy Sheets' house on Thirteenth Avenue. It was across some railroad tracks surrounded by weeds and trash and loud noises, but actually the west edge of the Horton Tuck sector was only a block away from the east side of the block that faced the Sheets's house.

"Andy," I said, "come in, why don't you? Sit down. You want a glass of water? Tell me about the dogs."

"Couple of weeks ago," he said, sitting down, crossing his legs comfortably, "no, thanks, I don't need any water—a woman in my section called me, very distressed. She'd owned her dog five years, and he had never run away. Now all of a sudden he was gone. I wrote down the dog's description just to be polite, but she'd already notified the pound, so what more could I do? And I mean, a lost pet, even for a POP cop it's a little bit trivial."

Rosie walked past my door. I held up one hand and said,

"Can you hold it right there a minute? I just have to catch—" I jumped into the hall and said, "Rosie!"

She pivoted in place. "What?"

"Will you come see me in about ten minutes? I've got a new job for you."

She opened her mouth to fire questions at me, but maybe I looked even worse than I felt, because after a couple of seconds she shrugged and said, "Sure."

I went back in my office, where Andy was standing by his chair. "You're busy," he said, "I'll make this short."

"It's not like that, I just had to—" I stopped and stared at my desk, where Andy Pitman had laid four spent bullets. "Where'd you get those?"

"After the third lost-dog report I started looking in the bushes and going through Dumpsters. Day before yesterday I found two dead dogs. We had a vet autopsy 'em, and she found these." He regarded them soberly. "They're a little misshapen from hitting bone, but I'm hoping they're still in good enough shape to identify the gun that fired them."

"Traditional rifling," I said. "Right-hand twist."

"Uh-huh. Probably a .22, don't you think?"

"If I had to say, that's what I'd say. But I don't have to say because BCA will do that. Andy, do you know that the little boy who died yesterday was shot?"

"That's why I'm here. Eldon Huckstadt told me this morning." He shrugged uneasily. "I know it sounds kind of crazy to suggest a connection—"

"Not to me," I said. "Will you let me have these, to get 'em tested?"

"Will you make sure I get 'em back if they're not a match? Because my dog owners—"

"Are gonna want some action. I know. You'll get 'em back with a copy of the BCA report, and we'll help you find your dog slayer if these don't match the bullet we took out of Billy Sheets."

"But if they do—"

"Then you and I are looking for the same sharpshooter, and we better hope we find him soon."

"Jesus. How long will the tests take?"

"Depends on what priority they give it. Let me get on the phone, see what I can negotiate, and I'll let you know."

"Okay." He turned toward the doorway and collided with Rosie Doyle coming in.

"Hey, Andy Pit Bull, where ya been?" She gave him a radiant smile. Rosie had become a huge fan of Andy's during his hard autumn days around Horton Tuck. She had raved about his courage, his moxie, his street smarts, so much that Kevin, accustomed to getting the lion's share of female approval, finally sneered, "Boy, you really got the hots for this guy, haven't you?"

"Watch your mouth," Rosie said. "Do you have any idea how abusive the men in my family would get if they thought I was falling for a married man?" Her expression conveyed only humorous irony, but later I reflected that she was the only one in the division who seemed to know that Andy Pitman was married.

"Hey, Rosie Posie," Andy said now, "ain't it a shame? We put those meth cowboys away, and now I hardly ever get to see you."

"Hey, yeah, dumb mistake," she said, dimpling attractively. She regarded him closely for a moment and said, "You brought us some juicy dirt today, though, huh?" Not even sexual titillation stifled Rosie's curiosity.

"You're gonna hear all about it, Rosie—come on in and sit down." I waved to Andy, saying, "Be in touch." He pointed a finger at the dimple flashing in Rosie's left cheek, waggled it suggestively, and galumphed off down the hall.

"Hang on," I said, dialing, "I just hafta do a couple of—" Darrell answered his phone, and I told him, "Unless your hair is on fire, I want you in here this minute."

"Okay," he said, "but don't you want me to—" I took a page from Lulu's book and hung up on him.

I speed-dialed BCA and asked for the ballistics section, amazed myself by getting Willy on the first ring, and asked him, "If I said I had a crazed gunman who I believe has recently graduated from shooting dogs to shooting children, could you give high priority to finding out if the four bullets I've got on my desk match the one we sent you yesterday?"

"High priority like this week, or—?"

"I was thinking maybe immediately." After a little silence, I said, "Or soon? Maybe quite soon?"

"I probably could get close to quite soon," Willy said, "if I knew for certain your crazed gunman wasn't standing on a pile of shit. Are you by any chance prone to hyperbole, Jake?"

"Absolutely not," I said. "I maybe sneeze a little sometimes in dogwood season, but—"

"Okay, smart-ass." He snorted a couple of times and then said, "So, you think you got something red-hot?" I explained my urgent need to know whether the bullets out of two dead dogs matched the bullet I had sent him yesterday.

"Uh-huh. Uh-huh. That's a .22 Long Rifle, by the way. We can tell you later today what make of gun fired it. Not going to be an exotic, I can tell you that right now."

"Good man. So if I send these bullets to you right this minute—?" Darrell was standing in the doorway, and I motioned him in.

"I'll get to them as soon as I can. Probably sometime today. Go nag somebody else now for a while."

I pulled on gloves, packed cotton balls around the four bullets, slid them into four plastic tubes with stoppers, and put the tubes in paper bags. I told Darrell to make up evidence sheets with the ICR number we were using for Billy Sheets, check the bullets in at our evidence room and right out again, and take them to BCA.

"And if you can," I said, "if they'll let you do it, check them in at the evidence desk there and then walk them over to ballistics yourself and hand them to Willy. If they won't let you take the bullets over there yourself, go over anyway and tell Willy they're out there. He promised me high priority, and I want to be sure he's reminded. Tactfully, of course."

"You got it," Darrell said.

"Be brisk," I said. "Eat later, okay?"

"Affirmative." He charged out of the room, looking like Overkill, Inc., holding up the tiny paper sacks with his weight-lifter's muscles.

"Now, Rosie," I said, "where are you with those search warrants?"

"Just finished the forms," she said, "haven't found a judge yet, but listen—"

"Give them to Lou. Tell him I said find the judge and get the warrants signed."

"Okay, but Jake—"

"*What?*"

"You said I was gonna hear all about what Pitman brought you."

"You will, but not now. Right now I want you to go back up to Central School." I told her about the conversation with the chief. "You're cleared to finish the investigation, he approved you."

"He did? Well, now." She gave a little shake of satisfaction and then grew thoughtful. "It never was clear to me yesterday," she said, "*is* this a police investigation? Or are we just helping the principal tidy up?"

"It wasn't clear because the chief was there both as the chief and as a parent," I said, "an ambiguity you're going to clear up today."

"I am? How?"

"By taking charge of the case. I don't think this is a police matter, really, but in view of the level of hostility involved, it seems reasonable to ask a few more questions. Begin by talking to the two hockey players nobody could find yesterday, what's their names?"

"Uh . . . Owen Campbell and Butch Ranfranz."

"Yeah, them. Better talk to P. K. too, and the kid who came to his rescue, the hair puller. Who else?"

"Well, Jason Hadley, of course. He went to the hospital shortly after we got there, nobody talked to him, but I hear he's in school this morning. And Brian Coe. The mouth. The chief may have talked to him, but I never heard what he said about the fight."

"Good. All of those."

"Are you looking for something specific, Jake, besides who hit whom with what, whose car is messed up?"

"I'm curious about what exactly Hadley said that started this mess. Tell them you've got to have a straight answer on that, don't let them buffalo you with this code-of-silence crap. Word for word, what did he say, and why did it make P. K. so mad? And where were P. K.'s two best buddies during the fight? What's their names again? Owen Campbell, that's it, and—"

"Butch Ranfranz."

"There you go. If they're such good friends of P. K.'s, why didn't they come to his rescue? Tell all these kids that if they can't convince you they're telling the whole story at school, you're going to bring them to the station and charge them with . . . uh—"

"Disturbing the peace?"

"Yeah, or something worse. Inciting to riot, how's that? Maybe assault, if we get really annoyed."

"I hate to bluff. Are you really ready to get tough with these kids?"

"If they won't tell us what's going on, yes, I am. Tragedies have been happening at schools all over the country. Afterward somebody always says, I guess we should have asked more questions, maybe we could have done something about it."

"Uh-huh. The principal is kind of a piece of work," she said thoughtfully. "One minute he's all over the kids threatening suspension, but then when *we* start interrogating them, he gets quite protective."

"Then eliminate him as an influence."

"What, you mean keep him out of the interviews?"

"Yes. Tell him you need to talk to the boys alone. If he protests, tell him you're ready to put every boy that was in that fight in front of a juvenile court judge, but if he'll leave you alone to do your job, you'll try to handle it at school."

"Whee. I can really say that to a high school principal?"

"Sure. You're a police detective, you can say whatever you need to. Listen to me, Rosie. I don't think this is anything serious, but I promised the chief we'd take care of it, and I want it taken care of, cleared up beyond question, and off everybody's desk."

"I gotcha."

"Good. Here's another thing I don't understand: if the cause of this fight is the rivalry for places on the hockey team, if P. K. McCafferty and Owen and Butch cared that much about playing, why have they been trying to quit?"

"They have?"

"Yes. They just couldn't get their dads to say okay. And the two big stars, Jason Hadley and Brian Coe, if they're so flamin' good they've got the top spots locked up, what are *they* mad about? A lot of what I've been hearing just doesn't make sense."

"Fights hardly ever do make sense, Jake."

"On the surface, maybe, but anger does, if you get to the bottom of it."

"So you think I should make everybody say what they're so mad about?"

"Yes. And don't let them blow any more smoke. Call for backup and bring them in here if you're not getting straight answers."

"Fine. Excellent!" She stood up.

"Remember, crying is also an evasion."

"Hey, you're talking to a Doyle, remember?" She smiled grimly. "We all went to parochial school."

"So?"

"You think those nuns were easy? The Doyle kids practically wrote the book on tricks and evasions."

"Is that why so many of you ended up in law enforcement?"

"Nah, we're mostly in it for the graft." She flashed a shit-eating grin and strode out of my office, bristling with competitive zeal. She knew the chief would have his eye on the reports from Central School, and she knew I could have sent Darrell back up there today.

I stuck my head into the small meeting room, where Kevin and Ray were bent over a chart, shuffling notes. "How's your map coming?"

"Taking a little longer than we figured. There's a lot of information to coordinate—"

"After lunch then?"

"Sounds good."

Lou was at his desk with his phone tucked into his shoulder, digging a cough drop out of a sack with his left hand and taking notes with his right. "Uh-huh," he said. "Uh-huh, sure." I made a time-out signal, and he put the caller on hold. I asked him, "You find a judge yet?"

"Caldwell. He'll be out of court in about ten minutes, I'm headed there after this call."

Back at my desk, the clock said 11:15. For no reason, I got a mental image of Trudy, working at her desk in St. Paul, and thought, This is ridiculous, we have to talk. My hands went sweaty as I dialed her number, so that I almost dropped the phone while I listened to it ring four times. Her recorded voice came on and suggested I leave a message. When the beeps stopped I said in a strangled voice, "Trudy, will you call me, please?" I put the phone down quickly and sat watching my hand shake, thinking, Well, that was brilliant.

Shamelessly in search of comfort now, I called Maxine. She answered with the brisk uninflected hello of the day-care provider. She usually has at least one toddler in her arms and several others yelling for attention, so she favors short words and simple sentences.

"How about lunch?" I said. "I could bring pizza."

"Oh, Jake, I've got a great big pan of soup on, just come over."

"Sure? I'll bring some cookies, then."

"That'll be fine, honey."

Maxine is my foster mother. Actually, she is one of six or seven women the state of Minnesota paid to raise me, but Maxine was the best, the one I stayed with longest and grieved for when they took me away from her. A couple of months ago, after years of fruitless searches, I found her by a lucky accident.

Since then I'd been seeing her often. She'd come out to the farm several times, and she and Trudy got along great. Lately I'd been indulging in idle daydreams in which I was beamed at from two sides by a clever mate and a doting mother. This stupid fight with Trudy didn't fit anywhere in that picture.

I tapped on my desk with an eraser, cracked my knuckles,

made a chain out of paper clips, and drank some more water. Finally I looked up a number in Owatonna, thinking, Not now, of course, but maybe I'll call her later. Then I dialed it quickly without thinking, and heard Trudy's sister say, "Hello?"

"Bonnie, have you talked to Trudy today?"

"Jake?" She made three syllables out of my name. "What's wrong?"

"Have you?"

"No. Haven't you?"

"No. She, um, decided to stay in town for a while, I guess."

"Jake, what did you do to her?"

"Nothing! She just—she got mad about something." Besides the awkward subject matter, part of my problem was that I had hardly ever spoken directly to Bonnie, who had made no secret of her opinion that Trudy was "throwing herself away" when she moved in with me. "If you see her," I said, "will you tell her I called?"

She said something under her breath that sounded like, "Mama."

"What?"

"I said I wonder if she's with Mama."

"Oh . . . I don't think so. They haven't, um, been getting along very well."

"Mama's been driving her bananas! Ragging on her about you, if you want to know."

"Oh, yeah? Why?"

"Well . . . she's just dead set against you, Jake, because you're divorced, and besides, you're . . . " Her voice trailed off.

I waited, and finally said, "I'm what?"

"You're not exactly white."

"Ah."

"See, Mama's got this real twitch about respectability, about what everybody's gonna *think*. So she hates that Trudy's living with a man she's not married to, but then she says it'll be even worse if she does marry you, that'll ruin her life for sure."

"Uh-huh. Well." I had never given Bonnie much thought, beyond being grateful that Trudy was nothing like her. She seemed high-strung and conflicted, a tense shrew like their mother, always ready to bite and scratch. Now all I wanted was to get off the phone.

"Well," I said again, "guess I'd better let you go."

"I'm sorry, Jake—"

"Not at all," I said. "Thanks for your time."

Lou walked in as I hung up the phone. He laid an envelope on my desk, and said, "Here you go."

I looked at him and blinked.

"Your search warrants, Jake."

"Oh! Yes! Very good. Thanks." He watched while I got up and began to button my coat. "Anything I can help you with, Jake?"

"Nope. This is all I need." I waved the envelope at him and walked toward the door, but I could feel his eyes on my back. Lou French was the oldest, canniest head in the section. If his asthma hadn't partially disabled him, he'd probably have had my job, and I'd be working for him. He'd never shown any resentment, but I'd always been careful to treat him right and keep him in my corner. So I closed the door from the inside, turned with my hand on the doorknob, and said, "I look like hell because I'm hung over. I went out and got totally plotzed last night after a fight with my girl. Now she's gone, and I'm trying to find some way to get her back, but in the meantime, the investigations in this office must proceed as planned. Okay?"

"Oh, absolutely." He coughed and said, "Glad it's nothing serious."

"Right." I decided not to even wonder how ironic he was being. "I guess, uh, we'll all be out of the office again this afternoon, except maybe Bo. So will you act as home base again, till we all get back?"

"Which will be when?"

"Later today. I think."

He winked and said, "Glad we cleared that up."

6

"GLAD to see you," Maxine said, and put her face up. I kissed her cheek and plucked a plump toddler off her chest.

"Jeez, this one's heavy," I said. "You should get down and walk, kid." He smiled shyly around the thumb he was sucking and buried his head in my chest.

"Here, let him get his coat off, kids," Maxine said. Two small but tenacious rug rats were already clinging to my knees. Maxine's house should have a sign on the door, "Caution, Great Need for Attention Inside."

I looked down and found Nelly Dooley smiling up at me. She is Bo Dooley's child and closely resembles him; she has his auburn curls growing close to the scalp, and the same air of poised self-possession, almost comical in such a small child.

"You can hang your coat on this first hook," Nelly said. "It's okay if it covers up mine."

"Thanks, Nelly. How you been?"

"Fine. My mom sent me a card, you wanna see it?"

"Sure." She streaked across the room to a row of shoe boxes on a bookshelf. She took a card out of the box with her name on it, ran back, and showed it to me. Bright-colored balloons were printed above the words "Happy Birthday!" and a big number 3. It was signed, in a shaky hand, "Mom," with no personal message added. Nelly's mother was in treatment for the third time in five years, trying to kick a cocaine habit that never seemed to turn her loose.

A small round mirror slid out of the card when Nelly opened it. She caught it and held it up to show me. "This is my Mom's mirror, see? From her purse. Dad says it's okay if I play with it." She looked at me searchingly and asked, "I don't think she'd be mad, do you?"

"I think she'd be glad to know you like it," I said. Nelly tucked it carefully back in the dog-eared birthday card and took the card back to her shoe box. When I lived with Maxine, I had a box like that, on the nightstand in the room I shared with Maxine's daughter Patsy. Patsy was a year younger than I was, and blind, so she wasn't in any position to snoop on my side of the room even if she'd wanted to, but even so the stuff in my box meant a lot to me. I kept my best marbles in there, a whistle and some prizes from Cracker Jack boxes, and for a while, once, a tiny turtle that I found by the river.

"Soup's ready," Maxine said. "Let's eat right away so you have a minute to sit afterward. Are these the—" She stopped herself before the dread word *cookie* had passed her lips, and stuffed the package quickly onto a high shelf. "Oh, and milk, good for you."

A variety of high chairs and booster seats crowded around her cheap plastic table. The bigger kids knew where they belonged and began climbing like Sherpas up the legs and sides of chairs. Maxine and I lifted smaller kids and tied on bibs.

"Watch your head, LeRoy, here comes the tray. Josh, are you sitting on your bib? Now, let's see," I said, "I don't think I know this handsome young man."

"That's Eddy. He just came to live with me, um, Sunday night," Maxine said. "Eddy, this is Jake, he used to live with me too. Can you shake hands with Jake?" A thin brown-haired boy put his left hand up, without moving his gaze from the edge of the table in front of him.

I held his cold, weightless fingers for a moment, said, "Happy to meet you, Eddy," and gave his hand back to him. He never looked at me or spoke.

"You can sit there, between Eddy and Nelly," Maxine said. "Eddy doesn't know anybody here yet, so he doesn't have much to say, but he knows when he's hungry, don't you, babe?" If he responded to her in any way it was too subtle for me to see, but she smiled at him anyway, filled her big ladle to the brim, and poured soup into his bowl. She was right about his hunger. He bent over his bowl and spooned soup into himself with intense concentration.

Maxine and I poured milk and passed crackers, picked up dropped spoons and mopped up a couple of spills. Finally they all settled down, and we started on our own soup.

"This is good," I said. "What is it?"

"Oh, kind of hamburger and leftovers." The table was quiet for a few minutes of peaceful soup slurping. Then LeRoy, the fat little clinger I had picked off Maxine's chest earlier, got full and began to beat on the tray of his high chair with his spoon, humming three loud notes over and over. That set off a general growing restlessness, and when Joshua started crushing his last cracker into Nelly's ear, Maxine said, "Anybody here want a chocolate chip cookie?"

All but Eddy yelled, "Yes!" and grabbed a cookie from her hand as if it might be their last. Eddy sat quiet, watching a space on the table in front of him. When Maxine laid a cookie there he snatched it and stuffed it in his mouth.

Maxine brought a couple of washcloths from the kitchen and wiped hands and faces while I lifted down and brushed off. She told them, "Today you can have a movie instead of a story before nap time," and put a cassette in the VCR. The smallest ones got propped against pillows on the floor, and Maxine dictated places on the couch for the bigger ones, putting Eddy on the end with Nelly between him and the other boys.

"Now," she said, sliding the divider within six inches of the doorjamb, "cup of coffee?"

"Wonderful." I was at the sink, rinsing bowls and cups.

"Leave that, now, come and sit." She was always trying to get me to rest. She seemed to think I kept up an exhausting pace in law enforcement, perhaps giving chase over shoulder-high fences like the cops on TV. Conversely, I had begun to feel bad about every minute I spent sitting down in Maxine's house, now that I had seen with adult eyes how much hard labor went into her day-care operation.

"Tell me about Eddy," I said. "Are you going back to foster care?" I felt an unreasonable twinge of jealousy, asking her that; from things she'd said since I found her, I'd concluded that she had not had a foster child since the calamitous day when I was nine, when her husband Lucas went to jail for kiting checks and drinking up my aid money and I got pulled, literally kicking and screaming, away from her household by my caseworker.

"Maybe. I lost my license when they took you away, you know, and for a long time I was so sad about everything. . . . Lucas was in jail, and you were gone. . . . I didn't care enough to try to get it back."

"How'd you manage?"

"I didn't. I went on welfare, can you imagine?" She pushed her hair out of her eyes, a gesture I remembered from when her hair was brown. It was nearly all white now, and today her mismatched eyes looked tired, the brown one shadowed and the green one lacking its usual sparkle. "Finally I came out of my fog enough to realize Patsy was finding one excuse after another not to go to school in the morning and then just lying on the couch all day, hugging a stuffed toy and singing to herself. So I made an appointment with the director of special ed, and he helped me get her admitted to the Academy for the Blind in Faribault."

"As a boarding student?"

"Yup. It's state supported, which was important because I didn't have squat in the way of money."

"Must have been hard to let her go, though."

"Tell me about it. She was all I had left. And she was scared to leave home. She cried so hard I almost couldn't go through with it."

I touched her hand. "The things we do for love, huh?"

"Amen. But it was exactly the right thing at the right time. She perked right up when she got in a place where everyone around her was blind. One of the main things they do is show the kids how to have fun and make the best of it. She learned braille and typing, and before long she was getting snooty with me because I didn't know how to work a computer. She was always bright, you know. And kind of sassy."

"I know. How's she doing now?"

"Fantastic. She got an education degree and went back to work for the school. Teaches computer skills, mostly. Helps with a handicapped riding program at a farm near there."

"Horseback riding?"

"Sounds impossible, doesn't it? But you should see them go."

"You see her often?"

"She comes to visit on the bus sometimes." She sat quiet a minute and then rocked her hand in an expression of ambivalence. "We don't see eye to eye much anymore. Pardon the expression. She's into New Age stuff. Crystals?" Her eyebrows did a little dance. "Anyway! After I got her in the school, I did housecleaning in Faribault for a while, just to stay near her. Eventually I got a job at a day-care center there."

"I figured that's how I'd find you, through your child-care license. But you never came up on any screen I could find."

"Well, for a long time I didn't even try to get my license back, I just worked by the hour for the owner of the center. Slave wages. But it was a way to stay close to Patsy, so I stuck with it till she got through school. Then I looked around for a town with plenty of working mamas and decided on Rutherford. Took the tests for a day-care license and rented this house."

"But about Eddy, now—"

"Well, lately I've been talking to CCRR—"

"Is that the supervising agency now?"

"Yeah. Child Care Resource and Referral. They're always short of people for foster care, and there's a Mrs. Armitage there, encouraged me to get reinstated. I was being sort of arm's length with her, though, because, see, there's a couple of things about this house that aren't quite up to code."

"What, plumbing, you mean, or—?"

"One antique bathroom, yeah. And some of the wiring. . . ." She squirmed in her chair. "Don't turn me in, now."

"Maxine. You're the best child care provider I've ever

known. I'm just trying to be sure I understand your situation."

"Well, my situation is there's two or three dozen little kids needing day care for every licensed operator that's available, so it's pretty easy to get a waiver from the supervisors. They're in trouble, too, they got all these welfare mothers that have to go to work to keep the country safe for politicians— Don't get me started on politics."

"I won't. So Mrs. Armitage asked you to take Eddy?"

"Yeah. Last week when the shooting happened, she said, 'I think I know somebody who'll take Eddy right now, and I'll figure out the paperwork later.' "

"Wait a minute. What shooting?"

Maxine leaned across the table and murmured, "Eddy's one of the Payson kids."

"The ones whose father—"

She nodded, grimly. "Eddy's the only one left."

I remembered, now: a despondent farmer on a failing acreage in the northwest corner of the county who shot his wife and four of his children before turning the gun on himself. The sheriff's department got the call, but I read part of the report. There was one survivor who hid in the cellar. They had quite a time coaxing him out.

"No wonder he won't talk."

"Or look at anybody. He watches the space in front of himself and a little on both sides."

"Is he any better when you're alone?"

"Never changes. No expression at all."

"Must be hard for you."

"He has trouble sleeping, that's what's hard. They gave me pills for him, but I don't like to give sleeping pills to a little kid. I made up a bed in my room, and I've been reading and singing to him till he can fall asleep."

"Are you going to be able to manage that and all your day-care kids too?"

"It's kind of tough right now. But Jason's going back to his grandmother after next week, and Nelly's mother should be home soon."

"I don't think Bo will leave Nelly with her mother for a while."

"Really? Diane has to get discharged and *then* pass the Bo Dooley test? Shee."

"She left Nelly alone in the house all day, went out looking to score."

"Oh, I know. We're all doing the best we can, aren't we?"

"Usually. I been falling a little short here lately." I looked at my watch. "I gotta go."

"Well, just a minute, now." She gave me her straight look. "You came over here to tell me what's wrong, didn't you? So tell."

"You a wizard now? I came to see you, what's wrong with that?"

"Nothing. I love it. So what's wrong?"

"Maxine—" I squirmed and waved my arms awhile. It was hard to say it out loud. "Trudy's—"

"What?"

"Gone."

"Gone, like gone visiting?" I shook my head. "Gone in a huff?" I nodded emphatically. "You know when she's coming back?" I shook my head. "You mean," Maxine said, watching me carefully, "you did something that made her really mad, and now she's gone somewhere to sulk till you crawl to her on your hands and knees?"

"Bingo. You have such a gift for precision, Maxine."

"I was married for some time," she said drily. "So." Her mismatched eyes searched my face. "You going to start crawling right after lunch?"

"I'm a police detective. I have an investigation to continue after lunch."

"But along toward five o'clock, you'll be getting down on your knees—?"

"I don't know." I got up and found my coat. "See, this isn't just some little spat, like I forgot a birthday or left the toilet seat up. Trudy got so mad she *attacked* me."

"Attacked—you mean she hit you?"

"No. She threw my boots out the door."

"Why?"

"I don't know! I was eating my cereal, as blameless as a new-born baby I thought, and I asked her if she'd like to go ice fishing—"

"Ice fishing? Why?"

"That's what she said. I gotta go to work."

"Now, wait a minute. After she threw your boots out, what did *you* throw?"

"Nothing! We both went to work, and when we came home we fought over the neighbor's dog."

"The neighbor's—"

"Don't ask. That time I got so enraged I went into town and got utterly shit-faced. So now I'm not blameless anymore, but for some reason I still feel mad as hell, and besides that I'm critically hung over and scared and sad. And Trudy's so disgusted she's left me."

"Wow." She had begun stacking the remaining lunch dishes in front of her place, absentmindedly replacing unused crackers in the box and wiping up cookie crumbs into a mound. "You two are moving right along, aren't you?"

"Whaddya mean?"

"You're already having the kind of fights married people have."

"Oh, Jesus." I buttoned my coat. "I was sure we could do better than that." I kissed her. "Thanks for lunch."

She followed me to the door and stood with her head out, watching me scuff through the salt she had spread on her icy sidewalk. When I was almost to my truck, she called, "Take care of yourself, Flaky Jakey."

I'd forgotten about the silly name game Maxine and I used to play when I left the house. I reached far back through shreds of other memories, searching for one of my old names for her. She was smiling in the cold doorway, and her breath made a great white plume of steam that rose around her head. I called back to the cloud, "You too, Waxy Maxy."

Kevin and Ray were bent over the table in the small meeting room, fussing over their chart, which had grown lumpy and colorful with Post-its, taped photos, and inked notes in three colors. I asked their backsides, "You about ready to take that thing for a test run?"

Ray's melancholy eyes peered around his arm; seeing me, he straightened, rubbed his back, and pointed at Kevin. "This man is a bottomless bucket, I can't fill him up."

"You're gonna be proud of us, Jake," Kevin crowed. "We got this neighborhood *nailed*." He asked Ray, "Where's the cover?"

Ray pulled a crackling sheet of butcher paper out of the closet and laid it over their complicated masterwork. They taped the top and put binder clips on the bottom. Kevin ran downstairs and checked out a car; they loaded their chart in the back, and I followed them in my pickup.

We parked in front of the Sheets house, which was still dark and empty, with tatters of crime scene tape flapping against its shabby green-painted door. Getting out of the car, Kevin nodded up the street, where three cars were parked in front of the pink stucco house.

"Mrs. Waymire's bridge club," he announced with great satisfaction, "meets every other Wednesday. They have lunch and then play cards all afternoon, and before they go home they have one drink, usually an old-fashioned."

"Okay, I'm impressed, Agent Smart. What say I put my tailgate down and we put your chart there?"

They folded the cover over the back and we lined the chart up with the street, weighting the corners with flashlights and cell phones.

"First," I said, "can you tell me who was around Billy Sheets when he fell down?"

"Yes. Here." Kevin detached one of the several handwritten lists taped to the upper right-hand corner of the chart and began to read. "Kids first. Jack and Mitzy Nordquist from the tan house on the corner. Two O'Connell boys, Troy and Shawn, live two blocks north. Their dad is Jim and Kay's third son. And Justin Frink, Benny Luntz, and Mary Lou Fitzpatrick, all from different sides of these two blocks. Seven kids from grades one through six, the usual bunch that waits for the bus here every school day."

"Nobody different?"

"No. Then the adults. Jim and Kay O'Connell, out for their walk. Joanne Horske waiting for the bus with her grandson Justin. Lyle Eickhoff walking his dog. And just before Billy fell down, Angie Sheets came out of her house and stood on the step."

"That's it? There were a lot more people around when I got here."

"Oh, well, everybody agrees that after Billy fell down and the police and ambulance arrived, a crowd gathered, and nobody's able to say who they all were."

"There was a girl on skates—"

"And the school bus driver, for a while, and half a dozen youngish men and two girls that nobody knew. They just came and went, sight-seeing. The TV truck was here. We were all here. It turned into a crowd scene. But in spite of the confusion, the stories I got from people in the neighborhood were remarkably consistent, regarding who was here just before Billy Sheets fell down. The answer is, all the usual people."

"Okay. Let's go on to the buildings on the block. Did you find names for all of them, Ray?"

"Yup. It's all public record, do the legwork and you got it." Ray started at the right-hand corner ahead of us. "Eighteen-ninety-eight. Tan stucco bungalow, occupied by owners, Herman and Bertha Nordquist, two children. Eighteen-eighty-eight, gray duplex, owned by Clagstad Realty, occupied by John and Tammy Mercer, she's the one got the hots for Kevin so bad she stood out in the cold with no coat on yesterday—"

"Come on," Kevin said, smirking.

"—and Willard and Mae Freeman, no children. Eighteen-seventy-eight is Sheetses—" He went on, talking his way to the north end of the street, pointing; at the end of the block he turned ten degrees and said, "Across the street—"

"Wait. Let's come down to the south end and work our way north again."

"Okay. Begin with the old two-story house on the corner, unoccupied," Ray said. "Belongs to Ernie Chisholm."

"Ernie Chisholm that owns Chisholm Construction?"

"Yes."

"You talked to him yet?"

"About what?"

"Aw, hell, we never finished our meeting this morning, did we?" I went over the results of yesterday afternoon's work with Ted Zumwalt's laser pointer. When I finished, we all contemplated the attic window on the dingy old house across the street. "Unoccupied, huh? That sounds convenient. Hold onto your chart here, I'm gonna use this phone and call Ernie." When I picked up the phone, Kevin grabbed the corner of the chart it had been holding down, and meticulously eased a photo back into its slot.

"If you've got a warrant," Ray said, "why talk to him? Why don't we just go search the place?"

"Ernie Chisholm's a very solid citizen. Been in business, well, what?"

Ray shrugged. "Twenty years. At least."

"Seems fair to assume if anybody's shooting a gun out of his attic, it's without his knowledge. Let's ask him to show us the house." I dug the phone book out of the pile of detritus that seems to accumulate of its own accord on the right-hand seat of my pickup and leaned into my cab to stay out of the breeze while I dialed the number. A secretary answered, asked me to hold, and in a few seconds Ernie's deep-chested baritone said, "Chisholm."

"Ernie, this is Jake Hines." He repaired a front step for me, once, in another life when I was married. He came exactly when he said he would to make the estimate, and sent his crew, just as he promised, two days later to do the work. When they were done, he called to tell me the job didn't take as long as he thought it would, and sent me a bill for thirty-six dollars and fifty cents less than I'd agreed to. Since then I've always thought of him as the guy who should be running the world. "You own the two-story house at eighteen-ninety-seven Thirteenth Avenue?"

"Yup."

"Nobody lives there, huh?"

"It's a pretty old house, Jake, it's not really in shape to rent. I use it to store records and small supplies, sometimes do a little prep work there. Why?"

"You know about the little boy that was shot on this block yesterday?"

"Oh by God that's right, that was in my block, wasn't it? I saw the story in the paper. Damn shame. What, uh . . . "

I told him about the search we'd made for the source of the bullet, and the way the red dot landed on the attic window of his old house. His silence lasted so long I thought I'd lost him somehow, and said, "Ernie?"

His voice had dropped about an octave by the time he answered me. "Are you suggesting I shot that kid?"

"Of course not. I'm saying the evidence points to a limited number of locations in the area where that bullet could have come from, and we have to search those locations."

"Well, you can put your mind to rest as far as my building is concerned. I keep it locked up tight, and I'm the only one who has a key."

"I still need to look at it, Ernie."

"Oh, come on," he said, impatiently. "Can't you take my word for it?"

"A child was murdered," I said. "If he was your kid, would you want the cops to take any shortcuts?"

"Mmm. Well. Okay, if you gotta see it, I can meet you there sometime tomorrow morning."

He was perfectly polite and reasonable, but something about the high-handed way he named the time made me want to raise the bar a little. "I'm sorry," I said, "I need to search that house this afternoon."

"Well, you can't! I'm too busy today."

"You don't have to be here. I'll send somebody for the keys."

"In a pig's eye!" I had moved toward the rear of my truck while I talked to him, and when he yelled at me, I touched Ray's elbow. Ray quit fiddling with his notebook and began to watch me. Kevin, seeing Ray's sudden stillness, stepped close and put his head next to my phone. "Nobody goes on my property when I'm not around! No, no, we're not gonna do that."

"Ernie, this is a courtesy call. I've got a search warrant, I can go in without you."

"Goddamn son of a—" Just in time, he remembered he was talking to the law. He sucked in a lot of air and went silent for a few seconds, muttered something to himself, and finally said, "I will be at that house in exactly one hour. And I better not find you inside." He punched off without saying good-bye.

I stepped away from Kevin, who had his right ear pasted to the outside of my phone, and said, "Well, now."

"Mr. Solid Citizen doesn't want us in his house just now," Kevin said.

Ray said, "We're not gonna stand here and wait for him, are we?"

"Hell, no. Put the chart in the department car. Drive it around the corner onto Nineteenth Street and tuck it up in the alley there. I'm gonna back up and park behind the bridge players. We can all sit in my cab."

It took Ray four minutes to park the car and get back. Three minutes after he joined Kevin and me in the truck, we heard Ernie Chisholm's diesel four-by-four coming east on Nineteenth Street very fast. He hit the pothole west of the intersection, bounced hard enough to loosen every bolt in his rig, skidded around the corner, and slid to a stop in front of his house. He hopped quickly out from under the wheel and hurried up the front walk, head down, so intent on finding the right key on his ring that he didn't notice us following till we bracketed him on the top step. He saw Kevin first on his right, said, "What—?" turned left, saw Ray, wheeled, and found me behind him. "What's going on?"

"We'll go in with you," I said, and watched his clear blue eyes darken with anger.

"What kinda bullshit—" For a minute, I thought he might swing on me. Then he controlled himself with an effort and turned back to the door. His hands shook a little as they unlocked it. We followed him into the dark, uncarpeted hall. "There, goddammit, see? It's just like I told you, a bunch of old records." The bare floor of the living room was stacked high with cardboard bankers' boxes full of hanging files. Across the hall, what must once have been a dining room held a ladder, a couple of sawhorses, some stacked lumber, and two cases of fluorescent tubes. "Some tools and equipment. What else do you want to see?"

"We're mostly interested in the attic," I said.

"The attic? Not much of an attic. More like a crawl space. Hope you're ready to do some climbing." He folded the ladder and Ray helped him carry it upstairs. He set it up in the hall, mounted halfway to the top, and handed down the cover from a hatch in the ceiling. As soon as Ray took it, Ernie climbed, with the ease of long practice, to the top of the ladder, reached through the hatch for an upright, and pulled himself up into the dark attic. After a few seconds a dim light went on in the space above the hatch, and Ernie's face appeared in the opening. "Watch your head. The tallest part's just over five feet."

Already halfway up the ladder, I looked down and met Ray's and Kevin's eyes looking up at me. I was sure we were all thinking the same thing—that he was calmer now that we had started up into the attic. Whatever was bothering him in this house was not up here.

The single hanging bulb lit an unimproved attic under the rafters, bristling with splinters and nails. The four of us, bent over in the dim cobwebby space, could barely move.

"Maybe you could sit on top of the ladder," I suggested to Ernie, "would you?" He leaned on his arms in the hatch opening and watched us bump into each other and bang our heads on rafters. We found only an open box of wallpaper, crackly with age and very dusty, and a set of rolled blueprints held by rubber bands that fell apart in my hands when I touched them. The only opening besides the hatch was the window in the gable end that we had seen from the Sheetses' yard.

"How do I open it?"

"Hook at the top," Ernie said. Ray put on gloves and tried it, but the hook had rusted shut, and the wood frame had swollen.

"Forget it," I said after a minute, "that window hasn't been opened in some time."

"You seen enough? Can we go now?" Ernie said. He kept looking at his watch; he really did seem anxious about the time, and I began to wonder if I had misread an irritable middle-aged entrepreneur with scheduling problems. I came back down the ladder wiping sweat off my face.

"You keep the house heated, huh?"

"Sure. Pipes'd freeze otherwise."

But why did Ernie Chisholm need to keep old records at seventy degrees? Living in an ancient farmhouse had sensitized me to the cost of heating poorly insulated spaces. "You don't have a water shutoff? Or a thermostat?"

"You worried about my operating expenses now?" He folded the ladder fast and said, "Let's go."

"What's in these rooms on the second floor?"

"Nothing. I'm not using the second floor at all."

"Are they locked?" I turned the handle nearest me, and a door swung open onto a bare-floored space with an ancient iron bedstead, and rolled shades pulled down to the window sills.

"Satisfied?" Ernie said. "Ready to go?" The pugnacious tone was back in his voice. He was anxious again as he had not been while we were in the attic.

"Sure," I said. Ray picked up the front of the ladder, Ernie took the rear, and they started toward the stairs. I stepped to the end of the hall and tried the door there. It was locked. "Let's have a look in this room first, though, huh?"

He had started down; he stood below me on the first step and roared, "Oh, for *Christ's sake*—"

"Ernie? What's wrong?"

The woman's voice came from the bottom of the stairs. She stood looking up at Ernie, anxious and uncertain. She was probably thirty, give or take, with light brown hair to her shoulders and big eyeglasses with clear plastic rims. She was dressed, like half the women in Minnesota in February, in wool pants, boots, and a quilted coat.

"Oh . . . Karen." Chisholm's face had flushed bright red. "Listen, thanks, but . . . uh . . . I won't be needing those records after all." He sent her a tiny head shake.

She waited just a heartbeat, pushed her glasses up on her nose, and said, "Oh. Um, okay. You want—shall I just take them back, then?"

"Yes. Take them back. And thanks." The four of us watched her turn and go out the door with her head held at an oddly painful tilt.

I was still standing one step above Ernie with my hand out. He turned and met my eyes, shrugged, and handed me the key ring with the proper key extended. I took it and opened the door at the end of the hall.

Inside this bare old shell of a house, Ernie Chisholm had created a fully furnished, comfortable bedroom and bath. It was made up with clean pastel sheets, a flowered comforter, and soft towels. A side table held a CD player and some jewel cases with titles like *Slow Dancing* and *Music for Lovers*. There was nothing tasteless or decadent about the place; it looked pretty and pleasant, like the brown-haired woman in the big glasses. Kevin and I made a quick search with gloves on and found no trace of firearms or ammo. I locked the door, handed the key back to Ernie, and said, "Thanks. I don't think we'll need to take up any more of your time."

Ray was still standing five steps down the stairway, holding up the front of the ladder. He turned and took one step down, and Ernie, responding to the tug on the ladder, followed. Ray helped him set the ladder up again in the bay window of the dining room, then turned at once and marched out of the house with his face a frozen mask. Kevin and I followed him across the street while Ernie was still locking the door to his house.

"What are you so mad about?" Kevin asked him when we got to my pickup.

"You ever spend fifteen minutes holding the low end of a

twelve-foot ladder?" Ray was massaging his upper arms.

"Why'n'cha put it down?"

"I was afraid he might heave it at me." He glared at both of us and asked, "Was that what I think it was? With the woman—"

"Correctamundo," Kevin said. "We were rocking Mr. Solid Citizen's dream boat."

"But it's got nothing to do with the shooting, right?"

"That's right," I said. "It might be a big problem for Mrs. Chisholm, but for us it was a waste of time. So let's see, what's next?" Shadows were already lengthening across the yards, and I felt a returning twinge of my morning headache, which had gone away during lunch with Maxine. "You got the info about that shed on Nineteenth Street on your chart?"

"Of course."

"Wanna go get the car then? Pull it around to the house with the shed, and I'll—" My glance caught on a vehicle in the street. "Whoa. What's this?" An old blue Plymouth passed us, going south on Thirteenth Avenue, and pulled into the Sheetses' driveway. When the driver turned off the motor in front of the garage, the car shuddered and belched black smoke. Fred and Angie Sheets got out.

Angie seemed to have shrunk. Her shoulders sagged forward, and her head was sinking into her chest. And she was drying up; her hair had gone stringy, and her cheekbones showed. She moved toward her house door cautiously, as if it hurt her to move.

Fred looked bloated, and his face was flushed dark red. He was wearing a gray suit jacket with the black pants from another suit. Neither garment fit him very well, and his blue shirt showed at the front where the jacket gaped open below the button. When he turned to close the car door, he stood with his feet set wide apart, swaying a little. I did not need to smell him to know he had been drinking.

They crossed the lawn with their heads down, absorbed in their own pain. Ray and Kevin followed me up the walk. When we met in front of their door, they looked up in dull surprise.

"Mr. and Mrs. Sheets." I put out my hand, and Angie took it and held on. "I'm sorry for your loss," I said, and she nodded wordlessly while a tiny trickle of water ran out of the corner of each eye and down the outside of her cheeks.

Fred looked puzzled at first. Then he remembered me and bristled. He grumbled a couple of words to himself and finally brought out, "Whaddya want?"

"We're in the neighborhood investigating your son's shooting," I said. "Have you decided to come back from Byron? Will you be living here from now on?"

"No use staying where you're not wanted," he said huffily. "We got our own place, we don't need no charity." He tugged at his ill-fitting coat. His wife looked at him and gave her head a tiny shake.

"Well. Since you're here now, could we agree on a time when it would be convenient to come in and take a look at your guns? We might as well get that out of the way—"

"Absolutely not!" He turned to his wife and said sharply, "Let go of his hand." When she didn't respond at once, he slapped our joined hands and said, "Let go of it!" Angie, without looking at him, pulled her hand back and tucked it inside the front of her coat.

"Mr. Sheets," I said, "I have a warrant to see your guns, if I have to use it. I was hoping—"

"You come at me with your warrant, Mr. Big Shot Policeman," he yelled, "and you better be ready to shoot your way in with it, because there's no way in hell I'm givin' up my guns to no dirty nigger!"

Angie rolled her eyes, mortified. Ray looked like he might be going to faint. Kevin took a step toward Fred Sheets, but I touched his arm and shook my head. We had better things to do than bump chests with Fred Sheets, and staging a donnybrook with a bereaved parent in his own front yard was not going to win any points for the department. I stepped between the Sheetses with my back to Fred and asked Angie, "Mrs. Sheets, when Billy fell down, which way was he facing?"

"Facing?" She came back from a long way off, wherever her mind hid out when her husband drank.

"Yes. What was he turned toward?"

"Well, he, uh, he was turned toward me, I guess. Well, yes, of course he was, because I had just called to him and told him he forgot his lunch money—" Remembering tapped some water source that her outward appearance suggested must be dry. Tears began to run freely down her cheeks. "S-so he was running back to me"—her last words were so garbled by grief I had to guess at some of them—"to ged the mo-muh-ey." She dropped her face in her hands and sobbed bitterly.

"Thank you." I touched her arm. "That helps us a lot, Mrs. Sheets. We're trying very hard to find out who did this to Billy, do you understand that?" Without raising her head, she nodded three times. "I'm going to type up a statement that says what you just told me, and a little later we'll be in touch to ask you to sign it. Will you be here?" She nodded again.

"Let's go," I said, and Kevin and Ray followed me back to my truck.

Fred yelled after us, "You come back here again, you're gonna be in a fight, you hear me?" When we didn't answer, he walked stiffly to his house door and tried several times to fit his key in the lock. After several fumbling tries he dropped it and began to swear. His wife leaned silently under his waving arms, snatched the key off the ground, and opened the door. She darted inside, and Fred wobbled slowly in after her.

"That bastard," Kevin said.

I shrugged. "He took a dislike to me somehow at the hospital."

"I'm gonna enjoy executing that search warrant," Ray said.

"We may not need it. You heard her say her son was running toward the house. I believed her, didn't you?"

"Yes," Ray said, "her I believe."

"Which means the shot came from"— I nodded across the street—"over there somewhere. So let's get back to Plan A. Ray, get the car, will you? We'll meet you in front of the house with the shed." Ray hurried north toward the easement into the alley; Kevin and I walked around the bridge players' cars and climbed into my pickup.

"So, Jake," he said, watching me quizzically as I drove toward Nineteenth Street, "you're cool with this racist shit, huh?"

"Fairly, I guess. Why?"

"You impressed me, is why. You didn't even blink at Fred Sheets. Been me, I think I woulda decked him."

I shrugged. "He's drunk."

"He'll still be a bigot when he sobers up." He stared at the horizon awhile and said thoughtfully, "I need to work on that."

"On what?"

"I still get mad sometimes when people get abusive."

"So do I, sometimes. You can't be an iceberg. But I try not to waste any energy on dinosaurs. I mean, the N word, in the twenty-first century? Please."

He laughed, a surprising, happy sound in the grim gray afternoon. "Maybe that's a good way to get on top of it," he said, "keep thinking how ridiculous most insults are."

"Whatever floats your boat." I parked the pickup in front of the house and lowered the tailgate. Ray pulled the department car in behind me and brought the chart up, saying, "Damn, that breeze is growing teeth." We all zipped jackets, turned collars up, and hunched close to each other over the back of the truck while the late-afternoon chill crept over the lawns and into our bones.

7

"HIRTEEN-FORTY-SEVEN Nineteenth Street," Ray said, reading his notes. "Owned and occupied by Mrs. E. B. Priestley. Given name Leticia. There's a notice on the record, though, 'Direct all bills and inquiries to James Priestley.' With an address and two phone numbers. The clerk in the tax office said he's her son, and he takes care of things for his elderly mother."

"Let me have it." I dialed the daytime number and got a CPA's office and then James Priestley.

"My mother's eighty-seven and a great-grandmother," Priestley said when I explained what we were doing. "I don't think we need to worry about her shooting at anybody."

"I understand," I said. "I just have to check out all the possible sources of those gunshots."

"Why is my mother's house any more likely than any of the others?"

"Not the house. The shed." I told him about the laser light.

"Oh, well, the shed, it's just a few old trunks and some spare furniture," he said. "It won't take long to search that."

"Okay if we just go to the door and ask her?"

"Oh, please, I'd rather you didn't," he said. "She gets upset very easily, and then she can't sleep. Can you hang on for ten minutes? I'll come right over with the keys."

He parked his spotless three-year-old Buick in front of my pickup and got out holding a key ring, a neat gray-haired man in rimless glasses, wearing rubbers over his wing tips. I said, "Appreciate your help," and we all shook hands.

"I called Mother and told her I was showing my old skis to someone," he said. "So she won't worry. *Too* much," he added ironically, waving to the anxious face that appeared between the curtains of the front window.

The cement walk along the side of the house was shoveled. We followed him into the backyard, ducked under some laundry lines, and waited while he unlocked the shed door and turned on the light.

"My boys and I keep some of our sports gear over here," he said, indicating snowshoes and skis on the walls, a canoe hanging from the rafters. "Otherwise, I think all that's in here is some gardening tools and a couple of trunks."

"It's mainly the loft we're interested in seeing," I said. It looked primitive, raw boards nailed to the top of rafters, and a ladder leading up.

"I don't even remember what's up here," Priestley said, climbing awkwardly in his overcoat. "Watch your step, it's pretty dark." We stood on the creaking boards around the open hatch, waiting for our eyes to get used to the gloom. "I'm sorry there's no light. You can see better over by the window."

The small wood-framed window looked out over the street, with a good view of the Sheetses' yard.

"I thought I left that locked," Priestley said. He reached out toward the rotating metal lock at the top of the lower pane. I caught his arm.

"Don't touch it. Please," I said, looking into his astonished gray eyes.

"What in the world—" he said, and just then Kevin said, from the corner, "Bingo." He had put on latex gloves and was standing by the open door of a tall cupboard, holding a rifle.

"Nice little plinker," he said, bringing it over to the light. "I had one of these babies myself once, Jake. Ten-shot with a scope. Lessee, this one's a Ruger."

"So help me," James Priestley said, getting agitated, "I have never seen that thing before in my life."

"You're saying it's not yours?" I asked him.

"Doesn't belong to anyone in my family. Doesn't belong *here.*"

"Two boxes of shells here," Kevin said, picking them off a shelf. "Remington .22 Long Rifles." He pulled the covers off the boxes. "One's full. The other one's about half used."

"Well, not by me," Priestley said, "and not by either one of my boys, I promise you. I've never been interested in hunting, and I haven't raised them to be. We do vigorous outdoor sports, but not—"

"Mr. Priestley," I said, "nobody's accusing you of anything at this time, you understand that? We're just trying to find out all we can about this gun and these bullets—"

"And this camera," Ray said, from the cupboard in the opposite corner, "this yours?"

"Of course not. Why would I leave my camera up here?"

"Sure? Digital camcorder, zoom lens? Damn nice rig."

"Absolutely not mine. What in hell's going on?" he asked me, plaintively. "My mother's going to have a *stroke*—" He stopped, put two fingers over his lips, and stared at me a minute, his eyes looking wobbly behind his trifocals. Then he asked me, "How did he get in here?"

"Who?"

"Whoever left this gun and camera. The door was locked. I've got the only key."

It was the second time I'd heard that claim in one afternoon, but I let it go. "Is there a backdoor?"

"Used to be. I nailed it shut and pushed an old chest in front of it."

"Let's take a look. Kevin, call the duty officer, will you, and see if there's anybody on duty who can dust the window and door here for prints. Ray, will you take care of the gun and camera? Better fill out the evidence inventory forms and get Mr. Priestley to sign them."

"I don't want to sign anything," Priestley said. "It's not my stuff."

"Gotta go by the book anyway," Ray said. "We found these

things on your property, so the chain of evidence starts here."

"I just don't like the idea of taking responsibility for something that isn't mine."

"It's just a formality," Ray said.

"Uh-huh. So's hanging."

I hunched up in the cold thinking what a pleasure it would be to tell him to quit being a stupid obstructionist pissant unless he wanted to find his own motherfucking break-in artist, and then I asked him, politely, "Mr. Priestley, you do want us to find out who's trespassing on your mother's property, right?"

"Of course."

"Good. Then sign the inventory form, and let's get on with it." He was accustomed to being in charge, and was so startled by a direct order that he bent over the paper and signed it. Ray and Kevin carried their booty tenderly down the ladder. Priestley and I went out the front door of the shed and kicked through deep snow to the back of the building.

"Why'd you nail the backdoor shut?" I asked him. "Did something happen before?"

"No. But my mother kept worrying that the shed was too close to the back gate, it might invite burglars." He sighed. "She thinks about burglars a lot. She hears people coming into the house at night. It's hard to be old." Turning the rear corner, he stopped. "Oh, damn! Oh, look at this."

In the two-foot space between the rear shed door and the fence gate, the snow was packed down in a welter of icy footprints.

"Don't walk in it," I said. "Stay right where you are, okay?" I took three photos over his shoulder, then made one long jump to the hedge and took three more pictures, of the alley outside the gate. "Chain-link fence all the way along the back of the property?"

"With this thick cotoneaster hedge right inside," Priestley said. "Supposed to make my mother feel safe. But nothing ever does. Boy, she'll be fit to be tied if she sees this."

The gate was the only gap in the hedge. Someone had plainly been jumping it, breaking off twigs from the top of the hedge on either side. A few cotoneaster stems and leaves were scattered in the snow on either side of the gate.

"They couldn't be getting in from out here, though," Priestley said. "The door is nailed shut, and I shoved a big old armoire up against it. Come back inside, I'll show you."

"Okay. But hang on a second." I jumped back across the unmarked snow to the corner of the building, pulled on latex gloves, leaned across the footprints to the old metal door latch, and pushed down on the lever. The strike slid back easily, and the door swung open about two feet before it stopped. I hopped onto the doorsill and looked in at a row of coats and suits.

Priestley said, "What do you see?"

"Coats and suits."

"I don't understand." He looked stricken.

"Looks like they broke the back out of the armoire."

"They? You think there's more than one?"

"Two different sets of boot tracks there."

"That so?" Priestley leaned over the tracks and stared.

"Let's go back inside and see how they did this." Kevin and Ray walked up to the shed door as we came around the corner, and I asked them, "Either one of you ever done foot casts?"

"I have," Ray said, "a couple of times."

"Good. Take the guns and camera downtown and check them in to the evidence room, pick up a casting kit and the video camera—what else do we need?"

"More help," Ray said.

"Right. Bring Darrell along too. Listen, though, show that camera to Bo Dooley before you put it away, tell him I said take a couple of Polaroid pictures of it and bring them out here and show them to Kay O'Connell. Ask her if it could be the one she saw."

"Gotcha," Ray said. Kevin followed me into the shed, asking, "What's happening?"

"Footprints by the backdoor. Looks like somebody's been getting in that way." We followed Priestley past the loft ladder to the big cupboard at the rear of the shed.

"Houses used to be built without closets in the bedrooms,"

Priestley said, "so they used these big old hanging lockers. Called 'em chiffoniers, armoires, chiffonades. Grandma had several upstairs in this house when I was little. Some had drawers on one side, and a mirror. Grandad put in closets when he added bathrooms, and the armoires got shunted off to attics and basements. But Mother hung onto this old turkey, because it held so much stuff. My boys and I had quite a job getting it out here."

It was stained almost black, ornately carved at the top and sides. He opened the tall double doors and said, "Well, what—" Light was streaming in around the garments.

"The whole back's gone," I said. "So the outside door swings into the chest."

"Somebody broke it out?"

"Not exactly." I pushed the coats and suits to one side. "See here?" The nails had been pulled out from the inside, and the boards stacked neatly at one end.

"What about the shed door?"

I showed him. "Same thing. Nails pulled out from the inside. Pretty neat job. They're all piled up here on the floor of the wardrobe."

Priestley looked about ready to cry. "I *always* keep this building locked," he said.

"Looks like somebody else has a key, then."

"No. My mother and I have the only keys."

"Your mother has one?"

"Well, of course. It's her building."

"I guess we better go talk to her then."

"Oh, do you have to? I mean, I doubt if she'll be able to remember where she put it. And obviously she didn't break into her own shed."

"But somebody did. So we better find out if she knows where the key is."

Ollie Green walked into the backyard as we came out of the shed. "I'm the only fingerprint tech on duty today," he said. "Can one of you lend me a hand?"

"I'll do it," Kevin said. "What besides this chest, Jake?"

I showed them the parts of the armoire I wanted tested, and the backdoor, imploring them to stay out of the footprints till Ray made his casts. "Then, Kevin, take him up in the loft. Be sure you do the cupboard doors up there, as well as the window."

At the front door of his mother's house, Priestley tapped once, stuck his head in, and said, "Mama?" He got no response but a distant rustling, so he gradually eased into the room, saying repeatedly, "Mother? Where are you? Mama?" Over his shoulder I could see a small foyer with a stairway on the right. Priestley opened the door wider and stepped in, and I saw a small head appear above the newel post on the landing where the stairs turned. Big eyes blinked down at us, and presently a dry, whispery voice said, "Who's there?"

"Oh, Mama." Priestley turned, relieved, and started up toward her. "I need to ask you a question."

He climbed toward her as he spoke, and when he stood in front of her, she touched the lapel of his cold overcoat and said, "Howard?"

"Come on, now, Mama, you know Dad's gone, we just went all over this yesterday. I'm Jimmy, and I need to ask you for the key to the shed."

"Oh, honey, I have no idea where that old key is," she said, suddenly flirtatious and devious. "What do you need it for?" Priestley hadn't given any thought to an excuse for needing the key. He stood there with his mouth working, and she looked down and saw me and said, "Is that the man that's buying the skis?"

"Yes," her son said, and then, in sudden inspiration, "and we need your key so we can unlock the backdoor. He wants to load his truck in the alley."

"Do you have to do this right now? I'm so afraid you're going to spoil the surprise," she said, and then clapped her hand over her mouth.

"What surprise, Mama?"

"Darn. I wasn't supposed to tell you," she said.

My phone rang. I had been standing just inside the door, and I stepped outside to answer it. Rosie said, "Will you be coming in pretty soon, Jake? A couple of these interviews today, I'd really like to hear what you think about them."

"You still at the school?"

"Just got back. I'm typing up my notes. Any chance you'll have time to talk?"

"Well—tell you what, put a copy of your notes on my desk, will you? It's four-thirty, and we're still pretty involved out here on Nineteenth Street."

"Um . . . okay. And we can talk in the morning?"

"Sure. See you then." I turned to go back in the house and collided with James Priestley coming out. He looked stricken.

"She gave it to my son Adam. He told her he had a present for me, and he wanted to hide it in the shed till my birthday."

"But you don't believe it."

"She forgets things," Priestley said. "My birthday's in November."

By the time Ollie Green was packing up his dusting gear, Ray was back. Darrell helped him with footprint casts while Kevin and I looked for trace evidence around the backdoor and the window upstairs. We found plenty of hair and threads, which hardly ever help find a suspect but gladden the hearts of attorneys when it comes time to convict. It was fully dark by the time we finished, so we were working by artificial light, which made us slow.

Priestley hung around, jittering and watching us through all this, because he was determined to reseal the backdoor of the shed. We helped him with that before we headed back to the station. The rest of the investigative team had already gone home, and our corner of the floor was dark and silent, though I could hear the clamor of day-shift street cops getting ready to check out on the other side of the hall.

I spent some time reading Rosie's notes, pondering especially the paragraphs that described the beginning of the fight. P. K. had finally told her what Jason Hadley said. It was, "You ready to die now, sucker?"

RD: Did you believe he was threatening your life?

PKM: No. He was just trying to scare me off the hockey team, and I got sick of it.

RD: You mean he's said something like this to you before?

PKM: Every day since preseason hockey practice started.

RD: Why does he want you off the team?

PKM: I skate better than he does.

RD: Why do you want to quit the hockey team, then?

PKM: I've decided that I like to skate, but I don't like to fight.

RD: Except yesterday you did, huh?

PKM: Yesterday I got fed up. Yeah.

Jason Hadley, asked to confirm or deny what he had said to P.K., said, "I might have known he'd narc on me, the stupid little worm."

RD: Did you mean to threaten his life?

JH: Get real. It's just a thing people say.

RD: They do? Who says that?

JH: Anybody, I guess.

RD: Most people only use threats if they mean to be threatening. If you didn't mean you were going to kill him, what did you mean?

JH: Nothing. It's just something to say. It doesn't mean anything.

RD: Are you mad at him about something?

JH: Why would I be? He hasn't got anything I want.

RD: I heard he's a better skater than you, is that true?

JH: Did he say that? That's a laugh. If he's a better skater than me, why isn't he captain of the team?

RD: I don't know. Maybe you're slower but meaner, is that it?

JH: Hey, I'm as mean as I need to be. And I'm as fast as I need to be, too.

The section on the separate interrogations of Butch Ranfranz and Owen Campbell was brief and straightforward. Each of them said they missed the fight because he was already in study hall when it started, and the homeroom teacher wouldn't let anybody leave the room until the shouting stopped. Their information seemed plain enough, but her last sentence read, "Follow-up queries tomorrow."

She had attached a handwritten Post-it to the top of her report. "Jake," it said, "Jason Hadley is an arrogant snot. I wanted to hit him with a backpack a couple of times myself. I didn't get the impression that P. K. is afraid of him, though. Something else is going on. R. D."

I typed very cursory notes of my day's work, made a copy for Frank and slid it under his door, and composed a list of tomorrow's most essential tasks. By seven o'clock I was back in my pickup, headed home.

As soon as I was out on the dark highway, the memory of Trudy's note came back like a kick in the gut, and the thought of walking into our cold farmhouse to spend the evening alone almost made me turn the truck around. For a minute I thought fondly about a couple of Rutherford bars where I hung in my bachelor days. I was tempted by the warmth I knew I'd find in them, the lights and music, and the easy conversations with affable strangers.

But I was tired and hungry, and I certainly didn't want to get drunk again. Besides, there was just a slim chance that Trudy might call, and an admittedly slimmer chance that I might say all the right things and persuade her to come home. So I drove north to the Mirium exit, rolled sedately down Main Street past the scenes of last night's follies, turned left at Burr Oak Avenue, and followed it to County Road 82. I tried to keep my mind a blank while I entered my dark yard, put the truck away, turned lights on in the kitchen, and built a fire in the wood stove.

I was staring into the open refrigerator, looking for something to cook and debating about a beer, when I heard an automobile with a familiar-sounding motor drive into the yard. It seemed to me then that all the blood in my body crowded up into my head and began to make a roaring noise. I held tight to the refrigerator door while steps approached the house and the kitchen door opened.

"Trudy," I said.

"Oh, good, you're here," she said.

"I thought—"

"We have to talk," she said.

I couldn't seem to get enough air in my lungs. "I didn't know you were coming. Your note said you were staying in town."

"That was last night."

"Oh." So she hadn't stepped over my comatose body on her way out the door. Then why did she leave?

She regarded me attentively. "You didn't know I wasn't here last night?"

"Oh, I—" The roaring noise was getting louder. I heard myself asking, "I guess you went to your mother's house, huh?" I slammed the refrigerator door shut. "Did she give you a fresh list of all the reasons I'm not good enough for you?" *Stupid, stupid, I never meant to say that.*

"I stayed with one of the girls from the lab." Her mouth had begun to take on that straight look it gets when she's becoming seriously pissed. "Who told you that about Mama? Have you been talking to Bonnie?" I got a sudden, horrid inner vision of the two of us actually fighting physically, throwing things and hitting each other with sticks of wood, and behind us in that image, a hungry-looking gray wolf stood watching us, slavering.

The gray wolf is a legacy of my roustabout childhood, when life quite often spun out of control. I saw him first when I was nine, just before my caseworker took me away from Maxine. He's not a friend. At best, he's a harbinger. Despite his impenetrable silence, I've always understood his message to be, "Jake Hines, you are just about to step in some very deep shit."

I took a big gulp of air and said, "Trudy, I got falling-down drunk last night, right across the road in Mirium, and somebody brought me home and I passed out on the floor. I woke up this morning so hung over I thought I was going to die, but instead of that I read a weird note from you that didn't make any sense at all, and then I went to work and had the craziest goddamned day you could ever possibly imagine. I've been insulted and threatened and lied to, and now I'm starving and exhausted and I'm sorry I didn't know you weren't here last night, but please don't yell at me about it right now."

She stood in the open doorway staring at me for a few seconds, and gradually her eyes took on a suggestion of a glint. She shook her head and clucked a couple of times, tsk, tsk, and said, "God, babe, you're just a great big mess, aren't you?" The corners of her mouth twitched. "You think you've got enough strength left to bring in a couple of bags of groceries from the car?"

I did a double shrug, opened my mouth and closed it again, and finally said, "Sure."

By the time I came back with the food, she had her coat off and a pan of water on the stove, and was tossing chopped onions into a sizzling pan. I set the table and built up the fire. She unloaded the bags and began stirring chopped beef in the pan with the onions. I poured her a glass of wine and fixed a big glass of ice water for myself. Ten minutes later she set two plates of linguini with meat sauce on the table, and the two of us got, as they say, right down to it.

"It's beyond good," I said after a couple of minutes. "It's the absolutely right stuff." She had just stuffed a forkful in her mouth, so she crinkled her eyes at me wordlessly.

When my hunger was mostly satisfied and I was just eating for the fun of it, I got up for another glass of water and asked her, "More wine?"

She shook her head. "I still want to talk," she said. "Are you about ready?"

"Yup." I came back with my glass and sat down. "I get to go first."

"You do? How come?"

"Because I think I know what part of the problem is." I snarfed another bite of pasta and chewed it thoughtfully. "As I see it, you've probably got an extra serious case of seasonal affective disorder. I've been trying to cheer you up every way I could think of— "

She suddenly sat up very straight. "You have?"

"You couldn't tell? I asked Maxine to come out Sunday because she usually makes you laugh, but you were barely polite to her and just kept doing a lot of cooking."

"She had two small children with her, remember?"

"Well, so? Let me finish. I passed up Monday-night football to show you one of those old tear-jerker movies that you usually like so much, but you hardly looked at it and stalked off to bed by yourself. Then yesterday morning I suggested we try a fun weekend at Lake Pepin, and instead of saying, 'Oh, goody,' you lost your temper about breaking a rubber band, and turned around and threw my boots out the door." I reached across the table and put my hand over hers. "Those are classic symptoms of light deprivation, Trudy. And there's help available. Pills and therapy—"

She pulled her hand out from under mine and pasted it firmly over my mouth. "Listen to me, you asshole."

I recoiled from her hand, startled. "Trudy! You never talk like that."

"I'm sorry, but I can't listen to any more of this pompous drivel." She tapped the back of my hand sharply with her index finger. "What did I say to you, Monday night, just before you turned on that sappy old movie?"

"Say?"

"Yes! Say! What thought did I express to you in plain English, the language of our tribe?" I stared at her and shook my head. "I said the same thing that I said to you yesterday morning, before you started rambling on about some stupid ice-fishing expedition on the Mississippi—"

"Not stupid! Not! People catch some of the—"

She slammed her fist on the table, making the dishes jump. "So help me God, Jake, if you say one more word about fish I'll break your face!"

"See, now, Trudy, there you go again, you're just being totally irrational—"

She came around the table in one lithe movement and put her face so close to mine that our noses were almost touching. "Before Maxine came out, before the movie, before all that talk about Lake Pepin, each of those times, what—did—I—fucking—SAY—TO—YOU?"

I watched her carefully, as much of her as I could see from so close up. If Trudy was using what she usually referred to as the F word, we were in unknown territory, where any answer might backfire. For lack of a better idea, I tried the truth. "I have no idea."

"I said, 'I need to talk to you.' " She drew back a couple of inches and asked me, "Can you hear me now? Do you comprehend the words? I said, 'I need to TALK TO YOU!' " She was looking at me hard-eyed, apparently convinced she had delivered a devastating topper.

"All right," I said carefully.

"Are you going to claim you never heard me say that?"

"No. I mean yes. That's correct, I never heard you say that." Her face was four inches away from mine, and I was trying to pay close attention to every word she said. But instead I found myself thinking what a beautiful mouth she had, and I leaned forward and kissed her on it. She made a small protesting noise, but her lips kissed me back a little and then a lot, and before long she had melted into my lap and we were kissing and groping each other as if we had just discovered this whole boy-girl thing.

She groaned, once, "No, Jake, listen—" but I whispered, "Sweet lovely," and kissed her some more on the mouth and then in some of the delicious places along her neck and down into her collar. In a short time we were on our way to our bedroom, not much troubled by the cold at all, because our bodies, which had known from the first time I ever touched her that they were exactly right for each other, were settling this argument in their own way.

Much later, coiled around her in the warm darkness under the quilts, I murmured in her ear, "Sweet love?"

"Mmm?"

"What was it you wanted to talk about?"

"Oh—" she slid her leg silkily across my belly, and I felt desire begin to rise again. "You sure you want to talk about it now?"

"Sure. Lay it on me."

"Well . . . I got a phone call from Texas on Saturday while you were gone to the dump."

"You did?" She was getting hard to follow again, but I wanted her to stay right where she was, so I kissed her hair and asked her quietly, "Who's in Texas?"

"The people who own this farm. Remember? Cammy and Jeff."

"Oh, yeah." I let my hand glide along the lovely curve of her hip and wondered if I had steam enough in the boiler for one more time. "What'd they have to say?"

"She. It was Cammy on the phone. She said Jeff got the deal he wanted from the company, he's gonna be manager of a whole division or whatever, so they've decided to buy a house down there, and they want to sell the farm right away."

"What?" I sat up, ruining our perfect arrangement of body parts. "Well, God, Trudy, why didn't you tell me right away?"

"I've been trying to. But I couldn't seem to find the right time."

"The right time? Since when can't you just blurt things out? All of a sudden you have to handle me or something?"

"Don't get so excited," she said. "For one thing, I wasn't totally sure how I felt about it myself."

"You weren't? How come? I mean, you're the one that picked this place to begin with. I always thought you loved it."

"I did. I do. But I thought . . . I was afraid it might affect our rela—Okay, I won't say the word, I know you hate to talk about relationships, but . . . a big mortgage like that . . . I was afraid you might feel like it was too much of a commitment."

"Too much of a—Trudy, what did we just do in this bed? Do you have any idea how bad I felt this morning when I woke up and found you gone? Christ's sake, woman, I couldn't get any more committed to you if you hung a stone around my neck and nailed my feet to the floor."

"Aw." She made a happy little chuckling sound. "My old sweetheart. Come back down here and cuddle. Although I suppose," she said, just as I was getting comfortable again, "we really should get up and do the dishes."

"Okay. In a minute." I slid my cheek along her lovely smooth arm and thought about the seasons I might be lucky enough to share on this funky old farm with this woman who would never be easy, and for a few beautiful seconds I thought my heart might explode with happiness.

"Jesus, though," I said, as the awesome difficulty of the details began to claw at me, "even if we could raise the down payment, how would we swing the repairs? I mean, I don't think I could face another winter here without better insulation."

"Or a furnace that works," she said into my shoulder.

"New wiring. Shall we get up? This is serious business." I put my pants on. "I mean, my God, Trudy, we really need to *talk* about this."

She said something I couldn't hear, inside the sweatshirt she was pulling on.

"What?"

Her face came out through the neck, looking flushed. "I said, 'Right again, Jake Hines.' "

8

EFORE we'd finished scraping plates, it was clear that we both wanted to stay on the farm, if we could. The location halfway between our two jobs was perfect for us, the little town of Mirium offered a few services without creating any nuisances, and owning some land of our own seemed exciting. Even the imperfections of the place had a certain appeal; I liked the thought of the tinkering and yard work it would take to make the place look respectable, and Trudy was dreaming of restoring the interior.

By the time we'd stowed the pans, we'd moved on to ways and means. Obviously buying a farm was a stretch financially, but trying to define the size of the stretch raised a dozen questions we couldn't answer. So I poured us each a glass of wine, and we sat down by the stove to make two lists of research chores. Trudy would explore the outer limits of our borrowing power, and try to determine the bottom price Tammy could accept. I was going to calculate the big-ticket repair items like wiring and insulation.

I made light of the worry Trudy had been brooding about since Tammy's phone call, that getting in a financial bind might take all the fun out of our relationship. "Everybody's in debt," I said. "And when the place is fixed up, it'll be easy to sell it if we decide it's a drag."

The next morning, Trudy stood in a pale sunbeam by the kitchen sink, humming something about being able to see clearly now, and dancing in place while she braided her hair. I patted her adorable gyrating buns as I passed her, and she chuckled and bumped me with a hip. We were both high on postcoital euphoria, and excited about the home ownership plans we were hatching. I could feel my ticker turning up at the thought of all the problems I would solve here, and I could hear, in Trudy's humming, the same giddy confidence building. We were lovers reading off the same page again; what could be so hard about broken heaters and bank loans?

My crew, when I got to town, seemed to be just as fired up as I was, though all for different reasons.

"Wow, have I got messages," Kevin said, coming into the meeting room with an armload of paper. "A lot of these are for you, Jake; you might want to deal with them before you start anything new."

"I need to talk to you before you start on *anything*, though," Rosie said.

"I might have to take the afternoon off," Bo said, "if Diane gets released today."

"Somebody's gotta kill the guy who keeps emptying the vacuum cleaner next to the air conditioning intake," Lou grumped, as he flopped into a chair and unwrapped a cough drop. "The air in this place is killing me today."

"We're kinda skating on thin ice here, legality-wise, aren't we?" Darrell said. He hung his jacket over the back of his chair and stretched before he sat down, straining the sleeves of his nice blue shirt in a mighty display of biceps. "I mean, confiscating stuff outa that shed before we even have a suspect?"

"It's evidence in a murder investigation," I said. "You think I should have left it there?"

"I'm just speculating," he said, "just using you guys for a bouncing board."

"Boy, Darrell," Lou said, looking pleased, "you do have a way with words."

"The man who owns the building says he never saw the gun and camera before," I said. "He was glad to get rid of them."

"Okay, I hear you. You want me to run 'em up to BCA before he remembers his wife gave 'em to him last Christmas?"

"You shouldn't run anything anyplace till we see what's on the tape in that camera," Ray Bailey said. He's quieter than anybody else in the section except Bo, so he often gets drowned out in meetings. Abruptly, now, he got my full attention.

"Tape?" I set down the stack of messages Kevin had just handed me. "Hey, you're right. That puppy's digital, isn't it?"

"So it doesn't need to be developed?" Lou said.

"No," Kevin said, "we can take it over to that guy on the support staff, what's his name?"

"Greg LaMotte," Rosie said.

"Yeah, he can upload it right into his computer, can't he?" Kevin said. "Play it back to us on his screen."

"We don't need Greg's computer for that," Ray said. "Where you guys been? We can plug the camera cable into the VCR here and watch it on our own TV."

"Damn straight." I made a stack out of yesterday's notes and the messages Kevin had just handed me, and pushed the whole pile out of my way. "Isn't technology wonderful? Go sign it out, Ray, and bring it in here. Don't unwrap it till you get in here," I called after his retreating back, and to my crew, "Who's got some gloves?"

"In my office," Kevin said. "I'll get 'em in a minute. But read that message from James Priestley while we're waiting, will you?" I scrabbled through the pile till he said, impatiently, "Here, here!" reached into the stack, and slapped a pink slip on top. It was a telephone message, stamped 7:46 A.M., that read, "Urgent I talk to you ASAP re: my mother's key."

Kevin said, "Is he talking about an extra key to that shed?"

"Yeah. I'm gonna call him right now." I walked back to my office to dial and heard, all around me, a talking frenzy erupt. My whole crew had run back to their cubicles to make urgent phone calls. Waiting for Priestley to answer, I began grinding my teeth —my new bad habit since I got the top job in the investigations unit. Sometimes the thought of all the things I don't control makes me want to kick out a window. I'm destroying my molars instead. I forced my jaws to relax as a voice said, "Priestley."

"Jake Hines."

"Oh, thanks for calling me back. I just wanted you to know that I talked to Adam last night—"

"That's your older boy?"

"Yes. The one who told that whopper to get the key. And his explanation—well, it doesn't make it right, of course, but it's a typical boy trick. He and some of his chums got it into their heads to form some secret society, and they wanted a clubhouse. Adam knew I wouldn't approve of his bothering my mother about it, so he went over there and talked her out of the key himself. He admits they took the back out of the armoire and pried the two-by-fours off the door. He planned to put the key back in my mother's house when she wasn't looking, hoping she'd forget she ever gave it to him. Meantime they could get in whenever they wanted to."

"To do what?"

"Oh, make up secret signs, I suppose, by-laws and all of that. Don't you remember being a boy?" My boyhood secrets mostly concerned tape decks and batteries lifted out of cars on the street. I decided not to share them with James Priestley.

He was going right on, anyway. "I told him, 'Adam, you lied to your grandmother, now that's just not right.' And he said well, he knew that, but she's getting so vague, half the time she forgets who we are and she never knows what day it is, so what's another little detail? I don't want you to think I approve, but I do think I can see his point of view."

"Uh-huh. Did you ask him what the secret society intended to do with the rifle?"

"Oh, he says he knows nothing about the gun."

"So one of the other boys must have put it there?"

"Well, I—presumably."

"You got their names?"

"Not yet. He's very reluctant to rat on his friends. That's honorable, of course, but I told him that I have to have their names; I'll want to talk to their parents. They all have to take responsibility for breaking into my mother's property, and there have to be consequences. My wife and I are discussing what's appropriate for Adam."

"Mr. Priestley, I need those names right away, and I need to talk to your son." Kevin was standing in my office door, beckoning. "Is Adam in school today?"

"Of course."

"Okay, I'd like to send an investigator from here to pick him up at school and bring him in here. I need your permission to do that, and I suppose you'll want to be present while I talk to him."

"I certainly will. But I don't know if I—when did you expect to do this?"

"A little later this morning. Maybe in an hour? Can you come over when I call you?"

"Does it have to be today? I'm pretty busy—"

"Mr. Priestley, a little boy was shot with a gun that could very well be the one we found in your mother's shed. I think it's in your son's best interest to eliminate him as a suspect as soon as possible, if we can."

"Oh, well, see here, of *course* you *can*. Adam's never been a problem child, he's never been in any trouble at all, do you understand that?"

"Right. All the more reason," I said. "I'll call you when we're ready." As I hung up, I could hear James Priestley still protesting, "He's a straight-A student—"

"Ray's got the camera," Kevin said, and we went back in the meeting room, where several personal agendas still vied for attention.

"The hospital called," Bo said. "They're releasing Diane right after lunch. I should leave about eleven."

"Okay."

"Mrs. Stokes got beat up again last night," Lou said. "I gotta get her into a shelter today."

"Get on it as soon as we're through here, okay?"

"The principal wants me to call him back," Rosie said, and Darrell, talking at the same time, said, "The boy-and-girl team I picked up for breaking and entering Tuesday is ready to plea-bargain. I gotta get together with Milo."

"You guys want to see this video or not?" I said, and then my own beeper sounded. I answered and got a message to call the chief. "Stay where you are," I told them. "Don't anybody move."

When I answered the page Frank said, "I'm going over next year's budget with two of the key people on the city council, this morning at ten. Since you're the one asking for the lion's share of upgrades, I'd like you to sit in on it, Jake."

"I can't do a meeting this morning, Frank," I said. "There's too much going on here."

"Jake, you've gotta start taking the administrative part of your job seriously—"

"I do, but—"

"You don't seem to. When are you going to start delegating more, and quit getting all bogged down in the hands-on stuff?"

"When you get me more people to delegate to. Do we have to have this argument right now? We've got a camera here that we think might have been at the scene when Billy Sheets got shot."

"You gotta realize—" He stopped, breathed once, and said, "You have?"

"Uh-huh. Just about ready to run the tape. You wanna come take a look?"

"You bet." Two seconds after I hung up, I heard his heavy footstep in the hall.

Ray had the gloves on and was cutting the tape on the evidence bag. As soon as he took out the camera, the whole staff peppered him with advice.

"The cable has to go to the video port—"

"Set the switch on the TV to video—"

"Wait, have you got the camera set for play?"

"You must not be on the right channel. It has to be Channel Three, doesn't it?"

"What we need in here," Frank said, "is a few more experts." The picture came up on the screen then, and we all stopped talking. Somebody turned off the overhead light, and the TV picture got brighter.

"Turn up the sound," Kevin said.

Ray fiddled and said, "There doesn't seem to be any."

"Has to be."

"Not if they turned it off. They musta turned it off."

"Let's quit fussing with it then," Frank said, "and just watch the picture." He had that hard edge of impatience in his voice that I'd been hearing a lot lately, and understood better and better the longer I tried to manage the complexities of the investigative department. He needed longer days. So did I. Ray started the picture again.

A small mixed-breed dog was sniffing a couple of pieces of red meat on the ground. He took a tentative bite, appeared to like it, and chewed contentedly for several seconds. Then a plume of dust and hair seemed to fly up from a spot behind his shoulder. He stiffened; dust flew up from another spot a couple of inches behind the first, and he fell over and lay still. The camera watched him for a few more frames before the picture went dark.

After a few seconds everybody in the room stirred, exhaled, and began to speak, but then the light on the screen came up again, and we all fell silent, watching. Another dog, bigger than the first and a little darker, entered the picture at the lower right, drawn once again to what looked like meat on the ground. The dog moved quietly to the food and ate, and dust flew up, and flew up again, and the dog fell down, and this time none of us made a sound except Lou, who began to cough. His hacking grew louder and faster and escalated to a choking crisis; he muttered apologetically and crept out of the room.

Pitman had brought me bullets from two dogs. I'd forgotten there was a third one missing. I felt a hot ball of anger form in my belly when a midsize mutt with a tawny pelt trotted onto the screen. I almost yelled, "No, go on! Get out of there!" Everybody had the same reaction, I guess; we were all glaring fiercely at the screen by the time the third dog fell down. The effect of the repeated shootings was cumulative. Each was more terrible than the last, and they were all made worse by dread of what was coming next.

When the scene in front of the Sheets house came up

on-screen, a subtle change took place in the room where we sat watching. Feet began to line up flat on the floor; shoulders pressed back against chairs, and hands were clasped tightly in laps. Soon we all sat at rigid attention, hardly breathing. We watched children running, playing, moving together toward the corner of the block. An older couple, the O'Connells, entered the top of the picture and walked toward the group. We saw Billy Sheets throw a ball to the child nearest him, and then Angie Sheets came out onto her front step and said something, and Billy turned and ran toward her. A plume of dust flew up from the back of Billy's jacket, and he fell down in the dirty snow with his hand out, reaching for his mother.

Darrell Betts made an agonized noise and lurched out of the room. I heard him retching in the hall, and then he went through the men's room door so fast it slammed against the wall. As the screen went dark, I stood up to turn on the overhead lights, and saw Rosie sitting with her head in her hands, tears leaking through her fingers.

"Wait," Frank said, "there's more." Jittery images appeared on the screen; people were running, pointing, calling to one another. The camera panned slowly across the confusion, found an opening in the crowd, focused on the figure on the ground, and quickly zoomed in for a close-up. The photographer lingered for a long moment on the still small figure lying there, before he zoomed out again and panned once more across the crowd. He caught Kay O'Connell as she turned from speaking to her husband, and for one eerie second she seemed to look right through the camera's eye and out at us.

The screen went dark then and stayed dark. A few seconds passed before Kevin stood up. He turned on the overhead lights and said thickly, "Dirty bastard went down for a close-up."

I took a deep breath and let it out slowly. When I was sure my voice would be okay, I said, "Bo, you think if you showed Kay O'Connell that shot of herself looking out, she might remember who was holding the camera?"

"Worth a try," he said.

"Oh, I don't think we should show this tape to anybody outside the department yet," Frank said.

"No, but Greg could make a still photo from that one frame. Take it over to him, will you, Ray? Don't let him touch the camera, keep your gloves on and do the rewinding yourself, tell him what we need, and let him pick the best shot. And then, come to think of it," I said as he started out, "ask him how long it would take to make a copy of the whole thing."

He flapped a hand back at me to show he'd heard and kept walking.

"Bo, you got anything else on your desk that won't wait till tomorrow?"

"Um—" He considered. "No."

"Then call the O'Connells, get them to wait for you if they will, get that picture, and go see them. Maybe it will jog a memory out of Kay. If she can't come up with anything, take her with you around the neighborhood, try again with the other people who were there that day. And let me know how you did, before you check out this morning."

Frank stood up and said quietly, walking out, "Come and see me as soon as you can spare a minute."

"I will. Rosie?" I touched her shoulder, and she turned her head halfway toward me without taking her hands away from her face.

"I've got a job for you. Come see me in about five minutes." She got up and walked away from me without a word.

Lou was dialing the phone when I poked my head in his office. His handheld respirator lay on the center of his desk, and I could tell from his gray-faced, sweaty look that he had been using it.

"You need to check out?"

He nodded grimly. "Soon as I find a social worker willing to get Bev Stokes in the shelter, I'm gone."

"Okay. I'll send somebody to debrief you as soon as I can."

Darrell met me in the hall, saying, "Jeez, I'm sorry—" He was still a little green, but suffering mostly from embarrassment.

"Forget it," I said. "That's about as bad as it gets. Remind me, was there something you have to do right now?"

"Uh . . . oh, yeah. Call Milo. About that plea bargain."

"You won't need any help with that, will you?"

"Nope, I got all I need."

"Go to it, then. Find me when you finish it. Lots of work here today."

"I hear you." Privately, I bet he'd be stopping by the arches for a Quarter Pounder with cheese on his way to Milo's office. Metabolism like Darrell's needs to stay fed.

Five minutes later Rosie stood in front of my desk, wearing fresh makeup but looking chastened. "I'm sorry, Jake. Five years a street cop, and then I cry over a video. Go figure."

"You don't need to apologize to me. I'd like to set fire to the damn thing myself; it makes me sick."

"What kind of a person could possibly—"

"I don't know. But I'm sure in a hurry to find out."

"So what's next?"

"I want you to call for a squad," I said, "go to Central School, and pick up a boy named Adam Priestley, and bring him in here."

"The honor student? Why him?"

"You know Adam Priestley?"

"Since yesterday. He's the one who was taking attendance in study hall the day of the fight, the one I think . . . it's the story I never get to tell you about."

"Tell me about it when you get him down here."

"Okay. But what do you want him for?"

"He jimmied the door to the shed where we found that camera."

"*Adam* did? Are you sure? Oh, I can't believe—he's this sweet little bookwormy kid, Jake, every teacher's dream student."

"Uh-huh. Bring him in here, and we'll see what kind of a dream he is."

"You want me to arrest him?"

"No. Tell the principal you need to talk to him, don't say a word to anybody else, go into his classroom and tell him we need to ask him some questions and he'll have to come with you. Have the officer stand by your side. He'll come. Take him to my office and call me if I'm not there."

"Son of a gun. I can't believe this. But okay." Restored to fighting trim by an interesting chore, she sailed out looking unsinkable again.

I walked across to the support-staff area, where Ray and Bo were bent over a desk, watching with rapt attention while images appeared and vanished on Greg LaMotte's screen.

"There," Bo said.

"Yeah," Ray said, "that's the best."

"Okay," Greg said, "we'll print that. Whaddya think, shall I try for a little more contrast?" In this universe, the picture has never been taken that Greg wouldn't want to buff up a little.

"Ray," I said, "soon as you finish here, go talk to Lou, will you? He's gotta go home. I want him to bring you up to speed on his current clients, in case he's still out tomorrow."

"Okay. By the way, Greg says we can make a copy through the VCR."

"You'll lose a little picture quality on the copy," Greg said, "but not enough to matter."

"Okay. And there's no danger of degrading the original?"

"Nah. Good for hundreds of plays."

"Good. Ray, will you do it as soon as you finish with Lou?"

"Sure."

"And then check the camera back into the evidence room. I don't know yet how I'll send it to BCA."

I hurried back to my office, called James Priestley, and told him I'd just sent a squad car to pick up his son. He said he'd talked to his lawyer, who told him he shouldn't let the police push him around, and should insist on an interview scheduled at his and his counsel's convenience.

"It's imperative that we talk to him right away," I said. "We have to find out whose gun and camera we found in your mother's shed."

"I told you, Adam doesn't know whose gun it is. Why are you so curious about the camera? There's nothing incriminating about a camera, is there?"

"There is about this one, yes."

"What do you mean? Are you suggesting it's involved in that shooting somehow? Of the Sheets boy? You think Adam had something to do with that?"

"I hope not. But I'm not at liberty to talk about this anymore right now. I'm sorry."

"Well, you've got to talk about it right now! If you're getting ready to arrest my son—"

"We're not. He isn't charged with anything, yet."

"Then why are you bringing him to the police station?"

"To find out who the other two boys are and what exactly they've been doing together."

"Well, you're not going to interrogate my boy without my attorney present. And he's not free to come over there right now."

"Mr. Priestley, do you understand what we're talking about here?" The image of Billy Sheets with a plume of dust flying up from his jacket was still devastatingly clear in my mind, I had a sick, sour feeling in my stomach from looking at it, and I wanted to get off the phone before I yielded to the temptation to vent some of my anger at James Priestley. "A little boy has been shot in his yard, and when we do charge somebody for that crime, the charge is going to be murder. Now I suggest you call your attorney back and the two of you think hard about how serious it might be if your son is mixed up in that, and then you come on over here and help us all you can. Now I gotta go." I hung up while he was still choking over his next protests, crumpled his earlier telephone message into a tight ball, and threw it as hard as I could into the wastebasket.

The next message on the stack was from Willy at BCA, and I dialed it, muttering, "Come on, Willy, amigo, tell me something I want to hear."

Willy did. "All five bullets were fired by the same gun. Almost certainly."

"How certainly is that?"

"Ninety-eight percent. Give or take."

"Probably close enough, huh?"

"To please a jury? Usually. You never know."

"From what make of gun?"

"A 10/22 for sure. Probably a Ruger. Bring me the gun, of course," he said, thinking he was being facetious, "and I'll tell you for sure."

"Funny you should ask. We think we've got the gun. If I send it today, can you get right on it?"

He made a noise that started as a snicker and ended as a groan. "Jake, Jake, why do you keep annoying me like this, when with just a little extra effort you could be a genuine pain in the ass?" He went on like that for a while, but I explained about finding the rifle and the camera in the shed, and after a while he got interested himself and said he'd see what he could do. So as soon as I hung up I called Russ Swenson, who was ramrodding the day shift, and asked him if he could spare a squad to run some evidence up to St. Paul.

"I'm spread too thin as it is," he said. "Send one of those jerk-offs in your own section; you won't even notice he's gone." When Russ reaches out and touches someone, he generally leaves a mark.

Frank was sliding spread sheets around on his desk in a fury of concentration; I stood in front of him for a few seconds till his eyes came up and refocused. He said, "That's a real poisonous sonofabitch took that video, Jake."

"I know. I want him bad."

"Or her? Guess we have to be PC."

"Jesus. Make me feel even worse."

"So where are we? You found the camera, your notes said, and a gun—"

"And now I've got the name of a boy who tricked his grandma out of a key to that shed. Rosie's gone to Central School to pick him up."

"Central School? This doesn't have anything to do with the fight, does it?"

"The fight? No. I don't see—why would it?"

"No reason. Just—damn funny coincidence."

"Yeah. But let's not get distracted by it. BCA says the bullets from the dogs match the bullet from the Sheets boy's body. Which isn't surprising, since we just saw all the shootings on the same video."

"And the gun—is the gun you found the one that did the shooting?"

"Well, naturally I think so. I'd like to send it to BCA today and find out. You think maybe you could light a little fire under Russ Swenson for a car and driver?"

"You don't have anybody to do it?"

"I'm short two guys as it is. Lou's going home sick, and Bo has to go get his wife out of the hospital at eleven. I explained that to Russ, but he wasn't feeling compassionate."

"Shit. You know I don't like to interfere between sections."

"Forget it then. I'll find some other way."

"No, this is important. I'll take care of it. But we gotta find a way to get you a little more heft so you can do your own arm wrestling. I'm working on a couple of ideas. Listen, are you thinking what I'm thinking, that there must be at least two people involved in these shootings?"

"Yup. One to shoot the gun, and one to take the pictures."

"Maybe taking turns?" We both winced. "Like some kind of a damn game. Jesus." He stacked some papers noisily. "I can't believe I'm saying this, but—kids, you think."

"It was kids got the key and made themselves at home in that shed. I have to go after them first. And it's gonna get messy, now, Frank." I told him about my conversation with James Priestley. "His parenting's on the line, he's got this smart boy he's always been proud of, and now he's gonna try to blame his troubles on us."

"If he's still in a mood to fight city hall when he gets here, let me know. I'll take him in my office for a frank and open exchange of ideas."

"That'll help." Strong men have grown feeble exchanging ideas openly with the chief.

I hurried back to my office and called Rosie's cell phone.

When she answered I said, "Answer yes or no to everything I say. Have you got Adam Priestley with you?"

"Yes."

"You're on your way back here?"

"Yes."

"His father's threatening to bring his lawyer down here and raise hell. The chief is ready to back us up if he has to. I'd like to get by without his help. Understand?"

"Yes."

"So I want you to go into the parking garage and come up the back elevator. Wait there in the back hall till I call you; I'll try to get his father and the attorney into my office first."

"Yes. Jake?"

"Don't talk, Rosie. Just get in here." I hung up on her. I knew she had something she desperately wanted to tell me, but I was beginning to think some of Lulu Breske's control techniques had their uses. I lined up four chairs in front of my desk, then found Kevin and stationed him at the head of the stairs.

"Bring James Priestley and his lawyer straight to my office," I said. "Don't let them start fussing around out here." I went back in my office and cleaned everything off my desk, put the tape recorder with a fresh roll of tape in the center of the blotter with a spiral notebook and two pencils beside it, and stood looking around, thinking, What else?

My phone rang. It was Amy Nguyen, sounding dubious. "Russ said I should call you to find out how to get ahead in law enforcement. Is it some kind of a joke?"

"Oh, Winnie, I'm sorry. Russ is just pissed because I did an end-around. I need you to make a run to St. Paul, will you do that? Good. I'll call you right back"—I ran and found Ray, who was still fiddling with the camera and VCR, and said, very fast, "Get that sealed up in an evidence bag fast, and check the rifle out of the evidence room. Then wait for Winnie and help her sign for both items, and see to it she has a map and instructions to get her to the crime lab in St. Paul. You got all that?"

"Yeah." I strode away from him, thinking maybe I'd invent a special commendation for the investigator on my crew who gave me the highest number of one-word answers in any given month. I called Winnie back and told her to get her instructions from Ray Bailey, who would meet her at the evidence room. Then I remembered the many times I have been lost in the unmarked halls of the Bureau of Criminal Apprehension, so I called St. Paul and got Ted Zumwalt on the line. I asked him, as a favor, to watch out for Officer Nguyen, who would be arriving in about an hour and a half, and help her navigate the many ambiguous turns of the great brick warren he works in. Ted did the best he could to contain his delight.

9

W/HEN Kevin brought a grim-looking James Priestley to
my door ten minutes later, I was relieved to see Wade
Rollie standing beside him. He's a solid middle-aged
attorney who heads his own small firm, always seems well prepared, and is not given to flashy moves. I had watched him in
court, where he seemed to keep his eye on the desired goal and
did not, like some of his colleagues, yield to the temptation to
showboat.

We shook hands all around. I seated them side by side in the
two chairs to my left and asked for permission to start my tape
recorder. Then I got Priestley's okay to spend a few minutes
telling Rollie about everything we'd found in the shed, including
the backdoor break-in. People aren't always entirely candid with
their attorneys. I didn't want any misunderstandings because
Priestley had tidied up the story. I gave generous credit, during
the narrative, for the full cooperation Priestley had given us in
the investigation.

Then I started on the hard part, asking for their help in the
interview to come. Using every euphemism I could think of, I
basically asked them to shut up and let me ask the questions.

"I'm afraid if all the adults start talking, Adam will feel
we're piling on, and he's likely to get defensive. Then we lose
time and information." Rollie nodded agreeably; Priestley still
looked apprehensive. "I'm hoping you'll monitor the ques-
tioning, and only stop me if you feel his rights are being vio-
lated. When I finish, if you still have questions, you can ask

them here, or I'll find you a private room where you can talk."

"Well," Rollie said. He cleared his throat in that my-throat-is-more-precious-than-thine way lawyers develop to stall for time. "Yes, that sounds reasonable enough." His glance had a little glint of steel in it when he added, "We'll just have to see how it works out." A small flick of his sword, to make sure his client knew he had a gladiator by his side.

"Fine. I'll see if they've arrived yet. Excuse me?" I took the shortcut through the storeroom and past the copy machine and found Rosie standing by the closed doors of the back elevator with a skinny, jug-eared kid, who looked a little uneasy but mostly quite interested. It is not all bad, when you're seventeen, to take a break from class and ride to the police station with a lively-looking redhead who's packing a Glock under her jacket.

"Ah, good, you're here. Your father and Mr. Rollie are already here, Adam."

"They are?" That shook him; his freckles stood out in his pale face. He rounded on Rosie. "You didn't tell me they'd be here."

"I wasn't sure about the attorney," she said. "Your father has to be here when we talk to you, Adam. That's the law."

"Okay, let's go this way." I led them back the long way, through proper hallways, with glimpses of busy people wearing badges, working at computers, and talking seriously into phones. It had the desired effect; Adam had sobered considerably by the time we reached my door.

Rosie said, "Uh, Jake—" and nodded toward the hall. I shook my head. Whatever was eating Rosie would have to wait; I couldn't stand out in the hall with her right now.

Priestley and his attorney stood when we came in. I introduced them to Rosie. Priestley remained grim and apprehensive, but Rollie brightened a little.

"Sit here, Adam," I said, indicating the seat nearest the wall. "Have a seat, Sergeant Doyle." She took the only chair left, between Adam and his father. I went around my desk and sat down, pointing out the working tape recorder to Adam. He looked at it the way a rabbit looks at a coyote.

I took a card out of my top drawer and said, "Now, I'm going to read you your rights. You have the right to remain silent—" I have the damn words seared into my brain so deep I'll probably still be reciting them after senility has robbed me of my name and address, but I've learned that people find the Miranda rules more impressive if you read them. Adam's father was impressed, too; he squinched his eyes and sucked in his cheeks when I got to the part about appointing an attorney if he couldn't afford one. He hadn't had time to consider, until now, that Adam's adventures might be costly.

When I finished I put the card back, laid my hands flat on the top of my desk, and looked at Adam Priestley a few seconds while the recorder hummed. Finally I asked him, "Why'd you break into your grandmother's shed?"

"She gave me the key," he said quickly.

"Which you used to get into the shed so you could jimmy the backdoor. Why?"

"Um—so I could get in when I wanted to."

"Why not just get the key from your grandmother whenever you wanted to use it?" His eyes darted around the room; he didn't want to look at me or his father. "Did you think she might start to notice if your dad had too many birthdays?" He hadn't known I knew that; he started to smile but quickly put his hand up to cover it.

"Okay, you broke out the back of the chest so you could get in when you wanted to. To do what?"

He twisted one foot around the other leg. "To have a place where I could come and go without asking anybody."

"You thought it was more fun if nobody knew where you were?"

"Yeah!" He grasped at fun, which sounded harmless.

"You and who else?"

"I'm sorry. I can't tell you their names."

"You have to."

"I can't. We promised each other we'd never tell anybody."

"Adam, you understand we're not playing games here?"

"I took a vow," he said, giving me a sort of Joan-of-Arc look.

He was in the police station, his father was there, and he was a little scared, but he was getting off a little on being noble, too.

"So you're ready to take the blame for shooting Billy Sheets?"

"For *what?*" He shook his head vehemently, without taking his eyes off my face, so that his eyeballs rolled in their sockets. "I didn't shoot anybody!"

In the same moment Wade Rollie raised his right hand off his briefcase and said, "Oh, see here, we're not going to stand for any bullying tactics—"

And Adam's father said, "That's not his gun you found, I told you that."

"I don't care whose gun it is. The shot that killed Billy Sheets came from that shed window. And so far, Adam's the only person I can place in that shed."

"But I wouldn't even know *how* to shoot anybody!" Adam wailed, "I've never even *held* a gun!"

"Guess you better give me the names of the other two boys, then."

"Where did you get that number?" James Priestley said. "How do you know there were two?"

"You told me," I said, "remember?"

"Did I?" He looked at his son. "Did you tell me two, Adam?"

"Yes. No, stop, I can't say any more!" Adam's voice was beginning to shake, and a couple of tears ran down through his freckles. He turned his face away and wiped it with the back of his hand, looking ashamed.

I remembered saying to Rosie, Remember, crying is also an evasion. I sat watching Adam Priestley, wondering if I was looking at a seventeen-year-old boy who was ashamed of crying but not of shooting dogs and children. While I pondered, Rosie unexpectedly leaned across her chair arm and asked him, softly, "How much did Butch and Owen pay you to fake the attendance records?"

Her question silenced everybody. Priestley and Rollie stared at her openmouthed. Adam, dumbfounded by this new attack, looked like a deer caught in the headlights. I did my best to look as if I had any idea what she was talking about.

Finally Adam couldn't stand the silence any longer and asked her, "What makes you think I did?"

"You take the roll in study hall Tuesdays and Thursdays, don't you? For Mr. Eliot?"

"Sure. Other kids take it too. At other times."

"Uh-huh. I noticed the handwriting didn't always match Mr. Eliot's. So I asked him how come. He said he has thirty students in most of his classes this year, so he got the principal's okay to have his honor students do some of the routine chores. Like taking attendance in morning and afternoon study hall."

"That's right. But I didn't—" He waved his arms awhile and tried again. "Why would I want money?" He tried to look contemptuous. "I always had more than they did, anyway." He stopped then, looking sick, aware he had said more than he intended. She watched him, smiling the awful smug little smile she uses when she plays poker, till he asked her, "What did you see that made you ask me that?"

"I noticed Butch and Owen were the first names on the list that day, but the last on Monday and Wednesday. So I looked back and saw that on Tuesdays and Thursdays, for the past couple of weeks, they were always first on the list, but they were always near the last on the other days. I asked Ellie Madden how come Butch and Owen never seem to be the first ones in the room when she's taking the roll—"

"Don't pay any attention to her. She's just jealous because I'm better at math than she is."

"She said Butch and Owen hate study hall, so they *never* come in till after the bell rings. But she said lately you've been putting them in the book first thing when you start taking the roll, even though some mornings they never make it to study hall at all."

"She'll say anything to get me in trouble. She wants to be valedictorian."

"That's right, she is your main competition, isn't she? The principal told me it's probably between the two of you, you've both got straight A's."

"That's right." He liked talking about his grades. He glanced at his father to see if good grades would help on that side of the room, but James Priestley's face had turned to stone.

"It's wonderful that you do so well in school," Rosie said, "but what I don't understand is why you'd risk it all for a couple of guys who aren't even friends of yours."

He sat up and said sharply, "Sure they are."

"Since when? Everybody else I talked to at school said Butch and Owen mostly hung out with P. K. McCafferty. And they said you didn't seem to have any particular buddies."

"Before, maybe." His pale face and neck were blotched with pink. "Because they were all in athletics. But this winter Butch and Owen decided to get off the stupid teams."

"Why?"

"They were sick of the other jocks. They wanted to try . . . they decided to learn about some of the stuff I knew."

"Like what?"

"Well, you know, astronomy, math . . . the Internet. I'm a whiz on computers." He looked to see if Rollie was impressed. Rollie was, but only by Rosie Doyle.

"So you three are buddies now? You and Butch and Owen?"

"I don't know about buddies. Friends, anyway."

"You were going to have a secret society or something?"

"You make it sound silly. We just decided to learn stuff together."

"Is that what the clubhouse was for?"

"I never said—"

"No, Adam, you never gave your friends away. We just figured it out, okay?" She waited a few heartbeats and summarized for him, "You just wanted a clubhouse where you and Butch and Owen could cruise the Internet, learn some neat stuff about the universe and so on, right?" She made it sound like earning another medal in Scouts.

"Well," he said, "yes."

"So the agreement was for Butch and Owen to skip first-period study hall to get the clubhouse ready—"

"Bring in games and stuff—" He could see, by now, that she understood.

"And your part was to fix the attendance records so they could skip school first period?"

"On Tuesdays and Thursdays. They never got much studying done, anyway." His ironic little smile invited us all to share the joke. Nobody shared, and his smile died.

"Let's see now. How many times was it that you did this?"

"Um—" he squirmed and twisted a button on his sweater. "Four times before. Tuesday made five."

"But not today?"

"Well, no. After—" He twisted the button some more and tried again. "I mean, the shed—"

Rosie sat back in her chair and looked at me. I nodded and leaned forward.

"Just the two of them and you? Nobody else was in on this?"

"No."

"So . . . they went to your grandmother's shed to shoot the gun?"

"No!" He shook his head hard. "I thought you understood—" He turned to Rosie, but she seemed lost in thought. So he hunched his chair forward a little, sat on the edge of it, and rested his arms on my desk. When he was as close to me as he could get, he made earnest eye contact and insisted, "That gun doesn't belong to any of us! I don't know how it got there."

I looked at James Priestley, and he said, "I'll vouch for the fact that it's not Adam's gun, and that he doesn't know—" He stopped suddenly, worked his mouth a couple of times, and said, "Well." He seemed to realize, then, the size of the loss he had just suffered. His shoulders hunched up a little, and his voice got hoarse. "I guess I should say, that as far as I *know*, he doesn't know how to shoot a gun." Adam sat back in his chair then, and looked down at his hands.

I turned to Wade Rollie and said, "I think we're about done here. Would you like the use of a room to confer with your clients?"

"And then he's free to go?" James Priestley asked me. It cost him to ask me politely, but he managed it.

"For now. You understand, somebody's going to be facing

charges in this case. And I can't say, right now, exactly what those charges will be or who's going to be facing them. At a minimum, I'll probably need to talk to Adam again, maybe several times."

"Will you"—Priestley looked at Rollie—"keep track of how this is going for me?"

"Well, sure," Rollie said, "I'll check with these folks right along. If"—he ventured a friendly smile in my direction—"if that's okay with you, Jake?"

"We'll give you any information we're free to divulge," I said. He understood I was giving him something to save face in front of his client, but he wouldn't get anything from me he couldn't read in the newspaper.

"Well, then," Rollie said, taking charge, "I think it would be a good idea if we all went to my office for a little visit. We won't take advantage of your hospitality here, Lieutenant Hines, but we certainly thank you." He got the other two out the door with little kindly seeming arm movements that were really calculated to keep them moving while establishing his identity as the alpha male.

James Priestley, moving away from us in his nice gray suit, with the light twinkling off his clean glasses, looked wrapped about as tight as a man can get. His son walked beside him like a stiff-necked stranger, more alone than ever, silent and pale. He slid a quick glance back at Rosie as he went out the door, but she was busy putting some papers in order. Wade Rollie, behind them, was looking at his watch as he went toward the stairs.

I closed my door and said, "That was a damn nice job, Rosie."

"Oh, thanks. Actually it was almost too easy; I was pretty sure of my facts."

"Well, but that's the part I mean, up there at the school, spotting that business of the two names being first on the list and figuring out what Adam was doing. The principal must have been onto this too, huh? Is that why he had them in his office when Darrell went back to school to talk to them?"

"You know, that's funny. He did have them in his office, and from what I could gather he was grilling them about exactly where they'd been during the fight, because he was uneasy about them not being down there with the rest of the team, and I think maybe Ellie Madden managed to slip him a little hint that they weren't in study hall. But he wouldn't talk to me about it. I don't want to mix any feminist rhetoric in here, but I think all the males in that building think Ellie's a ball-breaking little priss, and they're rooting for Adam for valedictorian."

"My, my. Do you think she's a ball-breaking—"

"Oh, you bet. But when she's right, she's right. And she was right about what Adam was doing with the attendance records."

"Okay. I say again, damn good police work." I smiled at her benignly. "And actually the interrogation was a nice sneaky con job, too."

"Why, thank you, thank you." She rearranged a couple of combs in her hair while she tried to look modest. When I went on watching her she said, "What?"

"Women do that, don't they? Fool with their hair when they want to blow off a compliment or an insult. Trudy does it, too."

She harrumphed some indignation at me. Rosie has a great harrumph, developed in a lifetime with mostly male relatives. When rude noises failed to stop my smiling, she said, "Well, so? Men jingle the coins in their pockets if something makes them unsure of themselves. And button their jackets and straighten their ties."

"True. Also shoot their cuffs and look at their watches and smooth their facial hair, if any."

She came off her high horse about an inch and said, "Smooth their facial hair? I hadn't noticed that one." I nodded. She relaxed the rest of the way and smiled. "It's all neat stuff to watch for, isn't it?"

"Sure is. You're getting good at this work, Sergeant Doyle. You have a real feel for it, I think."

"When it doesn't make me cry, huh?" she smiled ironically. "Keen-eyed Rosie Doyle, girl detective. That's what my Mom calls me. She thinks it's time I got married and started having babies. I told her being a police investigator is made to order for a good Catholic girl; I get to be on the side of the angels all the time and still ask all the nosy questions I want."

I laughed out loud, which felt good to my face. "Okay, Keen-eyed Rosie. Can you guess what our next job is going to be?"

She looked at me a minute, sighed, and said, "Butch and Owen."

"Uh-huh. Not as much fun as Adam Priestley, I bet."

"Parents first?"

"Yes. You can get the names and phone numbers from the school office, right? And I'll call them while you line up a squad. Make it two squads—I think I'll have Kevin go too."

"Oh, Jake, I don't need any—"

"Please," I said, holding my hand up, "these are large athletic types, okay? Let's not take a chance on any rough stuff. But say, come to think of it—"

"What?"

"They *are* big guys. And both seniors. Wouldn't it be convenient if they turned out to be over eighteen? Why don't you check on their ages before you do anything else?"

"Oh, what a nice thought. Listen, could I make a couple of other calls first? I've had some people hanging fire all morning."

"Sure, take your time," I said. "In fact, why don't we try to set this up for the first thing after lunch? Butch and Owen aren't going anywhere till school's out."

I took the tape of the Priestley interview to Rae on the support staff, because she's fast and friendly and she hardly ever transforms priceless information into meaningless garbage. Back at my desk, I looked at my watch, saw it was not quite eleven, and decided to type up my own impressions of the interview, to augment the tape. But when I pulled up yesterday's notes, instead of scrolling directly to the end I began reading them over, and soon I was filling in details I'd been too tired to include the night before.

Revising text is like weeding a garden; you never stop when you intended to. I had skipped the incident at Ernie Chisholm's house, believing that it had no relevance and was better not written down, but now I thought, You never know, and began typing in the sad little story, keeping my tone carefully noncommittal.

Kevin Evjan put his head in my door while I was still struggling with it and said, "Got time to look at something?"

"In a minute. Have a seat."

"Shee," he looked around, "plenty of choices in here today." He set the two extra chairs back where they belonged against the wall, settled himself comfortably in one of the two remaining, and began leafing through the folder he was carrying. One of the reasons I picked him for an assistant is that he doesn't take a lot of tending. He sat reading contentedly while I typed fast for five more minutes.

When I got to a good stopping place, I said, "Whaddya got?"

"Remember I said I'd search back files at the dear old *Rutherford Blat* for stories about Stearns?"

"Oh. Yeah. You found something, huh?" I had not thought about the retirement party since I mentioned it to him, and I didn't want to think about it now.

"Mmm." He gave me a strange, ambiguous look and slid a dozen copies of clippings across my desk. "Sure hope you weren't planning a roast," he said.

"Listen," I said, "I don't think today is the—" My eye was caught by an upside-down studio portrait of a much younger Al Stearns. I turned it around. "Son of a gun. He was really a good-looking dude in those days, wasn't he?" Even allowing for studio buffing, Al Stearns looked very attractive in an immaculate patrolman's uniform. And he was smiling! "When was this?"

"Date's on the margin." I read it; May 22, 1979.

"The old unis were a little more studly, weren't they?"

Kevin said, "I thought the shirts were white."

"The brass wore white. Street unis were gray with black epaulets and shirt flaps. Frank showed me his once."

"That's a Smith and Wesson revolver he's packing, isn't it? A .38?"

"Uh-huh. Model fifteen. See the speed-loader pouch on his belt?"

"We had a flat leather Sam Browne belt before we got the basket-weave ones, huh?"

"Yeah. I guess what made that lash-up so sexy was all the brass buckles and snaps."

"No Velcro," Kevin said. "Imagine enforcing the law without Velcro."

I noticed the headline under the picture then: "Rutherford Police Officer Hurt in Traffic Mishap." The story was just a few paragraphs long, a brief account of a traffic stop in which one of the two patrolmen at the scene was hit by a passing motorist.

Kevin said, "I'm sort of sorry I missed riding two to a car. How long's it been?"

"A dozen years, I guess. Since computer aided dispatch came on line." The story said Sergeant Stearns's injuries were serious but not critical; he had a broken leg and lacerations, and was in stable condition in Methodist Hospital.

I noticed the surprising part. "Stearns was a sergeant?"

"Wonders never cease in this story." He handed me another clipping. "Read on." It was dated the following day. Several readers had called the paper to ask why the motorist who struck a patrolman while he was issuing a speeding ticket had not been arrested or even cited. In response, a reporter asked some questions and was told that Sergeant Stearns had "inadvertently stepped into the traffic lane of the roadway." The chief of police was interviewed. He said a thorough review of the case was being initiated, but preliminary findings indicated an unfortunate accident that was nobody's fault.

The motorist who hit the cop corroborated the story. He had been obeying all traffic laws when he passed the two cars, parked one behind the other at the curb. Just as the passing motorist pulled even with the lead car, Sergeant Stearns stepped, "or fell," directly in front of him. The driver couldn't stop in time. Stearns had attempted to jump out of the way, and partially succeeded, saving his life but leaving one leg still in harm's way. The motorist, who was alone in the car, was only slightly injured. His vehicle had sustained damage to the right front bumper and windshield, and was being repaired.

"I suppose his insurance company wasn't happy, though," Kevin said. "Because somebody kept asking more questions, and it went on for weeks. Look at this." He waved a sheaf of clippings.

"Listen, I don't have much time. Can you summarize? Why did this turn into such a big deal?"

"He was drunk. Stearns. His partner had tried to handle the speeding stop alone, but Stearns got out of the car and began giving the driver a bad time, forgot where he was, and stepped right out into traffic."

"Wow. And then what?" I said, skimming through the next dozen clippings. "Looks like at first the department tried to deny that he was drunk on duty."

"Right. The press took to calling it Policegate, and like always the cover-up got to be much worse that the original offense. Other officers and clients began telling stories about times when they'd seen Stearns behaving erratically."

"So this wasn't a onetime thing?"

"Not at all. Stearns had a drinking problem that had been escalating for months. His partner and his shift commander had been trying to cover for him but urging him to get help."

"Hard man to urge," I said, "if he was anything like now."

"For sure. Looks like he was in total denial, till the whole thing blew up in his face."

"Who was chief then?"

"Clifton."

"Ah. Not a guy to go to bat for his crew, the way I heard it."

"Doesn't look like it. Made one or two tries at sweeping the whole thing under the rug, but he started throwing bodies over the wall as soon as the mess got close to his door."

"So Stearns wasn't the only one who got disciplined?"

"Aw, shit, no. Before Stearns got stripped of rank and seniority, he cost his partner and shift commander each a couple of long suspensions too."

"You remember Clifton?"

"Gone before my time," Kevin said.

"Well, mine too. But I met him at somebody's retirement

party. I could tell some of the older guys hated him, but they never wanted to talk about it."

"Anyway, I guess this explains why Stearns never has much to say."

"You think so? This much later?"

"A guy who lets his personal shit splash all over his partner? I bet nobody talked to him any more than they had to for a long time."

"I'm surprised he kept his job."

Kevin tapped one of the clippings. "At one point Clifton said he was going to be fired, but somebody must have stood up for him big-time. He lost almost a year's pay, but he got to keep his badge."

"Ah. Guess that's why he worked the extra year."

"To fill out his pension time, yeah. You never heard any scuttlebutt about this? Lou never mentioned it to you, or Frank?"

"Not a word." I sat and stared at the several newspaper photos that accompanied the stories, showing a slender, handsome Stearns smiling in an immaculate uniform. "Jeez, it must have been a can of worms." I stacked the clippings and handed them back to him. "What a way to blow a career." I stared at the wall a minute. "I see what you mean, no traffic jokes."

"Right. No buddy stories either."

"This party gets more hilarious all the time."

"We could hire a belly dancer."

"Or sell chances on a trip to Mars. Listen, thanks for looking that stuff up. Put it away where nobody else sees it, huh? We'll think about Stearns later. Right now I want you to get ready to go to Central School with Rosie." I told him about the information we had pried out of Adam Priestley.

"So now you want to talk to Butch Ranfranz and Owen Campbell."

"You bet. We want them to account for every minute of the time they've been out of school for the last three weeks."

"Whee. Is the Sheets shooting starting to look like it has something to do with the fight at school?"

"I don't see how. Although it is a freaky coincidence, huh? We go to stop a fight and stumble across two guys skipping school—"

"And they just happen to be the ones breaking into the shed next to the shooting? I feel like I'm making this up."

"Me too. But what can we do but follow the evidence?"

"Mmm. You think they conned Adam Priestley into helping them?"

"That's the way I read it. Unless he's pure evil and I just can't see it."

"Ooh, pure evil, there's a good movie title. When do you want to talk to these next two assholes? Not that I'd ever think of prejudging the little turds."

"Right after lunch, I thought. Rosie's getting their parents' names now, so we can call them and get permission. She's also checking on the boys' ages. We might get a break there; it's possible they're over eighteen."

"Breaks are nice. Well"—he looked at his watch—"I'll go see about—" He stood up and turned, and then Rosie walked in the door without knocking and stood there looking dazed.

"Butch Ranfranz and Owen Campbell are missing from school," she said.

"You serious? They must not know we found out—"

"No, something's different this time. They made study hall all right, and second-period social studies, then classes broke at ten-forty-five, and they never made it to trigonometry class at eleven."

"So . . . the janitors checked the johns and the locker rooms?"

"Yes, but somebody came into the principal's office while I was on the phone, and said Butch's car is gone from the parking lot."

"Maybe we better check the shed on Nineteenth Street," Kevin said.

"There's something else," Rosie said. She was fidgeting in front of my desk, turning a file folder around and around in her hands while she darted little quick glances at the two of us in turn. Finally she said, in a strangled-sounding voice, "P. K. McCafferty's missing too."

Then all the phones on our side of the building seemed to ring at once, and outside in the street, sirens began to wail.

10

S HULTZY said, when I answered my phone, "We got a Priority One, Jake." All around her at the dispatch desk, I could hear other voices repeating the same information, very fast. "Two shooters on the roof of the Merriott Hotel. At least two, maybe more. They've shot two people on the street and two inside the hotel. Russ says get everybody downtown ASAP. Can you notify your crew, or—"

"All but Darrell; he's out of the building. You'll have to page him." I put down the phone and told Kevin, "Get Ray in here." To Rosie I said, "Get your vest. Check your weapon, bring plenty of extra clips. We've got two shooters on the roof of the Merriott."

Ray and Kevin came back as I was getting into my vest. I repeated the information, adding, "Tell Lou he's our anchor again. Gear up and come downstairs. Rosie and I will go check out two cars."

Rosie and I took the shortcut to the back elevator. It was groaning away somewhere above us; I heard the doors open and loud voices yelling, "Hold the elevator, hold it!" and the sound of heavy wheels going in and out of the car. I said, "The stairs—" and we ran down.

"Only one set of keys left," Rosie said.

"Grab it."

"Rats, it's that miserable old Dodge with the bad starter. Shall we—"

"I don't want to take my pickup into a mess like that," I said. "Just sign for it, Rosie, we're not going far."

The parking garage was a nightmare of slamming car doors, squealing brakes, and gas fumes. All the radios were crackling, dispatch saying, over and over, "Code Three, in the area of the Merriott Hotel, two shooters on the roof firing into the street, two victims down in the street, two inside the hotel, see the officer in charge—"

Rosie said, "Could that possibly be P. K. up there? I can't believe it, Jake."

"Don't believe it. P. K. would never—" I was going to say "hurt anybody," but then I remembered the fight that started all this.

Two squads came in fast from the street, one right behind the other, squealing their brakes as they maneuvered into parking spaces. Both drivers jumped out and ran toward the small room under the stairs marked "ERU Supply Room." Three of the ERU team were already in there, gearing up. They banged into each other and swore as they pulled equipment out of lockers and began putting bulletproof vests and headgear on over their camouflage uniforms.

The ERU storeroom is, as the chief says, "ten pounds of shit in a five-pound bag," and it keeps getting worse as they add equipment. Watching five men wrestle big guns and extra ammo, radios and battering rams and scopes and tear gas canisters out of that little space, you have to wonder if the most dangerous part of their job isn't getting away from the station.

All their special clothing is hot, too, made out of industrial-weight artificial fibers, and the heavy gear they hang on it raises the inside temperature even further. I could hear Vince Greeley, manhandling his body bunker over a bench in his three layers of nylon and Kevlar, yelling, "Let's get outside before I fucking *melt!*"

"Look, they're loading the Peacekeeper," Kevin said, coming up behind me.

Ray stepped out of the elevator and stared. "They're really gonna use that thing?"

The Peacekeeper is an armored personnel carrier that the chief scrounged from the U.S. Air Force while they were having one of their periodic generosity fits. They send out circulars offering their old junk when they need to clear out parking lots for new equipment. The vehicle Rutherford PD got had been out of service and scavenged for parts for years, reduced to a rusty shell with bald tires and a pile of loose junk under the hood.

"They saw me coming," Frank said apologetically to the garage techs. "I'll get rid of it, guys." He reckoned without Vince Greeley, who took one look at its bulletproof windshield and rotating roof turret, and fell in love.

"I mean, gun ports in the bulkheads, for Christ's sake," he told me, grinning radiantly.

"Oh, well, if it's got gun ports we better keep it," I said. I thought the whole project was too off-the-wall to last, but I should have known Vince Greeley would keep the balloon aloft. Born with an extra squirt of testosterone and never happier than when he's going overboard for the ERU, Vince passes many happy hours working out in his home gym in what his wife calls the Taj Garage. As soon as he saw the Peacekeeper, he turned his prodigious energies to mustering every junkyard owner and shade-tree mechanic he knew. He put the arm on local entrepreneurs for cash and scrounged cut-rate tools and auto parts. Eight hundred volunteer hours later, he wheedled a paint job out of Frank.

"What's white and blue and incredibly sexy all over?" he demanded with his head in my office door, the day the Peacekeeper rolled out of the paint shop. He insisted I go down with him to view the results, and he found my reaction quite gratifying.

"Holy crud," I said, "this thing is awesome."

He cackled his high, manic laugh and yelled, "The burnin' end, right? Am I right?"

"Jesus, Vince. The radiator looks like a cattle guard."

"Quarter-inch armor plate all over the body," he crowed, "three-eighths on the doors."

"Who're we going to war with, for Christ's sake?"

"Pity the poor bastard, whoever he is," he crooned. "This baby'll stop a .308."

Today they piled their nylon bags of equipment into the back of the unlikely looking beast, climbed in wearing all their cumbersome garments, and rolled out with the rotating roof lights blazing and the siren going full blast.

"No use giving the bad guys any anxious moments, huh?" Kevin said. "This way they know we're coming for sure."

"We're going in the old Dodge?" Ray asked me, looking, if possible, more dubious than usual. "We may have to get out and push."

"Just get in," I said. I turned on the radio.

"Remember to set it to the emergency frequency," Ray said.

"I brought my handheld for that. Here, turn it on. I'm gonna leave my car radio on dispatch freq so we can transmit if we need to."

The motor on the Dodge started on the second try, one better than average. We followed the Peacekeeper toward Broadway, at a lengthening distance. We were almost two blocks behind when Vince pulled up at the outer perimeter roadblock three blocks south of the hotel. Casey moved a section of barricade out of the way for Vince, and I floorboarded it, yelled, "Wait, wait," and got through before he closed up again.

Once inside the perimeter, Vince slowed down and turned off his siren. He stopped in the intersection of First Avenue and Second Street, facing the Merriott Hotel, which occupied an entire block on Broadway, facing west. Vince idled in the intersection, hunched forward over the wheel and peered around while he talked into the radio. I pulled up a couple of lengths behind him and started my own survey.

The most dangerous thing about big crime scenes is that they quickly tend toward a circus atmosphere that can become almost impossible to control. Street cops start out in charge, and yield command to their patrol sergeants as they arrive. Before long patrol sergeants are taking orders, off and on, from detectives, who eventually relinquish control to their lieutenants and captains, and so on up the food chain. All this wielding and yielding of authority usually takes place in the middle of a crowd of people reacting to fear, pain, rage, hysteria, and simple curiosity, yelling, "What's happening?" and, "Where?" and sometimes "Help!" Trying to keep the bystanders from making matters worse during a crisis can be a chore in itself, and overlapping circles of authority don't make it any easier.

Bringing order to the chaos at crime scenes was part of the goal when the chief created the Emergency Response Unit. Not the only one, of course; as the bad guys got better organized and more heavily armed, it simply made sense to have the worst situations handled by a team of experienced officers with specialized training and equipment. But one of Frank's first rules when the team was formed was that whenever the ERU team was called out, the leader of the ERU team would be in command of all forces in the field until the emergency ended.

In the two years since the unit was formed, it had worked very well when it worked by itself. On bigger emergencies, its attempts to coordinate with the department as a whole had gained it one rave review, two so-sos, and one miserable screaming match. Today, I thought, looking at the mass of people and vehicles in front of me, might be its toughest test yet. To begin with, there were already victims in serious need of help.

A gray-haired woman in a tweed coat lay at the edge of the sidewalk half a block east of the hotel. She was not moving. A little trail of blood ran from somewhere under her body and across the sidewalk. Reaching the curb, it formed slowly into big drops that dripped into the gutter and pooled there.

A few feet past her, a young man in a tan jacket and khakis sat propped against a storefront. He seemed to be staring down the block toward us, but I couldn't tell if he could see us; his eyes looked glazed, and his lips worked aimlessly. He had clamped his left hand over his upper right arm. Blood seeped through his fingers, making a spreading stain on his pants.

Two ambulances were parked against the curb at the far end of the block behind us, with their roof lights going and their motors running. Patrolmen were deployed in defensive postures behind the five squads I could see around the block, and I knew there would be more behind the building. Their weapons were all trained on the roof of the hotel. While I watched, a puff of smoke appeared at the corner post of the retaining wall at the top of the hotel facade, and the three officers who were within range of the gunshot fired back.

Two blocks south of where we sat, I saw Ed Gray rousting a couple of cars away from the curb. As soon as they were out of the way, a big RV pulled around the corner from Fourth Street and jockeyed into the space. Ed climbed on board, and the motor home began to bristle with antennas, lights, and loudspeakers. He was activating the ERU command vehicle, an electronics junkie's dream.

I backed into a parking spot a few feet ahead of the ambulances, waited for a break in the radio chatter, and checked in with Ed on the dispatch frequency.

"Copy," he said, "hold one." Listening from another town to Ed's radio transmissions during emergencies, you might think he was directing a burn at the city dump. The crazier things get, the cooler it makes him. He came back in a minute and told me to find Russ. "He's managing the traffic around the hotel, I think he's by the bank there."

"I see him."

"Good. Check in with him, see if he needs any help."

"Copy."

"You got a radio that gets our freq?"

"Affirmative."

"Monitor that."

"Copy." I turned up the volume on my handheld a little. We could hear but not transmit; the ERU channel is for team use only. Ed Gray was talking on it now, telling Vince that job one was getting the victims off the sidewalk.

"What about the victims inside the hotel?" Vince said.

"Their injuries aren't critical," Ed said, "and there were a couple of doctors at a meeting in there who are taking care of them for now. We're gonna leave them there till this is over. Let's do the two on the sidewalk just the way we practiced, okay? Standard 'downed citizen' rescue."

"Affirmative," Vince said. "This job is made to order for the Peacekeeper. I'm gonna pull down past you—" When their strategy was settled, Vince turned right in the intersection and drove south past the command post, while Ed Gray told all the rest of us to get in place and ready to fire at the roof. He directed the ambulances to pull left through the intersection and park on First Avenue, in the shelter of the office tower, with their rear doors open and their stretchers out.

Vince drove two blocks south, turned left under the shelter of a six-story apartment block, rounded the corner onto Broadway fast, and floorboarded it back north toward the Merriott. He hit the brakes hard just as he pulled even with the young man in khakis, and squealed to a stop within inches of the gray-haired woman's hand. As soon as he stopped, puffs of smoke began to appear alongside two pillars near the south end of the roof, and a couple of bullets hit the armor plate of the Peacemaker with a noise like the crack of doom. One ricocheted and shattered glass somewhere, and a woman's voice screamed. All of us who were in range fired at the puffs on the roof.

When the backdoors of the personnel carrier burst open, Huckstadt and Cooper jumped out carrying body bunkers, and ran full tilt toward the two people on the ground. Cooper, heading for the man in khakis, had the farthest to run but was better placed when he reached his victim; the store's awning gave him partial shelter. He got his man on his feet and tucked in tight behind the bunker with him. Then he slid his own feet under the victim's and quick-walked him to the back of the personnel carrier. Arms reached out to help him hoist the victim inside, and he jumped in over the bumper.

Huckstadt's victim was partially sheltered by the vehicle, but she was unconscious and flat on the sidewalk, and he was already carrying the heavy body bunker. He covered both of them with the big shield, slid his arm out of the handles, and knelt, gathering her in his arms. I heard him yell, "Now!" and Clint Maddox vaulted from the back of the Peacekeeper, covered the distance to Huckstadt in two long leaps, snatched up the bunker, and covered them all with it as he and Huckstadt scrambled back into the armored car.

Somebody pulled the rear doors of the Peacekeeper shut

while Vince Greeley laid a stinking black trail of rubber on the pavement in a roaring getaway. He bombed straight north for two blocks, slowed for an almost sedate left-hand turn, turned again onto First Avenue, and stopped by the ambulances. Before his wheels had quite stopped turning, the ambulance drivers were at his backdoors with gurneys.

I had run the old Dodge forward to the middle of the block in front of the hotel, and my crew and I were sheltered behind its open doors, shooting up at the roof of the hotel whenever we saw anything move. All around us, from behind every door and pillar that offered protection, other uniforms watched the rooftop, firing when they saw a target. As soon as Vince crossed Center Street, Ed Gray said, "Cease fire." The sudden silence was as shocking as noise. I said, "Now!" and we all jumped back in the car.

I had left the motor running because I knew the Dodge would pick this moment to stall forever if I gave it a chance, and I demonstrated a little speed of my own backing out of there. When we were safely west of Second Avenue, I took my time finding a parking space.

"Jesus," Kevin said softly, almost reverently, "that went nice."

"Uh-huh," I said. "We got hit, though." I got out and took a look at my left front fender. Three inches in front of the door I'd been crouching behind, its jagged metal edges glinting, was a fresh bullet hole.

"Damn," Ray said, just behind me, "they wounded the Dodge." He stared at it sadly. "Shame they couldn'a killed it."

"Good work," I heard Ed Gray say, as we got back in the car. "Now let's get that window washer out of there."

Window washer? "God's sake," Kevin said, "I never saw him there." He must have been working on his platform when the shooting started on the roof. His rig dangled at the third-floor level, on the north end of the building near the rear corner. Too frightened to move, he squatted on his platform, with tools and cleaning rags dangling, his bucket upside down on his head. He seemed to be doing his best to believe that his whole body was inside the bucket that rested on his shoulders.

"Same drill," Ed said. "Come when I call you, Vince. The rest of you, get ready to fire again when I give the order."

I started the Dodge again, miraculously on the first try this time, and ran it forward in the middle of the street as I had before, and we got out and got behind the doors, which felt like very flimsy cover now. From this position I could see the stains on the window washer's coveralls, and the sign painted on his module—"Happy's Cleaning Services," with round yellow smiling faces around it.

A man in a blue suit leaned out a window in an office directly below the platform, looked up at the man under the bucket, and said something to him quietly. The window washer lifted his bucket a little, listened and nodded, and then pulled the bucket back down over his head and very cautiously raised his body enough so he could grope for the power switch on the cable.

"Start now, Vince," Ed said. "The rest of you, fire at will."

Vince roared past us going east as the window washer's fingers found the switch, started the motor on his hoist, and lowered his platform to the sidewalk. Vince slid to a stop with his rear doors even with the platform. The man unhooked the safety line from his orange vest and jumped off the platform with the bucket still on his head. Puffs of smoke showed near the pillars on the roof above him. Bullets hit the top of the Peacekeeper with a hollow *bong!* and ricocheted off. Huckstadt and Cooper jumped out the back of the blue and white vehicle and stuffed the window washer, bucket and all, none too gently inside. Vince roared away while they were still trying to get the doors closed.

"God," Rosie said, when we were safely back in our parking spot, "what ails these guys on the roof anyway? All these guns shooting at them, and they don't know enough to give up?"

"Let's get our own work organized," I said. "When this is over, we'll have to sort out what happened, so we should spread out now and try to gather information from different points of the crime scene. I'm going to work my way over to Russ—he's over there behind the pillars, at the side entrance to the bank, see him? He'll be the watch commander in charge here. I'll tell him you three are taking up positions at the back and both sides of the hotel, and you'll be ready to assist the cops he's got stationed there."

Rosie said, "How do you know—"

"They'll be there, Rosie. Russ knows what he's doing."

Kevin said, "And you're going to stick with Russ? What if he assigns you to crowd control on the outer perimeter?" He knew as well as I did how much Russ loves to stick it to investigators.

"He usually gives his sense of humor a rest in emergencies. Now. Got your phones and pagers? Check your ammo, take plenty. Stay safe."

Rosie said, as she climbed out of the car, "Will you try to find out if P. K. McCafferty is up there?"

"Yes. But he won't be." I watched them move off and then made my way to Russ, who was bunkered down comfortably behind a pillar and a garbage truck he had commandeered. He had jury-rigged a bench out of sawhorses and lumber from a nearby construction site, and had radios and phones laid out in front of him. He was communicating with his street crew on the dispatch frequency, monitoring the SWAT team's tactical frequency, and hectoring anybody he pleased by cell phone and pager. Standing beside him, I heard Ed Gray's voice from the command post saying, "Ready with the throw phone, Vince?"

"Affirmative. Cooper's gonna do the run. Tell 'em inside we're gonna use the door on the Second Street side."

"Copy that. You call the start."

"On my count," Vince said, and then, after a lull, "One, two, three." The Peacekeeper roared east on Second Street, aimed like a bullet at the side door of the hotel, as Russ raised a handheld megaphone. He clicked on the mike and boomed, "On the roof! On the roof! This is the police! An officer is going to bring you a phone so you can tell us what you want! He's going to throw the phone out to you from the access door by the chimneys. Hold your fire! He's not there to harm you in any way! Repeat, hold your fire so an officer can throw you a phone!"

Russ repeated the deafening message several times while

the big blue and white truck sped to the side door of the hotel and slid to a stop. Cooper jumped out the passenger side, made two running leaps, and disappeared through the open hotel door somebody was holding for him. Bullets rained down briefly toward the Peacekeeper from beside a pillar at the top of the building. I heard the hammerlike blows as they bounced off the armor-plated roof of the personnel carrier, and thought it must be noisy as hell inside. Three guns spoke from doorways across Second Street from the hotel. The firing on the roof stopped and then moved to the rear north corner of the roof, following the Peacekeeper, which was soon out of range.

We listened anxiously to crackling silence till Cooper whispered, sounding a little breathless, "Okay, I'm all set at the door." A few seconds of confusing noise followed, then a moment of silence, and then he said, "Phone's on the roof."

A few minutes of radio silence followed, till Cooper said, "Ready for pickup." Vince came on and murmured that he wanted to switch the pickup to the backdoor, and told Buzz Cooper to let him know when he was in place there. They muttered a few more exchanges, and then the Peacekeeper roared north in the alley, paused at the back door of the hotel, and sped on.

Meanwhile, Russ plunked the other half of the throw-phone system onto the bench in front of us and said, "You ever do any hostage negotiating, Jake?"

"Started the training a few years ago. Gave it up when I got the job I have now."

"You might get your chance to try it today, if Mickey Crowley doesn't get here pretty soon," he said. "I can't do everything here myself."

I stared at the radiotelephone in its sturdy case, and tried to remember anything at all about the course. The equipment was simplicity itself, but the people on the other end of the phone could be anything from hearers of phantom voices to screaming psychotics, and I'd read enough of the literature to know that negotiators needed a lot more than common sense.

"Here," Russ said, flipping a switch, "is the on button."

"Oh, good," I said, "that'll help." The receiver came to life with the harsh sounds of a mike being banged around. A young male voice said excitedly, "Whadda we s'posta do with this thing?" and another voice, farther from the mike, yelled, "Leave it alone! Don't touch it."

Russ clicked on his loudspeaker again and boomed up at the roof, "As soon as you're ready, pick up the phone, so we can talk." Actually, I knew, I would be able to hear what they said whether they picked up the handset or not. Cooper had turned on the mike before he threw the phone out onto the roof. It was going to broadcast every sound within twenty yards of itself until somebody turned it off.

A yellow light would show, though, on the set down here, to let us know when somebody picked up the handset on the machine on the roof. Then somebody down here had better be ready to talk, because that, I had been given to understand during the three sessions I attended, was the magic moment. It was vitally important to establish rapport with the "client," as we called him in negotiating school, as soon as he was ready to talk. If you made him wait a while, he might change his mind and never talk again. It had to be done exactly right, too; clients might be fragile as glass, emotionally unstable and ready to crack.

I felt pretty fragile myself as I stood by Russ Swenson, watching the unlighted lamp on the radiotelephone with growing dread. My imagination had begun to conjure headlines reading "Negotiator Blows It" when a dark, burly man in the uniform of a sheriff's deputy stepped out of the side door of the bank building and Russ said, "Well, Jesus, Crowley, where you been?"

"Just right where you'd think, Russ," Crowley said, "driving toward Rutherford at breakneck speed." He had a pleasant, ironic manner that was calculated, I thought, to keep people off his back. No taller than I was, he outweighed me by fifty pounds at least, not with fat but with massive muscles through the chest and shoulders, and a weightlifter's huge neck. I'd seen him a couple of times, bringing prisoners to the detention center. Somebody told me he had a farm near Elgin and raised game birds. I'd never have guessed him for a sensitive manipulator of unstable personalities, but I was glad to take him on faith today, having learned, in the three minutes since Russ turned on the radiotelephone, how far I was from being ready for the job.

The three of us watched the light awhile. A couple of times a fresh volley of fire erupted from the roof of the hotel and was answered by more gunfire from the street below. After each of these volleys Russ picked up his megaphone again and entreated the shooters on the roof to pick up the phone and talk. When his cell phone rang, he answered, said, "He's right here," and handed it to me.

"Come down to the command unit, will you, Jake?" Ed Gray said.

I sidled along the bank as far as the alley, turned east, and trotted past the backdoors of a dress shop and a Chinese restaurant, slid carefully around the overflowing Dumpsters of a couple of bars, squeezed by a beer truck to reach the sidewalk, crossed Third Street to get comfortably out of range of the Merriott roof, and followed sidewalks the rest of the way to the command center.

An extra noise had recently been added to all the other commotion on the street, and now I looked up and saw what it was: the Channel Four traffic helicopter, newly arrived from Minneapolis. We were going to be an item on the Twin Cities evening news. I stepped up into the command unit, where Ed Gray was watching TV.

The set in the command center was picking up the video from the helicopter, which was circling the Merriott. It showed a fairly clear picture of four figures on the rooftop. Only two of them seemed to be moving; the other two sat with their backs against the ductwork that connected the chimney stacks to a metal motor housing about the height of a short door.

Every third pass or so, the pilot would break off his circle to fly directly across the top of the building. He lowered his altitude a little each time he did so. As I watched, he made one of those passes, a little closer than before, and one of the moving figures raised his weapon. A puff of smoke flew up from the weapon, and the helicopter banked sharply and climbed away. We were treated to a vertiginously whirling view of buildings, vehicles, and upturned faces, till the helicopter leveled off and began circling the roof again, a little higher. I tried hard to identify any of the figures on the roof as he flew over them, but the picture moved too fast.

I looked around the RV. Schultzy waved to me from a desk where she was chewing gum, typing into a laptop, and reading the message that scrolled up the screen. Besides watching TV, Ed was talking on a cell phone and fiddling with the strap on a plastic helmet. Beside him, bareheaded, stood a tense-looking Al Hanenburger, wearing camouflage fatigues and a bulletproof vest. I stood in the stairwell just inside the door and waited.

"Jake," Ed said, still tinkering with Hanenburger's helmet strap, "come over here and try on this helmet for me, will you?" He handed me a deeply padded shiny black plastic helmet like the one he was fixing for Hanenburger. "Put this plug in your ear first," he said.

I pushed the plug into my ear canal and let the cord trail down to my shoulder. "Now pull the helmet straight down," he said. "Good. Pull down the face plate. Now buckle the strap. How's it feel?"

"It's fine," I said. "I can't see you or hear you, but the hat is fine."

"Hat," he said. "Jesus." They both laughed. Hanenburger looked as if it might have been his first laugh in a while.

Ed pulled a helmet like the one I was wearing out of a cupboard above the sink, fiddled with the earplug, and pulled it on. He plugged the wire into a transmitter clipped to his vest and plugged my wire into another transmitter, which he handed to me, saying, "Hold this a minute." Suddenly his whispered voice said, inside my head, "Can you hear me, Jake?"

"Yes," I said, and my voice came out of his helmet so loud we all jumped a foot. Ed and Al laughed merrily again. Ed said, "There's a radio in the earplug. Your voice activates it through the bones in your head."

"I remember this thing." I was whispering, now, inside the

helmet, and Ed was nodding brightly. "Vince showed it to me when you first got the ERU gear."

"It's for a silent approach, inside houses usually. You're not going to be that close to the roof, but you and Al gotta be able to talk to each other, and they might hear you if you use a regular radio."

"I'm going someplace with Al?"

"I hope so. Take off the helmet a minute. Now," he said, speaking normally, "are you still a good climber?"

"I guess. Whaddya mean?"

"Not scared of heights? I was telling Al here about the time you chased the purse snatcher up the water tower."

"Oh, the crazy climber, yeah." It was years ago. A junkie had mugged a woman and snatched her purse on the steps of her own apartment building; she called 911 within half a minute, stuttering with rage. Ed and I happened to be cruising a block away, so we caught up with the felon right away, but the fool wouldn't give up and let us arrest him. We cornered him against a thick hedge of holly; he jumped through the punishing thorns and ran bleeding across a creek before we were out of the car. We chased him on foot into Bryce Park, and Ed caught him by the tennis courts, but he pulled free while I was trying to put the cuffs on him; he was hurting for a fix and had the strength of a crazy man. In the end I followed him, purse and all, to the top of Malloy Tower and wrestled him all the way back down the fifty-foot ladder, both of us swearing and kicking, scattering lipsticks and canceled checks and small change over a wide area. Ed called me Spider Man for weeks afterward.

"What do you have in mind?" I asked him, not at all sure I wanted to hear the answer.

"We want to get Al up in the scaffolding of that construction that's kitty-corner across Broadway from the Merriott."

"Al's your sharpshooter today?"

"Yup. He's been waiting his turn, and this is it; Frye's out of town." Hanenburger concentrated on looking cool. "Now. Here's the plan. The framing's mostly up, and the hoist that the crew's been using is on the west side of the building. I think you'll have good cover all the way up. The crane is on the twelfth floor by the elevator shaft, which is mostly built. The base of the crane has a lot of boards and cement bags stacked around it. We think Al can fix himself a perch that will give him good cover and a good field of fire right across the Merriott roof."

"Okay, so what's the problem?"

"The lower portion of the building has flooring in and some walls, but there's only scaffold up on the top five floors. Al here," Ed said, not looking at him, "it turns out he's a little bit afraid of heights." Hanenburger studied his shoes. "But he's willing to go up there if you'll go along and help him figure out his route and maybe carry his gun. Think you can do that?"

He looked at me steadily for two heartbeats and said, "So far they're not talking to us on the throw phone, and we're not sure how many guns or how much ammo they've got up there. And we don't know the condition of the hostages. We don't want to storm the roof if we can help it, but we might have to. If it comes to that, it sure would help if Al could pick off one of them."

"Well . . . ," I said, and then the chief walked into the RV, looking more somber than I had ever seen him. He nodded to each of us and then stood silently watching the TV set with big knots moving in his jaw. I said, "Sure. I can do that. No problem."

"Good," Ed said. "Let's get you geared up then." He found me a Kevlar vest and hooked my transmitter to it, saying, "Don't turn this on till you're ready to go up. And once it's on, remember, you'll be talking to everybody on the team. So speak only when it's essential."

He helped me figure out where to put my Glock so I could get at it, and how to use the sling on Al's big Remington 700 so I could have both hands free when I crossed the girders. Then he rechecked all of Al's gear, moving deliberately, the way he always does, each thing just another job, no hurry. By the time he was satisfied that we were ready, we were so hot we were desperate to get outside.

"I've got an unmarked car waiting for you," Ed said. "It's gonna take you to the hoist on the First Avenue side of the building. The main thing is to stay out of sight, remember." He followed us down the steps, still advising us as we walked to the car. "We want to get you in place without them knowing you're there."

His phone rang. He sprinted back up the steps, and I heard him say, before the door closed, "Chief, Russ wants you down at the bank building where he is. If they get one of the shooters on the line, Mickey thinks he might need to consult you about options." Frank came out of the RV and got into his own car, looking ominously grim.

Mary Agnes Donovan was in the car. "So you got the new Crown Vic," I said. "If I'd known where it was, I'd have arm-wrestled you for it."

"You must be driving the old Dodge, huh?"

"If *driving* is the right word. More like herding. Mary Agnes, do you know why the chief is so bummed out?"

She shook her head and shrugged, but Hanenburger said, "His son is missing from school, they think he might be one of the ones shooting from the roof."

"Oh, bullshit," I said. "P. K. would never do that."

"That's what I said," Mary Agnes said.

"Whatever," Hanenburger said. "You know him better than I do, I guess." He looked like a man with other things on his mind.

We took off our helmets, but even so it took us a while to wedge ourselves in the car. As we passed the Second Street intersection, I looked toward Russ's station and saw Frank standing by the pillar. Mickey Crowley was leaning close to him, talking to him intensely. Frank had his right hand clamped tight over his right ear, trying to block out the rest of the noise in the street so he could concentrate on what Mickey was saying.

Mary Agnes stopped the car by a section of metal scaffolding that was draped in heavy black plastic sheeting. "This is where Ed thought you ought to unload," she said. I got out of the car holding my helmet, and she said, "Here, let me help you with this," lifted Al's gun off the seat, and said, "Uff-da, this thing is heavy, huh?" I was very worried about how heavy it was, so I grabbed it from her, trying to show Al, who stood waiting with his helmet under his arm, that I was not bothered by the weight.

"All set now?" Mary Agnes said. "The construction super's over there; he's going to run the hoist up for you. Good luck, guys." She flipped us a little wave and drove away.

I started to move toward the man by the hoist, but Hanenburger caught my left elbow in his right hand and said, "Wait a minute, huh?"

I watched while he took a deep breath. Then he stood up very straight and said, "I'm a helluva good shot, Jake. I can put a bullet inside a circle the size of a silver dollar at a hundred yards. I've trained for this and I'm ready, but I never thought I might have to do it from a high place." He licked his lips. "It's something I can't—" He had been going to say, "control," but he stopped. "You get me up there today," he said, "and I'll find a way to lick this. I want to stay on this team."

"Sure," I said. "Don't worry. It's easier than you think. Just don't look down, okay?" I knew it would get worse the more we talked, so before he could say any more, I walked toward the man in the hard hat who was waiting by the hoist.

There must have been a whole crew here working when the shooting started, but a lean red-faced man in jeans and an orange vest stamped "Adams Construction" was the only one around now. I wondered if Ed had found him and got him back here, or if he'd never left, and I felt a sudden, irritable need to slow everybody down and get some questions answered. I walked over to the red-faced man and stuck my hand out. "Jake Hines."

"Bill Orsello." We shook hands, and then he shook with Al Hanenburger. He looked at both of us quizzically and said, "Well, you boys about ready to go up?"

"You're going to run the hoist?"

"Yep. She's not fancy, but she'll get you where you want to go." He showed us the steel wire cage, lifted by a cable that unwound off a motor-driven drum at the bottom.

"You open this gate here, see?" We stepped into the steel-floored cab. Our footsteps made a loud, hollow sound. The walls of the cage came up only to our hips. There were signs everywhere telling us not to smoke, not to exceed a load of two thousand pounds, and not to put our hands outside the walls while the car was moving. Who would want to?

"Then to get out, of course," Orsello said, carefully casual, "you'll want to use the gate on the other side." Good point, Orsello, I thought. We'll be hanging out over nothing at all on this side, won't we? He walked into the cab and showed us how to open the other gate from the inside. "Don't worry about closing it," he said. "You can do that on the return trip." He could see from the way we looked at him that we had not even thought about getting back down and did not want to think about it now.

"So," Orsello walked out and closed the gate gently between us, "how high do you want to go?"

"The crane's on the twelfth floor, right?"

"Yes."

"That's where we want to go then."

He raised his eyebrows. "Well, now," he said, "on the twelfth floor there's a platform around the hoist, but after that—there's no way to get to the crane, you know, except across the girders." He waited a few seconds, blinking at us, and said, "You understand what I'm saying? There's no flooring in yet on the top five levels."

"We understand," I said. "We're going to put our helmets on now, and after that we can't hear you or talk to you, okay? When I nod to you, you send us on up." I knew if we stood there and talked about it much longer, we would not be able to go.

When I had my helmet strap fastened, I looked at Hanenburger and whispered, "All set?" and he nodded.

I told Ed Gray we were good to go. He said, "Okay, here's the situation: the shooters have never picked up the phone, they're not talking to us. They're talking to each other about never getting off the roof alive, then one of them thinks maybe they could use the hostages to demand a car and safe passage, but it's very disorganized and panicky up there, and we don't know what they'll do. We're still hoping to negotiate with them, so we're hoping you can get to the crane and under cover without us doing any more shooting. The more we shoot, the less they'll be likely to talk. But you'll have to tell us when you get up there if that's possible, understand?"

"Affirmative," Al said.

"Tell me what you see when you reach the top. Everybody else, stay off this line now."

I met Orsello's eyes and nodded. He flipped a switch, a humming noise began, and in a couple of seconds the car began to rise. I'd expected a lot of clanging and lurching, but Adams Construction must have bought the top of the line. The cage slid smoothly up the metal guides, not too fast. Soon I was looking into the second-floor windows of the buildings across the alley, enjoying the startled eyes of a girl looking out. I looked at Hanenburger to see if he was also enjoying the girl, but he was getting a green, wormy look, like a man about to puke.

"We better turn around," I whispered, "so we can see where we're going." We did some careful jockeying of our padded parts in order to turn in the small space. The view the other way was less interesting but more secure; we slid past the raw edges of the third-floor ceiling, saw the coils of foil-wrapped ducting between floors, and then fourth-floor chipboard flooring. Several more raw edges of plasterboard and flooring slid by, and then we were suddenly looking at the top of the library building two blocks away, framed by the girders we were climbing through.

"Find the horizon," I told Hanenburger. "You see it there, beyond the library?" I looked at him; he nodded back. I wanted to keep him busy, responding to me instead of to his fear. "Keep your eye on that horizon," I told him, "and don't look down."

He did as he was told, so he did not see, as I did by the time we passed the eighth floor, that most of the obstacles that had been providing visual separation from the Merriott Hotel were gone now. The hoist was gliding smoothly up into a Lego world. Except for metal girders, the only impediments to the three-hundred-and-sixty-degree view were a few piles of building materials stacked on planks laid across the girders here and there.

"Ed," I muttered into my jaw, "we're not gonna have much cover up here till we get over to the crane."

"Okay, we'll get ready to give you some cover fire," he said, "how soon?"

"Now," I said, because I could feel the hoist slowing down. There was a silence, during which he must have talked to Russ on the dispatch frequency, and then his voice came on again inside my head, telling the ERU boys what was up and then telling us the firing would begin in five seconds. I didn't listen closely because our cab had come to a stop and we were looking across the tops of girders and a few piles of construction debris at the Merriott roof.

"Aw shit," Hanenburger said, as his gaze moved from the horizon to the rooftop, "they can see us plain as day over here!"

"We'll keep 'em busy," Ed said, as guns began firing from the street below and from a couple of fourth-floor windows in buildings around the hotel, where I hadn't seen cops before. The two active figures on top of the Merriott ran, crouching, to pillars on the front and side of the roof, knelt in the shelter of the retaining wall, and peered down over the edge. They were getting good at the game; they knew just how high they could raise their heads without becoming a good target.

"Let's get to that crane while they're busy," I whispered, and Hanenburger nodded, looking fierce. He opened the inside gate, I walked out onto the platform, and he followed me. Adams Construction had done a nice job on the platform; it was sturdy and didn't bounce, and there was plenty of room for the two of us to stand there side by side. I had not noticed any wind on the ground, but it was windy up here, breezy enough to blow flaps and the ends of straps around. The whirling air played on the metal uprights like a giant Jew's harp, making a hateful moaning noise. I wasted two seconds cursing the wind and then told myself to forget it, and pretty much did.

I picked my route, stepped out onto a girder, satisfied myself that it didn't bounce or sway, and walked quietly toward the first upright, twenty-four feet away. I could feel the emptiness under me compressing my spine, making my toes curl. When I got to the first pillar, I turned to say, "Don't look down," expecting to have to coax Al Hanenburger across. He was right behind me, watching the Merriott roof as he moved toward my pillar. I sidled around it and went on.

A couple of killers with rifles had cured Al Hanenburger's fear of heights. He had been shot once, in an ERU raid on a crack house, and he must have remembered exactly how much it hurt. He crossed those metal beams like a mountain goat. I had to hustle to stay out of his way.

The crane had been installed on a concrete slab by the elevator housing. As soon as I got in its shadow, I relaxed; I couldn't see the roof anymore, so I knew they couldn't see me. I stood still a few seconds by the last pillar, debating whether I wanted to cross to the crane the short way, along a girder, or take a little detour and cross on the nice big metal plate that covered the elevator shaft. Then Hanenberger hissed, behind me, "Go on, for chrissake!" and I realized he was still two feet out in vulnerable open territory, staring at shooters. So I minced quickly across one more stretch of nothing to the crane.

Hanenburger was right behind me. Just as he stepped up onto the cement, the wind caught one corner of the metal plate over the elevator shaft and flipped it up. I watched, horrified, as the plate I had thought was solid collapsed into several sheets that tilted, slid, and then crashed into the shaft. They must have hit every obstacle on the way down; the noise seemed to go on forever. I imagined myself falling through that pain-filled darkness with the metal plates banging into me. For a moment, I was too terrified to move.

Hanenburger said, "Christ, they'll hear that—" He dropped to his knees, crawled into the crane mounting, and peered through.

I laid the Remington carefully on the cement and pulled myself into a space beside him. "We need some more cover here," I said. "I'm gonna slide these cement bags—"

"I'm afraid they'll see them move," Al said.

"I'll take it slow," I said. "Watch now—" The sacks were heavy, and I was almost immobile in my heavy vest, so taking it slow was not a problem. The shooters never even glanced at me; they were preoccupied with firing back at the cops on the ground. Our building was going to be one story higher than the Merriott, so we were looking down on them from about seventy-five yards away.

When we had our pile of sacks in place, I crawled out and got Al's Remington. He took his gun from me and ran his hands over it like a man caressing a woman. He dug a bipod out of one of the many pockets in his vest, found a secure rest for it, set up his gun, and sighted through the scope. When he was satisfied, he stretched and wiggled till he was as comfortable as possible and whispered, "All set up here, Ed."

Ed told his other shooters, "Cease fire." The intermittent gunfire stopped, and in the windy silence that followed it, Ed said softly, "Al, tell me what you can see."

"Two shooters, kneeling by the wall at the front of the building. They've been alternating between handguns and rifles, but they're not firing at anything right this minute. Two heads on the other side of the ductwork that connects the chimneys to the motor housing. Looks like people sitting down."

"Yes, they are sitting down. Pretty sure they're hostages. The hotel manager says the shooters brought one hostage with them and kidnapped the other one in the lobby as they went through. We've had an off-and-on view from that helicopter for some time, and we haven't seen either of those people move or pick up a gun."

"That's the way it looks up here, too."

"Okay, Al, just stay ready there, we're going to do some deciding now. I'll get back to you soon. Nice work getting up there, by the way."

"Copy," was all Hanenburger said, but he looked pleased.

And he had better take all the pleasure he could get out of the compliment, I thought, because the hardest part of the sharpshooter's job, the wait, lay ahead of him. He might lie where he was, stretched across cold cement and steel, for five minutes or the rest of the day. Nobody was going to ask him if his muscles were cramped, or if he was hungry or needed to pee.

Snowed on, rained on, frostbitten or sunburned to a crisp, he would stay where he was till he got his shot—or didn't. If, at last, after unknown stretches of unutterable boredom and neglect, his moment of opportunity came, he was supposed to hit exactly what he fired at and nothing else, and then go home and shovel the walks.

Without a doubt the worst job on the ERU team, I had always thought. Today I was going to sit up here in the freezing wind and watch him do it. Lucky me.

We watched as Mickey Crowley picked up Russ's megaphone and blasted another message toward the hotel roof, pleading with the shooters to pick up the phone and tell him what they wanted. "This doesn't have to be all or nothing," he told them. "We can figure something out here if you'll talk to me."

Now that we were sitting still I could see, to my immense relief, that neither of the shooters on the roof was P. K. McCafferty. I wanted to convey that information to the chief without acknowledging that his son had ever been suspect, so I said, "I can see both suspects clearly. I don't recognize either one."

"Do you know them, Al?" Ed said.

"No," Hanenburger said.

One of the two figures on the roof, the one in the baseball cap and green fleece jacket, was inclined to use the phone. He had dragged it over near the chimneys, and he looked at it now and said, "Why don't we find out what he's offering?"

"Screw it," the second shooter said, "it's just another trick. Can't you hear our voices down there?" That one was wearing a shearling vest and chinos, and suddenly I remembered where I'd seen him last: in the yard at the Sheets house the morning Billy got shot. When we divided up witnesses, I had left him for Kevin to interview. Maybe I'll add Palm Pilots to my wants list in the chief's new budget, I thought; it would be handy if I could bring up Kevin's notes right now. On the other hand, if we got very much more gear to carry along, we'd have to give up chasing bad guys entirely.

Crowley's harangue went on for some time. Then there was

silence, during which I assumed the ERU team and the chief were debating options. Before very long Ed Gray said, in our helmets, "Al, have you got a good shot right now?"

"Yep. I can get one for sure. Maybe both unless the second one's quick."

"How about you, Jake?"

"I have an excellent view. Can't guarantee to bring anybody down at this distance."

"Understood. Hang on a sec." When he came back, he said, "We want you to decide on targets and each take your best shot."

"I better take the one in the vest," I said, because he was closest.

"Agreed. On my count. One, two, three." Al's big gun spoke, and the kid in the green fleece jacket fell over, rolled once, and lay still on his face. I fired my Glock at the boy in the vest. Dust and junk flew up from his right arm, and a stain grew on his plaid shirt as he leaped for the shelter of the motor housing. Al fired again as his feet disappeared; dirt and chips flew up where his bullet landed. I couldn't tell if part of what flew up was foot parts from the kid in the vest.

"One down, Ed," Al said. "Jake winged the other one, and I mighta hit his foot."

"Where is he now?"

"Behind the low metal housing on this end of the ductwork. Out of sight."

"All right. We're getting ready to go up now. In the meantime if you get a good shot without endangering the other people on the roof, Al, take it."

"Copy," Al said.

The voice of the kid I had shot, yelling at the top of his lungs, carried across the roofs, suddenly; I heard it in an echoey way, coming from him and from the throw-phone base on the ground.

"Go get the phone, McCafferty," he screamed. "You want to die right here? Go get the phone then."

There was no mistaking the ill-fitting shirt and funny, awkward stance of P. K. McCafferty when he stood up. He walked to the throw phone, picked it up, and carried it behind the housing. I saw everybody lean forward around the radiotelephone on the ground; the yellow light must have gone on. Mickey Crowley picked up his headset.

"Okay, asshole negotiator," the kid in the vest yelled, "you ready to deal?"

Crowley began talking into his headset, but the kid in the vest cut him off.

"Watch and learn, asshole," he screamed, and then, in a quieter voice to someone nearby, "You're going over to that pillar on the front and get up on it. Get up on it, you heard me." He began to scream again. "What are you waiting for, Altar Boy? Start walking."

P. K. came out from behind the housing and started toward the front of the roof.

"Ed," I said, "P. K. McCafferty is one of the hostages, and he's moving toward the front of the roof." He was walking steadily across the wide windy open space, looking young and terribly alone. "Ed?"

"I hear you. Be quiet now and let me talk to the rest of the team. Vince?"

"We're inside a doorway, just across from the backdoor of the hotel," Vince said. "Ready to go up."

"Good. Al, is the shooter still behind the chimney?"

"No, the housing. That's the lower structure at the other end of the ductwork from the chimney. You understand?"

"Yes. You got that, Vince?"

"Copy," Vince said.

"Good. Go in when you're ready, Vince," Ed said, and at the same time I heard the shooter yell, "Get your ass up there, McCafferty, or I'll shoot you right where you are!" I watched in disbelief as P. K. walked to the right front corner of the building, held on to the pillar to steady himself, and stepped up on the facade. He turned to face the pillar, which rose a couple of feet higher than the facade, stepped up onto it neatly, and turned to face the street.

A strange sound rose up from the street, like wind through the trees, a mass intake of breath from the hundreds of people who were watching the roof.

"Okay, asshole," the shooter on the phone yelled, "negotiate that!"

Hanenburger poked my arm. When I looked at him, he put his finger to his lips and pointed at the north end of the building, where Al Stearns was standing on the window washer's platform, fiddling with the button on the hoist.

I mouthed, "What is he doing?" and Hanenburger raised his eyebrows and shrugged and went back to watching the metal housing, with a glint in his eye like a red-tailed hawk. Stearns got the hoist going and began to glide quietly up the outside of the building.

Crowley said something into the throw phone, and the shooter cackled and said, "He's up there to get me what I want. Understand? First you bring a car to the north side of the hotel, all gassed up and ready to go, and I mean right up on the sidewalk by the door with the car doors open so I can walk right out the door of the hotel and into the car, understand?"

Stearns was passing the fifth floor, standing quietly on the platform, not looking up or down.

Crowley talked a minute into his handset, and the shooter yelled, "Never mind all that bullshit, just get the car! And it better be within three minutes because my arm's hurting a lot now and I'm thinking maybe it would be more fun to shoot P. K. McCafferty off that pillar and see if the chief of police could catch him as he fell, you wanna see that, Asshole Negotiator?"

Stearns passed the tenth floor. As he neared the top he began to crouch, trying to stay out of sight, but his knees were stiff and he had begun to look bulky and awkward up there. People behind the barricades of the outer perimeter had noticed him now, and were pointing upward.

"Ed, we're ready to go in," Vince said in my helmet.

Ed said, "Hold on. Al?" The platform carrying Stearns reached its highest point and stopped. He stood up with his

Glock in his right hand, rested his arms on the facade, and got ready to fire at the kid in the vest who crouched behind the housing. The kid saw him and rose to fire back, and Al Hanenburger blew the top of his head off.

Four men in speckled suits burst onto the roof and ran toward the two shooters lying there. Stearns threw his head and shoulders over the facade and began trying to haul the rest of his bulk up over the obstacle. He hung there, kicking his boots at space, and there was an awful queasy moment when it looked as if he was going to fall back, till Huckstadt ran and pulled him over, and he collapsed onto the roof like a sack of suet.

Greeley and Cooper left the prostrate bodies and ran to the pillar where P. K. still stood, staring down at the crowd below, appearing unaware of the carnage around him. Without a word, they reached up and grabbed him off his perch.

"He's okay, Ed," Vince said. To Stearns, as he led P. K. past him, Vince said, "You ever pull a crazy stunt like that on one of my operations again, old man, I'll shoot you myself."

Stearns raised his head and said something I couldn't hear, and then Vince's high, cackling laugh hurt my ear, and he was yelling, "Are you *serious*? Oh, for chrissake—"

Ed said sharply, "Quiet on this frequency! What's going on?" There was total silence for a few seconds, and then the mop-up chatter began. Huckstadt bent over the second hostage, talking softly. Cooper told Ed to send an ambulance to the side door and a hearse to the back, and a squad to pick up Stearns. Owen and Butch lay still on the roof, growing cold and stiff, looking like castoffs. I wondered if their parents knew yet.

Hanenburger began mumbling unhappily. I said, "What's the matter?"

"Aw, shit," he said. "We gotta go back down over them same fucking girders."

I knew how he felt. It seemed to me we deserved to have a rescue helicopter appear above us and hover protectively, calling down cheery messages like, "Don't worry about a thing! An experienced cop-carrier is coming down to pluck you off that roof and take you to the nearest beer!" But nothing like that showed any signs of happening, and after a couple of minutes we got on our feet and faced the descent.

It wasn't pretty. The wind was stiffer and colder than when we came up, and we were tired and pretty well drained of adrenaline. I hated every foot of it myself, and Hanenburger quit cold once, at the second pillar from the last, and said, "I can't."

"Al," I said, from the safety of the platform where I stood smelling my own sweat, "you already did this once. You know you can do it."

"Nobody's holding a gun on me now," he said. Abruptly, he realized how ridiculous that sounded, and burst into hysterical laughter that forced him to cling to the pillar for three minutes. I thought of saying, "Actually, you know, it's only the top five stories that aren't filled in," but I was afraid he might start laughing harder and not be able to stop, and I knew I didn't have what it would take to go back and get him. He pulled himself together finally and came across the last two girders looking me right in the eye.

Bill Orsello gave us a nice trip down in the hoist. We stood side by side, getting braver with every foot we sank, enjoying the view over the rooftops on the west side of town. At the bottom Orsello opened the little gate for us, and we shook his hand and thanked him. Then we walked together, feeling like heroes, to Russ Swenson's bunker by the pillar. He was breaking it up; he handed us each an armload of gear and said, "Carry this stuff to the van for me, will you? I can't do everything here myself."

In the street nearby, oblivious to us all, Frank McCafferty stood holding his son in his arms.

11

"HE chief is hot to debrief everybody," Kevin said Friday
morning. "You got any objection to a CID about ten
o'clock?"

"Hey, it beats doing anything useful," I said.

I was just blowing smoke; I knew, after yesterday's series of
critical incidents, that the chief would want to get everybody together to talk while their memories were still fresh. And it probably wasn't a bad idea, but on principle I resist anything
resembling a counseling session. I figure I got enough counseling, growing up as a ward of the state, to keep my head
straight for a couple of centuries. Now that I'm a grown-up, I try
to keep my thoughts to myself.

Frank got the large meeting room on the third floor and we
all filed in together, the ERU team, all my investigative section,
plus Andy Pitman, Russ Swenson, and Marlys Schultz. P. K.
McCafferty had been given an excused absence from school so
we could debrief him too, but we kept him waiting in his father's
office for over an hour, because it turned out everybody had a lot
to say.

"I keep hearing gunfire," Rosie said, after the main parts of
the story had been filled in. The whole room, almost with one
voice, said, "Me too."

"It did get noisy sometimes," Ed Gray said, "but our policy of
firing whenever a target presented itself worked well. We kept
the shooters pinned down on the roof. They never did any more
significant damage after we got the inner perimeter in place."

"Yes. And there was good separation between the inner and outer perimeters, Russ," the chief said, "crowd control was very well managed. And the handoff to Ed, that worked okay, didn't it?"

"Been better if the command center got there ten minutes sooner," Russ said, "and we need to sort out where the investigative section belongs during emergencies. If anywhere," Russ said, with a delicate lip curl.

"Ed?" McCafferty turned to Gray's upraised hand.

"The RV got there as fast as it could without killing anybody in traffic, and I thought the handoff went very well. The cooperation between the ERU team and the rest of the force was excellent. Your help was decisive, Schultzy." She beamed at him and snapped her gum. "Also, we sure appreciated your help with the high work, Jake."

"What was that all about, anyway?" McCafferty asked.

Hanenburger cleared his throat. "Turns out I suffer from a touch of acrophobia," he said. Everybody stared at him, dumbfounded; it was the most complicated word anybody'd ever heard him use.

"Hell you say," the chief said. "How long you had that?"

"Didn't know I had it till yesterday," Hanenburger said. "Didn't know what it was till I looked it up last night."

"So that was you up there with him? Jake?"

"Yes. All I did was carry his gun. Next time he won't need me."

"I'm gonna get help from the sports med shrinks," Hanenburger said. "But I owe you a big one for yesterday, Jake."

"You already paid me back," I said.

"I did? How?"

"By not sneering at me when I missed my shot."

"Hey, for a Glock at that distance, and with the wind? That was good shooting." Hanenburger and I were buds now. Maybe I should climb a tall building with Russ Swenson.

"Okay! What else, now, about ERU operations?"

"Chief, you haven't said anything about the Peacekeeper," Vince said.

"Oh. Yes. The pickups were very well executed, you're all to be complimented on your saves. Looks like the woman's going to be okay, too."

The ERU guys tossed a couple of thumbs-up around, and Cooper said, "Can you believe that window washer? Sitting there under his bucket?"

"He may have looked pretty comical with that pail on his head, but he presented a very difficult target from above, so it wasn't a bad plan at all on his part," Frank said. "And the way you scooped him off that sidewalk, that was very nice work. So tell me: what do you think of that vehicle now that you've used it in a real emergency?"

"It's noisy as hell inside," Cooper said. "When those slugs hit the top? Major, major headache."

"Yeah, if we wanna fire out of those ports," Huckstadt said, "we better wear ear protection or we'll all be deaf."

"Let's give credit where it's due, though, huh?" Vince said. "I don't see any of you wearing bullet holes this morning."

"And no holes in the bod is *good*," Cooper said. "Lotta scrapes and bruises, though." He showed us his elbows. "We need some padding in there for when Vince executes his hairpin turns." Vince glowed proudly.

"And we gotta practice closing the backdoors while we're under way," Maddox said. "Those are some heavy sumbitches."

"All right. Well—you want to keep it?" Frank asked, and was almost blown out of his chair by five men saying in spontaneous unison, "HELL YES we want to KEEP IT!" They looked at each other and laughed.

"Guess that settles that," Frank said. "Now. I just want to say that in my opinion, this department performed at a high level of professionalism during yesterday's emergency, after all our other options closed off. The rest of my questions are for the investigative team, so I'm going to excuse everybody else. With my thanks," he added, standing up, shaking hands and patting backs as he ushered them out the door. He closed it and came back saying, "Let's all move down here together, huh?"

We moved, but when we sat down again, we were not together. All the faces on my crew had closed up. We'd all hated pretty much everything that happened since Tuesday morning, and yesterday's shoot-out had felt like unearned punishment. If Frank was going to take us to the woodshed now, we were going to have a few words to say in our defense.

Frank rubbed his face wearily, leaned forward on his elbows, and gave us his pop-eyed stare. "I didn't sleep much last night. Well, rightly so. I mean—this all happened on my watch, so of course—but at first I was so damn glad to have my son down safe, it was all I could think of. My wife too, she made me promise to express her thanks to all of you. She's already started baking up a lot of treats to send down here." He smiled rather stiffly and then rubbed his face again. "But ever since things quieted down a little, I've been going over and over the same question: Could any of these deaths have been prevented?"

I sat still while he considered. I'd been going over the same ground myself without finding any firm answers, so I was beginning to hate the question.

"We've been moving more and more toward proactive policing," Frank mused. "Setting up POP areas, giving out cards with pager and cell phone numbers so people can call their area cop personally if they feel they need to. The guys on the street think those moves have had some positive results. But *this*"—he raised his arms with his palms turned up—"it feels like a nest of snakes grew under a rock in my front yard, and I never noticed."

He searched our faces. "It may be too early to ask this question. But do any of you see places where we might have been quicker off the blocks, and possibly saved some lives?"

Follow procedure, do it by the book, he's always told me. Leave the soul-searching to daytime TV. Hadn't we been doing that? "You think we missed some things?" I asked him, not looking at my crew.

"I'm not trying to blame anybody," the chief said. "I'm looking for some help here."

"The kid in the vest," Kevin said suddenly, "has been bothering me. That first morning at Billy Sheets's house, the kid in the vest, in the yard there, that was Owen Campbell, wasn't it?

We had him right there. And he just—dropped through the cracks."

"There were so many people around," I said, "I assigned him to you in a hurry—"

"And he was gone by the time I turned around—"

"So neither one of us ever thought about him again."

"He must have been there to take the pictures, huh? The ones we watched later?" Kevin raised his eyebrows almost to his hairline and shuddered.

"They started to get off on the killing," Ray said, slowly. "That's what I think we saw on that video. They shot the dogs for practice, right? Then they shot the little boy to prove to themselves they could do a human. And they must have told each other they were just documenting their practice shots, at first. But Owen going down for that close-up, that makes me think they were beginning to enjoy killing for its own sake."

"That's what Andy Pitman thought," I said. "That's why he brought the bullets to me. As for that last piece of videotape, I think going down into the crowd for the close-up may have been the ultimate thrill for Owen. A great bit of bravado, you know? To be right there and not have anybody know—"

"Like an arsonist at a fire. Yeah," Bo said. "I got very sick of you hounding me to find that camera, Jake, but you were right, the camera was the key to everything."

"But not the only one," Rosie said. "If we had pushed harder on the questions at school, that first day—" She sent a sidelong glance at the chief.

He shifted in his chair and said, "Yes. I wish I'd insisted on more precise answers that day. I was trying not to offend any of the authorities at school, which in hindsight should have been the least of my worries."

"But then it's discouraging when you think about it," Rosie said, "that even when I did find out what Jason said to P. K.—about killing him—it didn't help a whole lot, did it? Because we didn't know whether it was serious, or just a nasty joke."

"Still don't," Darrell said.

"Well, communication's always going to be a tough nut," I said. "But looking back I wish I'd zeroed in earlier on following the trajectory of the bullet that killed Billy Sheets. It was when we nailed that and really went after it that the investigation started to move." I looked across the table at the chief. "Hard evidence, that's what gets the job done, right?"

"Always." But then he rocked his big right hand in an ambiguous gesture and added, "Although—" Frank's eyes, this morning, had a lot going on behind them. He stood up. "I think you better hear what P. K. has to say."

He brought him in with somewhat formal courtesy, his hand under his son's elbow, and led him to a seat next to Rosie. Amazingly, P. K.'s shambling gait and apologetic stoop seemed unchanged. I don't know what I expected, but it seemed as if there should be some outward and visible sign that the teenager in front of us was the incredibly poised boy who'd stood quietly on that dizzy perch yesterday, waiting to be blown off into two hundred feet of emptiness by his childhood buddy.

But he was the same slouchy kid with the surprisingly appealing smile; only a little puffiness around the eyes betrayed the storms he had weathered. He slumped in the chair Frank led him to, laid his big-knuckled hands on the tabletop, and waited.

"I know this isn't easy," Frank said, directly to him, "but everybody in this room needs to hear what you told me about the hockey team. See, we're trying to figure out if there were things we should have done—"

"It had nothing to do with you," P. K. said.

"Tell us anyway," his father said. P. K. studied him for signs of an ambush, apparently decided there was none, shrugged, and began to talk to a spot on the table about six inches ahead of his hands.

"Jason Hadley and Brian Coe decided to, you know, rule? In school sports. They were both seniors, it was their last chance to star. Brian needed the scholarships to go to college, and Jason just wanted the, you know, glory?" He had the teenage tendency to insert question marks randomly. "Jason's girl dumped him just before the prom last spring, and he wanted to make her eat—" His glance slid to his father; he shrugged and said, "You know."

"Denise?" Frank said. "That nice blond cheerleader?"

"Uh-huh. Well. They had a little clique, with Dan Finseth and Chris Hyland and Noah Schellhammer, big guys, you know, pump a lot of iron and stuff? They made like a pact or something. To work together, grab the top spots on the teams, win a bunch of big games, and get their pictures in the paper all the time." He made an exhaling sound like, "Shee-ee."

"Couple of guys last fall got sick of it? Moved the ball away from them on a punt once during a scrimmage and ran it all the way for a touchdown. The next day they got hurt bad in practice. After that Brian's Bruisers, that's what they called themselves, they pretty much had things their way in football and basketball."

"But hockey—" He was getting more relaxed as he talked, and the question marks were farther apart. "I'm too light to do much in football and too short for basketball, but I've always known how to skate and I like it. I made the team every year since seventh grade, and I'm beginning to be, like, you know," he squirmed, "a pretty fair hockey player?"

Frank said, "He made high point—"

P. K. said, "Dad," and made a shushing gesture with his hand. The chief of police sat back in his chair and shut up. The rest of us checked our shoelaces.

"Butch and Owen—we've played together a lot the last couple of years, so we had some moves worked out, not totally ill, you know, but still—"

"Ill means good now," his father said, "don't ask me why."

P. K. rolled his eyes up, gave his head a tiny shake, and went on "The Bruisers cornered us in the showers during the first week of hockey practice this year and told us to forget the first team unless we wanted to get hurt. We told them to stuff it. After that it was war on the ice, every day at practice.

"I'm a faster skater than any of them, so they never hurt me seriously, but they messed up plenty of my plays. Jason took Owen to the boards one day and banged up his knee and elbow pretty bad; he's mostly been on the bench ever since. About a week later Chris got Butch's jersey over his head and Noah chipped a couple of his teeth and sprained his shoulder. That's when Butch and Owen said fuck hockey—" He looked momentarily shocked when he realized what he had just said to his father, but then shrugged and went on. "All they wanted after that was to get even.

"I still wanted to play. But Jason and Brian started coming up to me about ten times a day, going, 'You ready to die?' With these freakish stupid grins? Saying how much fun it was gonna be to kill me, I'd never see it coming—" He stared at his spot on the table while he swallowed a couple of times.

"I was mad too and I wanted to get even, so yeah, I admit I talked to Butch and Owen about how we oughta bust their balls—but then one day Butch and Owen started talking to me by the lockers, saying they had this *plan* . . . they could get guns and stuff. At first I thought they were kidding and I went, 'Sure, why don't we swipe the cannon out of Meade Park, and load that up?' But they went, 'Hey, we're serious, we got a plan.' I went, 'Get outa here,' and just walked away. I never thought they'd go through with it, but anybody could see they were, like, beyond pissed, they really hated these guys now.

"That's when I began to see how completely *crazy* everything was getting. I mean, you know"—P. K. sat back and looked around the table—"hockey is just *a game.*"

For a few seconds he seemed like the most grown-up person in the room. "That's when I told you I wanted to quit," he told his father, "and we had this—uh—sort of a fight."

Frank moved his hand and whispered something that sounded like, "Sorry."

"That's all right. I did it, anyway." Frank's jaw seemed to grow a couple of new muscles. "But Munger got so pissed, and he did this utterly dweeb thing. He called my house and got Mom on the phone. I couldn't believe—" P. K. shook his head. His glance caught his father's, and he almost smiled. "Little did he know, huh?"

Frank nodded ironically, and for a moment they looked alike.

"He started to lay a big trip on her about how unfair it was of me to leave the team with the season just starting. He hardly got into it before Mom just—blew him away. She told him he better find out what was going on in his own team, or he was going to be facing a season with Brian's Bruisers and nobody else."

"See, I find out now that my wife knew all about this," Frank said, "and she and P. K. both say now that they tried to tell me, too, but I said I didn't want to hear anything about him squealing on his teammates. I've always had that rule," he said miserably. "I thought it was right."

My crew and I studied our shoes again, and then P. K. said, "Anyway, the coach started trying to find out what was up with Brian's Bruisers? That was pure bullshit he was giving you," he told Rosie, "about competition being good for both teams. He knew by then he had a problem."

"I kinda thought," Rosie said.

"So after that," P. K. said, "Brian and Jason said they didn't care if I quit the team or not, they were gonna kill me anyway." He shrugged a huge, loose-jointed shrug. "They didn't really mean kill. They meant hurt. But five of them? They could hurt me plenty whenever they got ready, and I could see it was just a matter of time. They were putting it off, enjoying the threats and looking for a good time and place. Finally I couldn't stand the suspense any longer, so I creamed Jason Hadley with my backpack."

When the second hand had crept halfway around the clock, I said, "I still don't understand why Owen and Butch took you for a hostage. I thought you were friends."

"We were. All our lives." He choked up for a minute, pulled his knees up, and wrapped his arms around himself. "See, but yesterday morning they told me, 'This is it, this is the day we're gonna kill Brian's Bruisers.' They thought I'd be really pumped for it after that fight. They came up to me in the parking lot during midmorning break and said, 'Put your books in your car and come on with us, we got the guns and ammo in Butch's car. We're gonna get those guys right here in the parking lot.'

"I went, 'Are you crazy? There's kids everywhere, some of

them are gonna get hurt,' and Butch just looked at me and smiled this creepy smile and went, 'Ain't that a shame?' "

P. K. unwound his arms, let his feet fall on the floor, and gave a sharp uncharacteristic bark of laughter. "But even after he said that, I still thought I was talking to my two best buds. They might have temporarily gone nuts over violence, but they were still Butch and Owen, right? So no matter how crazy they talked I just looked right at 'em and said this really sucks and I'm not gonna let you do it." He threw his hands up over his shoulders and said, "And they were shocked! They were so *into* it by then—they just couldn't believe I wasn't going to go along and help! They both said to me, 'Listen, whose side are you *on*?'

"Butch opened the trunk of his car and showed me the pile of guns he had there under some sacks. Four or five of them, a freaking *arsenal*, I have no idea where they got 'em all. He said something then, like, 'You better get out of the way if you're not gonna help.' And all of a sudden it was, like, time's up, you know? No more fooling around, they were going to get busy and start killing people right then.

"I grabbed the keys out of the lock of the trunk and went and jumped in the driver's seat and started the car. I don't know why one of them didn't shoot me right then, except they were like . . . in shock, they had this plan and I was messing it up, and it took them a while to decide what to do about it. Anyway I started backing out of the parking space, and they ran after me and jumped in the car. By the time they got the doors closed, I had the car in forward gear and I drove out of that parking lot about seventy miles an hour.

"I didn't have a plan. I just started driving toward the station." Frank nodded at that, looking pleased. "Then they started yelling they'd kill me if I didn't turn around, so I opened the window on my side and screamed out at the street, 'This car is full of guns and ammunition!' But people just stared and shook their heads, like, 'Kids today!' So I drove crazy, all over the street. And I couldn't get arrested! Why can't you ever find a cop when you need one?" P. K. McCafferty asked his father.

Outrage and amusement chased each other around Frank

McCafferty's face while P. K. curled up around himself again and stared hard at the table. "Finally Owen seemed to kind of get hold of himself. He grabbed the steering wheel away from me and drove the car into a light pole. I bumped my head bad, and I guess I kind of blacked out for a couple of minutes. When I came to enough to know what was going on, Butch was driving the car, and I was in the passenger seat. Owen was behind me with that stupid revolver pressed up against the back of my head. It seemed like we were all playing parts in this incredibly bad movie, you know? Owen said I had messed up the killing they were planning to do, so now I could just watch while they killed everybody they could find."

He kept hunching his head deeper into the neck of his sweater; it was over his chin now. "Owen made me walk in front of him into that hotel lobby downtown, and Butch grabbed the bellman to use for his shield and they shot two people right there, in the lobby, on the way to the elevator. Just pointed two handguns at total strangers and went blam-blam. Then they took the elevator to the top floor and made the bellman show them how to get out on the roof."

He closed his eyes for a while. When he spoke again, the sweater was up around his nose and his voice was coming out muffled through the blue wool, sounding worn out and sad. "After that I guess you all know more about what happened than I do. For me it all got—unreal. Because as far as I could tell, Butch and Owen had changed into two people I didn't even know." He was silent so long we all started to look at each other. Then he said, "I'm sorry they're dead, though." He put his hands in front of his face, and I thought he might be going to cry, but instead he gave his cheeks the McCafferty rubdown, sat up, and asked his father, "Can I go now?"

"Yes," Frank said, and added formally, "We're very grateful for your help, son." He walked the boy out to where his mother was waiting to take him home. By the time he got back, my crew and I were gathering up notebooks and looking at watches, and he could see we'd had enough debriefing for one day. He said something halfhearted about taking another look at this information after the dust settled, and we all mumbled vague agreement.

I left the room without meeting his eyes. I knew what he wanted, but I wasn't in the absolution business, and it wasn't my place to say how much he should have heard or understood at any given time. Besides, I had recently flunked listening myself.

Kevin followed me into my office afterward and said, "You know what's funny?"

"Oh, please, Kevin, do tell me something that's funny."

"Well—nobody said anything about Stearns."

"I know. It seemed like somebody should, but I thought if the chief didn't bring it up—"

"Yeah. Well, one thing, it should be easier to get people to come to his party."

"Except Vince. Is he still mad? That Stearns interfered?"

"No. Didn't you hear him laugh up there? Vince told Stearns he'd shoot him if he ever got in the way like that again, and Stearns said, 'I guess there's no danger, this is my last day.' Vince thinks that's a hoot."

Kevin stood fidgeting in the doorway. "Why'd he do it, do you think?"

"Who? Stearns? Maybe he decided to go out in a blaze of glory."

Kevin made a face. "In starkest contrast to the rest of the career, right?"

"Well, you know what they say, it isn't over till it's over."

I had an idea, though, why Stearns had gone up the wall, and even though it was none of my business, strictly speaking, I had an itch to find out if I was right. So when Kevin left, I went down the hall to Lou French's cubicle.

He was wheezing into the phone, making rapid notes while a female voice went tearfully on and on. He lifted one finger in a wait-a-minute signal, listened a while longer, saying, "Uh-huh. Uh-huh," and finally, "Joyce, I'll tell you what, lemme call a couple of people and see what kind of action we can expect on this, and I'll call you back, okay?"

He put down the phone, sighed, and said, "Why couldn't

Joyce Mangan's husband happen to be walking past the Merriott Hotel yesterday when the firing started?"

"Wouldn't that have been convenient?" I closed the door.

Lou pushed his glasses up and said, "Aw, shit, what now?"

"Relax, just a question. Frank didn't even mention Stearns in the meeting today—"

"Well, he could hardly give the guy a commendation for breaking every rule in the goddamn book. Way I heard it, Stearns left his post on the perimeter to pull that stunt on the hoist."

"I know, but—Lou, I know about the mess-up, years ago. Kevin found the newspaper clippings. But I didn't see Frank's name in any of those stories."

"So?"

"So do you know why Stearns went up the wall yesterday?"

Lou juggled a pencil a few times and said, "I don't mind telling you what little I know about it, Jake, but I advise you to keep it to yourself."

"Of course."

"Frank and Al rode together for a couple of years, before Frank made sergeant and began his . . . meteoric rise to power." He wrinkled his nose and said, "Why am I making fun of it? Frank earned every rating he ever made, times over." He considered a minute and said, "You know, Al was a damn good cop, too, before the bottle got him. And I guess in their times together they got in one or two tight situations where Frank had reason to be grateful to him. So when Clifton decided to hang ol' Stearns out to dry, Frank got up a committee of guys who thought he deserved a little better than that."

Lou cleared his throat and pushed a few notes around on his desk. "I was one of the guys Frank recruited. We went in and made our case to the chief, and got told, none too politely, to butt out. When we got out of there we all said, 'Well, we tried,' but I could see Frank wasn't satisfied. He never said any more to me, but I saw him going in the chief's office a couple of days later, and a week or so after that Clifton told the media that Stearns had been stripped of rank and suspended the maximum amount of time without pay, but he would resume duty as a patrolman at the end of the following month."

Lou leaned back in his chair and whistled a tuneless little ditty at the ceiling light for a few seconds. Then he sat up with an ironic smile. "Clifton was quite a swordsman, you know. And I don't believe all his conquests were outside the department. That's pure conjecture, and if you quote me, I'll deny I said it. But Frank had something. It worked for Stearns, but it stalled his own career for several years; he didn't advance in rank again until Clifton retired."

"Did you ever ask him what he did?"

"I tried, once. He said, 'Who wants to know?'" Lou shrugged. "I didn't say anything, and he just walked away."

12

I S this a polka or a schottische?" Trudy asked me.
"The way I do it? Probably both," I said. "Just keep twirling, huh? And bouncing up and down."

"I've never danced in snow boots before," she said. "Do winter festivals always make people so crazy?"

"Yup. Especially if breakfast is a shot of schnapps with a side order of beer." The music stopped, and she perched on a snowbank, fanning herself with a folded twelve-pack carton. The temperature was hanging right around twenty-five degrees, so dancing in snowmobile suits had made us steam. The ice was littered with jackets and scarves that everybody pulled off when they got too hot, and put back on when they stood still a minute and chilled down. We were all wearing Polaroid sunglasses, too, and as much sunscreen as our faces would hold; Lake Pepin was covered with fresh snow, glaring in bright sunshine.

"Let's go check our lines," I said. We picked our way through the chattering groups of red-faced people clustered around fishing holes cut in the ice. They sat on upturned buckets, jigging their lines and telling long, tall stories about fish they'd caught here other times. When they got cold, they'd get up and pace around, still talking, every so often erupting into loud laughter and telling each other to get out of here with that bullshit.

Our fishing site was almost embarrassingly luxurious. Vince Greeley, when he agreed to come along, suggested trailering his fishing shack. "It's got a floor in it, and a little heater," he said, "so we can take turns fishing inside where it's warm. Whaddya think?"

"If you want to," I said. My original Winter Fest plan had been simplicity itself: toss some fishing tackle in the back of the pickup and drive to Lake City. It began getting more complicated when I asked Trudy, "Shall we ask Maxine to ride along? Seems like she's overdue for some fun."

"Hey, good idea," she said. "I can talk to her while you slaughter fish." Trudy still saw ice fishing as a primitive masculine ritual, and suspected that guys only wanted their mates along to cook and drive home. She was humoring me about this trip because she was happy about the farm and determined that our pledge never to fight again should last more than three days.

Maxine said, "I'd love to, kids, but right now I can't leave Eddy."

"Bring him along," I said. "I'll teach him to fish."

"Isn't that too much trouble? I don't want to spoil your fun."

"You won't. I'm gonna be teaching Trudy anyway. Rigging one more tip-up isn't that big a deal."

Then Bo Dooley decided it would be good for him and Diane to be alone for her first weekend home, and asked Maxine if she could keep Nelly.

"I didn't want to say no to him," she said apologetically when she called. "But I think, now, with two kids—that's just too much, isn't it?"

"No, it's really better," I said. "Nelly can teach Eddy, she's a whiz at baiting a hook." Bo had been teaching her to fish, and she was learning fast because she loved doing whatever her father was doing.

But Trudy said, "This is getting kind of top-heavy with women and children, Jake. Why don't we find another couple?" So I called Vince Greeley Friday night, and by Saturday morning he had transformed the weekend into an Eddy Bauer catalog demo.

"There's room on the trailer for my big cooler, too," he said, in his fifth phone call. I'd seen his cooler; it was the size of a small dinghy. In a few minutes he was back on the line saying,

"I'll bring my Coleman lanterns, too, huh? And we might as well have the propane grill."

Then the food conversations started. Vince's wife Laura contributed a monstrous pan of lasagna, Maxine brought a vat of potato salad the size of a snare drum, Trudy made double her usual peanut butter cookie recipe, and Vince and I each bought beer and pop and chips and salsa enough for a platoon. Vince and Laura's two kids never left home without books and games, bags of extra clothing and a toy apiece, and then there was all the bait and gear.

Sleet began to fall in late morning. Packing food and gear into two vehicles and a trailer while cold sleet pelted us in the faces took up so much of Saturday afternoon that by the time we reached Lake City there was just time before dark to check into motel rooms and set the kids up with pizza and movies on the VCR.

"But tomorrow," Vince said, "them fish better watch out for us, huh?"

"Why am I so tired?" Trudy said, collapsing into bed. "We're only forty miles from Rutherford."

"Maybe because we brought supplies enough to stay all winter," I said, stretching and groaning. "God, just think, tomorrow we have to haul it all home again."

In the morning, though, as soon as I looked out the window I forgot all that and yelled, "Oh, Jesus, Trudy, come and look."

"What? What?" She came running to the window, looked, and said, "Oh, Jake, did you ever see a more beautiful day in your whole life?"

The wind had blown the clouds away, and sunshine poured out of a bright blue sky. The buildings and trees looked new under a fresh dusting of snow. While we watched, a train came around the bluff, across the lake on the Wisconsin side, and ran right along the shore, blowing its whistle. Trudy laughed with joy and said, "It looks like a toy!"

We collected Maxine and the kids from next door, bought cinnamon rolls and coffee and cocoa from a food stand, and hurried out to the lake. Vince and I had set up the shack the night before. He was already there with his family, working his auger hard to cut the first fishing hole. He popped open a beer apiece for us and held up the schnapps bottle, urging, "C'mon, you better have some of my loudmouth soup before you start to fish!"

"Uh-*huh*," Trudy said, when I showed her how to push the hook through the dorsal fin of a wriggling minnow, "this looks doable. Pretty gross, though. I better have another one of those beers to help me through this." She had started glowing when she saw the sunshine, and the schnapps was turning her wattage ever higher.

"Gosh, this is a pretty place," Maxine said.

"You've never been here before?"

"Isn't that crazy? Living so close? But no, I never have."

"You want me to rig a line for you?"

"No, I'll just watch." She nudged my shoulder. "Wouldn't it be great if Eddy caught a fish?"

"Or if he'd even try," I said. He still seemed inaccessible, staring at that mysterious spot a foot ahead of his face. Suddenly, he made me think of the dog Darby; I shivered and turned to talk to sweet, pretty Nelly. I rigged her up a line on a short pole; she baited her own hook and stood by a hole, jigging her line patiently, keeping herself amused by watching Vince's boys fight. They were only a year apart and relentlessly competitive, arguing over every detail of tackle and bait and even, to their father's chagrin, about who got which side of a round hole.

They were close to Eddy's age but ignored him, having sensed something about him that they probably couldn't even put into words. Nelly asked him, "You want to hold my line, Eddy?" He shook his head quickly without looking at her. Even a head shake, though, meant that Nelly had established more communication with him than the rest of us.

We put all our lines on tip-ups then, little wooden rigs with a red flag on a thin strip of metal that was rigged to flip up if a fish pulled on the line, and we took turns watching them with people at neighboring holes so everybody could fish and still see some of the events. The kids loved the snowmobile parade, which was noisy and colorful. They brought back balloons that the snow-mobilers handed out, and Maxine and Trudy tied them to their tip-ups. Vince and Laura each caught a fish, and then we all went to watch the shooshing contest.

They took their places at the starting line, six teams of four people each, randomly mixed as to gender. Earlier, each team had nailed old boots or sneakers to two two-by-fours eight feet long. Now they laid their boards side by side, slid their feet into the shoes, and laced up. Somebody fired a starter gun, and the predictable happened: four people on each team tried to lift the heavy boards by moving all their feet in unison, quickly lost their balance, and turned turtle. Soon there were six piles of people on the ice, all nailed to boards, flailing helplessly and calling each other unspeakable names. Now and then a team would right itself and move, urged on by their cheering section, a few feet forward, before crashing onto the ice again.

The teams all survived the race without serious injury, but some of the spectators got so weak from laughing they had to be carried from the field.

Just as we got back from the race, Nelly's red tip-up flag popped up. She ran to pull it up, calling to Eddy, "Will you help me?" To my surprise Eddy grabbed hold of the line behind her, and they pulled it up together, hand over hand. She had a nice northern pike, three pounds plus, with two rows of razor-sharp teeth.

"Stand back a minute, kids," I said. I got it off the line and put it in a bucket for her; she held it out to Eddy and said, "Feel it!"

He pulled the mitten off his slender right hand, reached out carefully, and touched the cold, slimy fish. His eyes came alive; he looked at Nelly, and something close to a smile crossed his face. Maxine saw it, and nudged me.

I laid Nelly's fish in a makeshift cooler of snow, checked her hook, and handed her a fresh minnow. While she baited her line, I asked Eddy, "Whaddya think? Wanna try a line of your own now?"

He looked at Maxine quizzically, actually moved his head

forty-five degrees and looked up at her. She nodded, and he looked back at me and repeated her nod.

I showed him how the slender metal strip with the flag should be bent down and caught in the wire hook, and how the spool of line at the bottom had to be turned so its flange would turn the reversed hook at the other end of the wire and trigger the tip-up if a fish pulled on the bottom of the line. Then I brought a fathead minnow and showed him how to thread the hook through the dorsal fin so the fish could still swim. He blinked a few times. Nelly said, "You want me to do it?" He shot her a quick little head shake and did it himself.

While he baited his hook, I cut a hole in the ice and skimmed the shaved ice out of the water at the bottom of the hole. We fed twelve feet of baited line and lead sinker into the hole, and I laid the two crossbars of the tip-up carefully across the hole at right angles, stood up, and brushed off my cold knees. Eddy stood transfixed, watching the slender metal strip for signs of movement.

"Now, you gotta realize," I said, "the key to successful ice fishing is the plastic bucket." He looked at me, blinking.

Maxine said in my ear, "I don't think he's quite ready for jokes yet."

I found him a bucket, upended it by the hole, and said, "Sit here while you wait." I got another one for Nelly and left them there, watching their fishing holes with single-minded concentration.

After a while Vince and Laura wandered downstream to the "golf course." The hotel staff had plowed fairways on the ice, setting up dozens of recycled Christmas trees in the heaps of snow that bordered the open areas. They were selling tickets that entitled the players to a golf club apiece and several bright green tennis balls. A tennis ball, built to travel across a net and sink, won't go far no matter how hard you smack it with a golf club, and it skitters around unpredictably when it lands. Vince's shouts of frustration began drifting back over the ice, alternating with his bragging claims for how far the next shot would go.

Trudy and I got a fresh beer apiece and strolled toward the hotel, where a crew was setting up a platform. A round-faced man with a big voice climbed up on it, set up a portable sound system, tested the mike with some terrible blowing and screeching noises, and said his name was Norm. Just that, no more, got him a big round of applause and shouts of, "Go, Norm!" He said he was going to be our deejay for the rest of the day and give away some prizes, and he got a second, even bigger round of applause. Obviously ice fishing was losing its edge a little, and people were ready to let Norm show his righteous stuff.

Norm played a Wynona tune, gave a prize to the best-decorated snowmobile in the parade, played some Willie Nelson, and awarded four silver cups to the one shooshing team that had actually crossed the finish line. Everybody clapped and stamped and yelled whether they knew the winners or not, because it was getting a little colder on the ice and stamping and clapping felt good. Norm played Kenny Rogers singing "The Gambler," and a thousand voices sang the choruses about holding and folding, loud enough to shrivel a couple of trees behind the hotel.

The man, woman, and child who'd caught the first fish of the weekend each got a sweatshirt, and then Norm said, "Okay, let's get serious here," and announced the minnow-eating contest.

"I think I'll enter that," Trudy said. She'd had a couple more beers and a blackberry brandy, and was feeling really frisky.

"Are you serious?" I asked her.

"Sure. I ate a goldfish once, right out of the bowl."

"You did? Why?"

"On a dare. I'm gonna do it." She squeezed through the crowd to the platform and gave her name to the judge, a white-haired guy in a plaid mackinaw and four-buckle overshoes, with a bait pail at his feet. I ran to get my camera, yelling to Maxine and the kids to come right away. We listened while the judge took the microphone and explained the rules: each contestant, in turn, would swallow as many minnows as possible; the judge would keep the count; "and all my decisions will be final," he said gravely. He handed the mike to the announcer, then took it back and told the contestants, "You gotta keep 'em down, remember. No barfin' allowed." The crowd whistled and stamped.

I held up my camera so Trudy could see I wanted a picture, and she sent me a grin a yard wide. Vince and Laura had somehow got word what was happening and were running madly across the ice toward us.

There were only two other contestants: a burly six-foot biker type with a red curly beard and a Harley stocking cap, and a waiter who had come running out of the hotel at the last minute with a coat over his uniform.

The announcer played a drumroll, and the waiter stepped up to the bucket. He reached in, pulled out a wriggling minnow, and screamed, "Omigod, these things are *alive!*"

"Well, sure, kid," the judge said. "Whadja think?"

"I thought they said *raw*," the waiter said. "I never thought— Jesus!" He dropped his fish and ran back into the hotel, followed by hoots and whistles. The biker stepped up to the bucket then, and for the first time we saw he was carrying a can of beer and a giant go-cup. He scooped up a dip net full of bait, held it high, and began dropping minnows, one at a time, into the cup. Spontaneously, the crowd began to count along with the judge.

"Nine, ten, eleven," they screamed, and the bearded man stooped and delicately, precisely, picked out one more minnow, held it up, and dropped it into the cup, as the whole crowd roared, "twelve!" He poured most of his can of beer over the fish. When foam began to run over the top, he put the can down on the announcer's stand, raised his cup in a salute to the audience, and began to drink. They cheered him on with whistles and stamping and plenty of free advice like, "Faster!" and, "Not so fast!"

He tilted his head back so we could all see his big throat working as he swallowed. When the tall cup was almost tipped level, he lowered it suddenly, stared over the crowd like a man who has just seen a truly remarkable vision, clapped his hand over his mouth, and bolted for the open space behind the stage.

"Well, shoot," the announcer said, "I guess that kinda eliminates him, doesn't it? How about you, little lady?" he said, smiling fatuously at Trudy. "You still think you wanna try this?"

She gave him a smile so radiant he almost fell off his stool, stepped to the bucket, and picked up a nice plump minnow. She held it high so we could all see that it was wiggling plenty, laid it gently on her tongue, and held it there for a few seconds with the tail flapping between her lips, while the crowd went mad with applause. She swallowed it, flashed another ten-gigawatt smile, and raised her fist in a power salute.

Vince was simply babbling with delight by the time she got back to us with her Winterfest sweatshirt. "Incredibly cool, just sensational the way you held it in your mouth there like a puffin!" he kept saying. "Tell us what it felt like, tell us, tell us."

"Sort of like an ice cube," Trudy said. "Not as bad as you'd think."

"Was it fishy, though?"

"Not very," she said, and then, firmly, "Now I don't want to talk about it any more."

Suddenly, voices were calling from around our shack, "Tip-up! Tip-up!" and we all ran toward our holes. When I could see which flag was flying I yelled, "Eddy, come on, you've got a fish!"

I pulled the wooden frame up; line was whirling off the spool, and I grabbed it and felt a mighty tug. "Pull!" I told him, handing him the line. He actually slid toward the hole a few inches before he got his feet set; then he pulled hard, but whatever was on his line was too strong for him. I helped him, and the line began to yield.

Vince came running to help, saying, "What in hell have you got there?" Maxine panted to a stop by the hole and watched anxiously. Then Trudy was there holding Nelly by the hand. Nelly said softly, "Keep the line tight, Eddy."

We fought the cold, wet line out of the water, hand over hand. The fish made a final dash just under the water, and I caught a glimpse of white on the lower tip of the tail. "It's a nice walleye," I almost whispered, desperately afraid we might lose it. But we kept up the pressure, and suddenly it was sliding up through three feet of ice. As it cleared the hole and flopped in front of us, a collective sigh of relief whooshed out of the small crowd gathered around us.

"Holy Moses," Vince said. "Look at that monster." Everybody was dancing and laughing around the fish.

Eddy looked at me, worried. "Is something wrong with it?"

Maxine's eyes glistened; Eddy had talked! "No, it's fine, Eddy." I knelt and put an arm around his bony shoulders. "Vince just means it's huge. You caught a really big fish, Eddy, you're a lucky guy!"

We got it off the line and into a bucket and took it to the stand to be weighed.

"My stars, young man," the woman at the scales said, "looks like you might have yourself a winner. Toby? Looka here." Her partner, who was writing stats in a ledger, turned and looked over his glasses and said, "Well, Celia, is that a walleye or a whale?"

People began to gather around. Celia put Eddy's fish in her oval pan, balanced the pan on the scale, and began pushing the little weights along the weighing arm while more and more observers crowded in, telling her not quite far enough yet, a little farther, oops too far, until she yelled at them to get away and leave her alone. Finally Eddy's walleye was declared to weigh six pounds, one and a half ounces.

"Is that pretty good?" he asked me.

"That's better than good," I told him. "That's a trophy-size fish. I bet you win a prize for that."

He got the sweatshirt for the biggest fish caught by a kid, and then—"Oh, my," Maxine murmured—he won an electric trolling motor for the biggest walleye of the weekend. We were all deliriously happy by then; we agreed to pony up enough cash to get the fish mounted for him.

Laura and Trudy went into the warm shack, which Vince had given up trying to tell them was made to fish from, and began passing out plates of potato salad and grilled fish. Vince and I drank our last beers out in the chilly sunset while we gathered up scattered, half-frozen clothing and fishing gear. Three or four guys still standing around their holes helped us heave the shack and cooler back on the trailer, and before long we joined the long line of headlights boring holes in the dark on Highway 63, headed home.

"Look, even Eddy's sound asleep," Maxine said happily as we carried the two kids into her house.

"He actually talked a little," I said, "didn't he?"

"Hey, he talked my arm off on the way home," she said.

"I couldn't hear," I said. "What did he say?"

She giggled. "He said, 'My fish was the biggest one, wasn't it?' about five times, and when Nelly finally told him to quit saying that, he said, 'Jake says I'm a lucky guy,' every couple of minutes till he fell asleep."

At home, in the kitchen, Trudy said, "Let's break all the rules and leave this mess till tomorrow night, huh?"

"Well, usually I'm very fussy about how I leave my kitchen on a Sunday night," I said, piling evil-smelling boxes and bags on the table, "but I'm willing to make an exception for a woman who swallows live fish."